*Books by* Will Henry

# ONE MORE RIVER TO CROSS

# ONE
# MORE RIVER
# TO CROSS

*The Life and Legend of Isom Dart*

# Will Henry

RANDOM HOUSE · NEW YORK

To **LESTER LINSK**
and the searchers for
the other shore

# FOREWORD

Isom Dart was not his real name. Nor can any accountant of those shadowed times declare in truth that his is the real story of the Arkansas slave who became a legend. He was born without a name, took that of his white master, Huddleston. He called himself Ned, a simple name for a simple man. Yet he raised it to stand beside the tallest. He has not been remembered. He was a black man. And white men have written the records, kept the rolls of honor. Yet there is a justice in Time, a Truth in folklore. From years long dead the dim trail is pointed by a trapper's lie, a cowman's yarn, the tribal spinnings of Yampatika and Shoshone old ones who knew the once far lonesome Basin of the Green, the Little Snake and the Yampa. The trackline fades. To follow it in spirit, to mark it in memory, to restore it to its rightful place among the classic strange true tales of the American heritage, these are the dedications of this work, the inspirations for the redemption of the Legend of Isom Dart.

W.H.
Brown's Park, Colorado
1966

Isom Dart drew rein. He sat on the old mule looking over the river but his hand was again with that of his white master dying in the twilight of Manassas. In his heart the words returned.

"You're all I have, boy, the same as my own son, the same as you were white. You must do as I say, you must get over the river to the other side."

Black against the last sunset, Isom Dart straightened. What had been given him with his freedom he did not know; what had been promised with it, he must always believe, must never forget.

Very gently he touched a spur to the flank of old Jeff Davis.

"Go long, mule," he said. "Over the river is free . . ."

*The Life and Legend of Isom Dart*

# 1.

In the Arkansas Ozarks the times were uneasy that war summer of 1861. Since April and the cannons of Fort Sumter no man of the South who dwelled near the North could feel safe. While slavery was a fact of life below the Arkansas border, the Ozark hill country was much too close to the centers of Union loyalty for property owners such as Squire Huddleston to know true rest. Gathering his belongings, including his few slaves, hill farmer Huddleston left Siloam Ridge and went south. Riding with him upon the seat of the lead wagon was a small Negro boy of twelve. The boy's name was Ned. No man knew his father or his mother. Huddleston had bought him as a baby for four dollars and fifty bars of lye soap against a guarantee by the seller that the foundling would winter-through safely on a diet of raw cow's milk and warmed sugar water, a gamble which Ned repaid by thriving like a brown and happy weed amid the rocks and hard-scrabble of the homeplace.

From the beginning Huddleston understood he had taken to shelter no ordinary boy. Unfailingly cheerful, instantly willing, lithe and handsome as a Nubian lion cub, the youth stood apart not only as an offspring of a shackled people but as an extraordinary individual by any judgment.

He had a magic hand with all animals, wild and domestic. Birds called to him and were answered. No fish hatched from mortal roe might elude the sorcery of his line, nor flee the hook and hackle of his home-tied flies. And he was like the animals: no white-tail buck trod more lightly in the thicket, no black bear hid with greater cunning in the bottom timber, no rabbit ran so well, no bobcat stalked the meadow's edge with greater stealth or keener cast of eye. Even with all the happiness of his foster home, it was the river's run, the ridge's crest, the wooded slope and grassy clearing where human voice fell not, nor clumsy booted foot, which were his true habitats. Within their spell he was secure, a natural child claiming nature as his only mother.

Adults liked the boy, favoring him for his alert, sunny spirit, and for his inherent wish to help all about him. For himself, Ned reserved two special loves—those of horses and of other children smaller than he, a twin devotion which he never changed, or failed.

He showed an early aptitude with firearms, and with all aspects of the hunt; by his tenth year he was steadily supplying game meat to leaven the otherwise monotonous menu of brined fat pork, grits and collard greens which was the daily fare of the Huddleston slaves.

Ned herded the farm's scant flock of sheep, tended and defended the band of scrawny chickens which gave eggs and an occasional fryer. He milked the cow, saw that the heifer stood to the bull, that the calf was not lost from the mother, nor taken by the catamount, the wolf, or the canny bear; he reported the labor of the mare in foal, the fleshing of the beef steers, the location and numbers of the half-wild herd of razorback pigs littered and ranging on Huddleston land. All of these things and half a hundred more he accomplished gladly and skillfully. In sum, he was of such use to everyone within the benediction of his instant smile or reach of his ready dark hand that when he was twelve his owner gave the boy his own name in formal declaration.

Thus it was that Ned Huddleston sat upon the driver's box of the southward-rolling wagon with the Squire of Siloam Ridge that long-ago day, outward bound upon the singular adventure that was to become the legend of Isom Dart.

# 2.

The war went forward three more summers and a spring. Inescapably Ned became a part of it, serving as personal forager for his owner, who had taken a commission in a Confederate regiment. A forager in war is many things—cook, valet, mess boy, runner, jack-of-all-officers—but primarily he is a thief, his first duty being to beg, borrow or steal from the countryside whatever might be useful and return it to his camp.

The assignment might appear simple for troops based on their native lands, as were the southern forces; but the young Negro lad soon learned one of the truths of war: people who would offer their lives in a cause would not willingly give up a Confederate dollar's worth of personal property. They would *sell* the hoarded food or clothing—for Yankee money—but contribute freely no crumb or thread.

Ned pondered this discovery in his friendly, trusting way, and was soon to ponder it more painfully. He was captured five times in his first year of foraging. Three times he was severely flogged by irate Confederate householders, once badly beaten by a plantation overseer, once incongruously rescued by a Yankee major and a raiding squadron of Union Cavalry from being run down by a pack of redbone hounds set on his trail by the loyal southern landowners.

As the great struggle wore on and its tides of battle washed farther to the North, the boy found that stealing from the enemy was infinitely less dangerous than attempting to "borrow" from the southern friend. Billy Yank seemed by far better able to understand than was his Confederate counterpart, Johnny Reb, that war was war and that foraging was as natural to it as wet, cold, cannon fire, misery and hope.

But yet young Ned decided, it wasn't really the soldiers of either side who made survival difficult, it was the people who were too young or too old or too cowardly to get into the fight, who behaved meanly behind the backs of their brave soldiers. They were the ones who made all the talk about dying for the cause, yet they would beat you with a club, or fire a gun at you, or turn the foxhounds loose on you if you so much as tapped on their doors at broad noon and asked for a cup of water or shard of stale bread.

This strange selfishness made a lasting impression on Ned. So did the soldiers for whom he rustled and crept and stole, who claimed that in the name of war any act of theft or deceit or force was fair. It had no moral meaning. The only thing that counted was to survive, to somehow live through whatever menace loomed at the moment. Once safely past that moment, a man might tell himself that whatever he had done, or ordered others to do, had to be done. The only other choice was destruction, or defeat for the cause. If a farmer or townsman did not understand his patriotic duty to support his troops then he might have to be persuaded by a bayonet at his throat, or the throat of his woman or child, or by whatever naked ugliness was necessary, to surrender his chickens, eggs or milk, bread, warm blankets, good clothing or dry boots.

It was war. All things were fair.

Young Ned quite plainly did not see these forces at work in patriotic terms; nor did the still unbreakably good-natured Negro camp thief comprehend in any real sense the issues of the bloody fratricide which brought his master's southern white folks to kill and be killed by their northern friends and kinsmen. Had he been told that he, a slave, was the central if somewhat unadmitted cause of the terrible waste, he would have refused to believe it. "Me, suh?" he would have said to the by-then Colonel Huddleston. "My people to blame? Why, we ain't done a thing." And the Colonel would have smiled and patted him on his head and told him not to worry, that a "nigra" couldn't be expected to understand anything that complicated.

But even though Ned would not understand that the War between the States had been emotionally ignited by the issue of slavery, he had already learned another aspect of the white man's military reasoning which was to stay with him for the rest of his life: it did not matter what a man did, it was being caught at the doing which brought shame and punishment. A man or a mere youth like himself, might lie, cheat, steal, wound, even kill another man, or burn down his buildings, or defile his women, and it would be forgiven if it was brought off undetected. The entire idea was to do the deed and escape. Admit nothing. Always lay the trail away from the scene to avoid pursuit or capture. Sneak and thieve and deceive, but do not call it that. Call it war, and forgive yourself the trespass, because to the winner went the absolution, to the loser damnation because he had lost.

# *3.*

In the second summer of the war the rumor grew that Abraham Lincoln was preparing to issue his Proclamation freeing the slaves. Colonel Huddleston, with his command in the Confederate lines gathering for Second Manassas, called Ned to his tent. The Negro boy found his master in poor condition; his leg was mutilated to the hip by a charge of chain-shot suffered in a forward skirmish some hours gone, and the surgeon did not believe the wounded man would survive. He was of no further military use and the brigade general had already signed his honorable discharge. A wagon train of captured Union blankets and medical materials was being sent back that same night. All southern wounded unable to walk or sit a horse were going out with the wagons, Colonel Noah Huddleston among them. It was of this fact the officer now apprised Ned. He then went on quickly to explain the particular urgency of the situation for his young forager.

"Lad," he began, "did you know the Yankee President, Mr. Lincoln, is said to be readying a paper freeing all the slaves?"

"No, suh," answered Ned. "I never. What's it mean, Colonel? What slaves Mr. Lincoln talking about?"

"All of them, Ned. That means you, too, boy."

The Negro lad shook his head. "Yes, suh, if you say, Colonel.

What's it going to mean, though, suh, this here freedom paper?"

"It will mean, Ned, that if you can slip up through our troops and get to the river and on across it into the Union lines, you will be free."

"Free from what, suh?"

Huddleston, tooth-gritting pain aside, smiled wanly. Freedom was an empty word to the boy. He must be given another view of the term.

"It means, Ned," he tried once more, "that if you can get over the Rappahannock tonight you can do whatever you want to after that. You'll be free, just like a white boy."

Ned nodded and scratched his head. He was trying hard to help out the injured master. Clearly his leg had him fevered, was interfering with his mind's work.

"How am I going to do whatever I want, suh," he finally asked, "when fust off I got to do whatever you want?"

"All right, Ned," Huddleston said, the pain very great. "Since that's the way you understand things, that's the way we will have to do it. You will know the truth later, God being kind to you meanwhile. Bring me that pen and those writing sheets. Hurry, lad. The hospital wagon will be by at any minute to put me aboard."

The officer wrote with great difficulty, but in a clear hand he stated he, the legal owner, freed the boy known in his own name as Ned Huddleston, and requested any who might find him by the road to give him aid and comfort to reach the North, where his freedom would mean something and he might have a chance to learn a trade and be a self-sustaining man of respect. The reason cited in the letter for freeing Ned was not Lincoln's forthcoming Proclamation, but rather the fact that in two hard summers of war the Negro lad had bravely earned the right to some better life away from the battlefield.

Huddleston knew, of course, that the honoring of his document would depend upon whim and pure chance should Ned be apprehended south of the river. But he affixed his name, rank, location of the family home and the dates of his commission, term of service and discharge, with the instruction that if Ned were captured he was to be returned to the Huddleston family in the South and under no circumstances punished for doing what his legal owner had ordered him to do—to try to reach the Federal lines beyond the river.

Sanding the letter, the wounded officer sealed it in a vellum envelope and told Ned not to reveal it unless to save his life.

"Make yourself useful around here after they take me away," he told the boy. "Let on like you mean to stay and forage for the troops as before. I've already told my friend Major Gainesford that he can have you. Go to him and behave as you would with me. But, Ned, come tonight, you go. You understand that, boy? You take out and hit for the river."

Ned frowned. There were too many shades of meaning and maneuver here for his uncomplicated nature. Again he shook his head. "You want me to serve the Major but to skin out the minute he turns his back? Then shag over the river, suh? Who am I going to serve yonder?"

"Nobody," explained Huddleston wearily. "You'll be free."

"No suh," Ned denied. "You can beat me when you're well, or set the dogs on me, whichever, Colonel. But I ain't never going to leave you. I ain't never going to serve no Yankee Gen'ril, nor no other man alive, less it's you, suh."

"I don't want you to serve any other man, Ned. That's what the letter says." Lying on the cot, he propped himself up on his elbow. "I hear the wagon coming. I want your word, Ned. You do what I have told you, boy. You have my name, and it's a proud one. Now you're free, as well, if you can get away to the North. You do it, you hear? After the war, I'll try to find you. Meanwhile, you go north and make a life for yourself up there." The officer put a cold hand on the arm of the Negro lad. His fingers gripped and tightened, and Ned put his other hand to Colonel Huddleston's. "Ned," the latter said, "you're my boy the same as you were white, and you got to do what I tell you. Goodbye."

Ned was crying then and he fell back into the tent shadows as the ragged and filthy work troops came into the shelter and took up the Colonel and bore him out to the wagon. When the vehicle had rattled on, Ned came out of the tent to watch it until it disappeared into the trees.

Then, as he had done all his life, he did what he had been told to do.

[9]

Unable, however, to find Major Gainesford immediately, he wandered around camp helping where he could until another Negro lad, older than himself and a fellow-forager, told him that his own officer had been killed that same afternoon in a cavalry brush at Raccoon Ford.

"You mean," asked Ned, feeling his stomach grow small with dread, "that Major Gainesford done got kilt?"

"Well, I allow you know he was my master," replied the other. "So ain't that what I said?"

Ned then told the other youth his own similar dilemma, but nothing of the freedom paper in his shirt. When both boys later heard that a terrible fight was forming up along the banks of Bull Run, not far away, they decided to flee the Confederate camp together. With both their masters gone, it seemed to the two lads that crossing the river and seeking asylum with the Yankees now made considerable sense.

"Lookit yonder," directed Ned, pointing. "Twilight's shut down hard along the river. Them bottom shadows twixt the willers and the bank ought to hide us safe as two charcoal cats."

"Sure enough," agreed Snakehead, a youth of lean reptilian look. "You take out fust, Ned; you're the sneakiest nigger I ever seen."

Ned bobbed his head in dubious accord. "Likewise the scairtest one you ever seen," he said, and slipped off noiselessly through the settling dusk toward the willow brakes of the Rappahannock.

## 4.

The two Negro youths came to the river. It flowed silently through the summer night, seeming far wider than by day. A great restless moving of troops was going on in the darkness which shrouded both banks. The boys shivered with the fear that a southern patrol might step upon their hiding patch of reedy brush before they could quit it. They lay close as common flesh, and each could feel the heartbeat of the other, wild and fast, like a bird or rabbit. At last, as there came a lull in the calling back and forth of the Confederate pickets, Snakehead stirred.

"I reckon we had best go, happen we mean to go," he whispered. "Ain't no Rebs near. You nerved-up yet, Ned?"

"My knees and teeth ain't," answered the other boy.

"That's all right," assured Snakehead. "When you is in the water that shaking will make you go like a speckle trout."

Ned started away from the brush heap. Both boys crawled belly-down. They were nearly to the stream when Snakehead thought he heard a footfall off to their right. For one instant he took his eyes from the silhouetted beacon of Ned's buttocks humping along in front of him. When there came no second footfall, he looked back but could not see the other youth's rump. Writhing to the right, then the left, then forward along what he thought was their path toward the water, his desperate hand reached through the pitchblende gloom of the bottomland, but he felt no touch of his friend's flesh. Forgetting everything, Snakehead stood up against the starlight and called out Ned's name, hoarsely, urgently. An answer came, but not from Ned.

"Hold!" challenged the Rebel picket. "Stand or be shot!"

Snakehead could see the picket now, up against the maples in the little bend above the brush clump. He could see, as well, the murky forms of several other gray-clad troopers moving in the starlight behind the first soldier.

Snakehead was not afraid, but he whirled in confusion. Where was Ned? Had he made it to the water? Was he hiding in the cattails of the bend, breathing maybe through the hollow stem of one of the tails, like any slave knew to do?

"Sing out!" said the picket. "Friend or enemy?"

Only one word would come to the mind of Snakehead, that was "nigger." That was all he was. He wasn't friend or enemy, he was just a nigger. He would tell the southern soldier boys that and it would be password enough for them.

Snakehead did not call out, however. He just started toward the pickets unthinkingly. He thought to grin and tell them who he was—Major Gainesford's forager—and that he had legitimate affairs down here by the river. But then he remembered that the Major was dead and that these boys would know that—maybe—

[ 11 ]

and they might get hard with him for lying to them. They might even say he was trying to run away, and they could shoot him for that. Snakehead stopped moving. As he crouched and half-turned away, the voice of the picket rang out again, and then the shots: one, three, five, seven of them. Snakehead felt only six. The last one missed and sang onto the surface of the river only an arm's length from where Ned lay half-submerged in the reeds. It skipped and skittered like a thrown flat rock over toward the Yankee side, from where the Federal pickets fired at it nervously and yelled for lanterns and a scout patrol.

The Confederate troopers laughed at them and called them blue-bellies. Then Ned saw the Confederates go through the starlight to the huddled form of Snakehead; he saw the first picket lean down and strike a match, heard his companions ask tensely who it was they had brought down, heard the first man say the word Snakehead had not said, "nigger," and that was all.

For an hour Ned lay in the reeds in the ebbwater of the river, and then he remembered with a start the letter given him by Colonel Huddleston. He was glad then. That paper gave him strength. It made him like a white boy, the Colonel had said; he had only to show it to anyone, and they would know he was Ned Huddleston, and help him on his way.

He arose from the muddy water, cleansing himself in its current. He didn't need to cross the river, nor explain to the pickets who he was. He wasn't like Snakehead, a nobody. He was Ned Huddleston, Colonel Huddleston's boy, and he had the paper to prove it.

Those southern boys hadn't killed Snakehead because he was a Negro. They had shot at him because he had failed to answer their hail. They hadn't known what color he was. Snakehead had died for nothing, but Ned didn't need to die like that. He had only to go up the bank and show the nearest Confederate officer his paper. Then everything would be right.

In only a few minutes he found a tent with lantern light and voices to announce it as an important meeting place of officers. He went toward it and was barred by the sentry outside, but he raised his voice to the soldier because he was the same as a white boy now.

The soldier seized him and dragged him, still dripping water, into the big tent.

"Begging your pardon, Gen'ril, suh," he addressed the white-haired officer at the crowded map table within. "This boy says he's got an important paper to show."

The slight man in the long gray cavalry coat and high jack-boots came around the desk. He looked at Ned and put a slender, fine-veined hand on the Negro lad's sodden shoulder. Ned looked up at him unafraid. "Suh," he said, "I'm Ned Huddleston, Colonel Huddleston's boy, suh."

"Yes?" said the sad-faced officer. "I believe you."

"Yes, suh, thank you, suh."

"You have an important paper for me, boy?"

"General, sir," interrupted one of the gilt-encrusted staff, "we must get on, sir. General Jackson is waiting to go forward to cut off Pope, and General Longstreet is wanting to know about moving on your right, sir. Please!"

"Colonel Malvern, I am doing my best, sir. Precisely as this small lad. It is the same war for all of us. The paper, boy."

Ned dug into his muddy shirtfront, brought forth the precious envelope. The gentle officer took it from him, extracted from within it the limp mass of Colonel Huddleston's letter. He unfolded the missive, studied it, passed it to the impatient colonel on his right. "What do you make of it, Malvern?" he asked quietly.

"Suh," said Ned uneasily, noting the looks exchanged between the high officers, "that there is my freedom paper. Colonel Huddleston, he done writ on there that he was setting me free, that I wasn't no slave no more, that I was his boy same as had I been white. Ain't you see that there, Gen'ril, suh?"

Colonel Malvern handed the paper back to his superior. The latter took it and looked at it once more. Then, with a deep sigh, he held it down for Ned to see. The Negro lad squinted and peered, and reached forth to turn the paper in the officer's hand, examining the hidden side. He felt his heart stop beating within him.

"It's not legible, boy," said the white-haired general.

"Suh?" said Ned, puzzled and afraid.

"You can't read it any more," said the officer. "It has been spoiled by the water."

Ned tried to stand straight, but his shoulders drooped. He knew what had been said, and what the running ink spelled out for him. He would not see the other side of the river that night, or the next. He was not as free as poor Snakehead lying in the summer mud. His name was nothing again. He was just a nigger now, like all the others.

He let the sodden paper drop, the tears shining against the dark wet of his face. The officer reached out and touched him. "Don't weep, lad," he said. "I believe you."

The boy blinked upward, awkward in the lamplight and the restive silence of the listening staff. "What, suh?" he asked hesitantly.

"I said that I believe what you say, Ned Huddleston," answered the officer. He bent and picked up the ruined letter from the floor. Brushing the dirt from it, he returned it carefully to its envelope, gave it back to Ned.

"Keep it with you," he said. "Carry it next your heart, where you had it." He paused, his patient glance finding the boy's frightened dark eyes. "*You* know what it says, Ned," he told him softly. "That is all that counts."

With the quiet words, Robert E. Lee went back to his waiting officers and the map table and march orders which would send Stonewall Jackson and J.E.B. Stuart racing hard around the Union flank of John Pope to fall upon the great Federal supply base at Manassas Junction, fatal stage for the Second Battle of Bull Run, called Manassas by the South.

## 5.

The kindness of "Marse Robert" was a brief candle in the night of Ned Huddleston's war. It lit the boy's spirit for a moment, but great men cannot stay, and Lee was gone with daylight. Ned's fortunes returned to those of camp forager for the Confederate army, and his life was to follow one regiment after another, now cavalry, now infantry, now artillery, as the South was driven back upon her last defenses.

In the process Ned became something more than thief and scavenger. During those final days when the great armies of the Confederacy were but rotten shells and food was the very name of survival in the field, all men became something different. The gallantry was gone. The great heroes, Jackson, Albert Sidney Johnston, Jeb Stuart, all were dead. The cause was now a curse and men sought to avoid it. Murder, arson, rapine and pillage were the secret military order of the day. Soldier lived in terror of soldier, and the people feared their own army as a plague.

Ned Huddleston lasted out this desperation because of the pride Squire Huddleston had given him with his name, and with the freedom paper. He was able to live because his master had said to him, "You are my boy, Ned; same as you were white." That was the grandest thing. A man could walk a long road mighty tall with those words in his memory.

The lonely Negro youth was sixteen years of age in that final spring of the war. Over six feet in height, he was as indestructible as a swamp oak fencepost. The bright handsomeness of boyhood was now a tightened mask of suspicion and vigilance. Eyes that once shone, now glittered. The wide smile, in the past so friendly, would gleam as quickly, but with a set configuration of the lips which wise men would read as anything but reassuring. Yet one warmth did remain to him, and it was not the gift of Squire Huddleston but a thing of his mother-blood, his birth-right: his will to be of help to anyone who seemed in need of help. It survived, untouched by war, in the freed slave's broad breast, setting him apart from his fellows, making other men uneasy in his presence. No matter how menacing his outer form, good still lingered in the heart of Ned Huddleston. And men have always misunderstood such good, or simply feared its truth.

With the April of Appomattox and the Confederate surrender, Ned, as so many camp-followers of the lost cause, turned westward. Somewhere out there toward the sunset, men said, a new land waited, and a new life.

And something more. Out there beyond Red River, past the Sabine and the Neches and the Trinity, where the winds of Texas wandered—out there, somewhere, freedom waited.

[15]

# 6.

By the time Ned came to the Red River of Texas at Shreveport, Louisiana, he was weary, for his travels had been hard. There was no honest work available, as there were a hundred freed slaves for every menial or manual chore. The countryside was moving with what the South called "gitalong niggers," whose approach to a white house with the plea for work—any kind of work—was universally met with one hand on the family shotgun, the other pointing on down the road, and the advice to "get along, nigra" issued in hard-eyed warning.

The attitude was that the emancipated people ought to have stayed loyally with their old masters. The fact that not one in a score of these former masters could care for his slave establishment after the peace was never considered. Neither was the fact that most of the liberated Negroes wanted and tried to stay on the lands of their birth or purchase, but were in most cases quite literally driven off them. The war had proved that slavery, if not the ultimate cruelty advertised by the radical northern abolitionists, was certainly the most monstrous economic luxury. But for Ned and thousands like him, it was not a moral or commercial question, it was the possibility that freedom was worse. Did a man choose to starve and yet stay loyal, or would he suffer the pangs of his shrunken belly and tortured mind unfettered?

Ned, reared in kindness and treated decently all his boyhood life—even with the four years of hell and hardness between Sumter and Appomattox added on—could see but one way for himself. "You're my boy, Ned," the old Squire had said. "You got to do what I say. Get on over that river and go free." So the wary youth, driven and "gitalonged" and starving, did not give up at Shreveport. He stood looking out over the great muddy tide of the Red River, surging through a misting rain and omi-

nously high with spring-flood, and he looked back on the lights
of the city and the baying of the dogs in the friendless dark of the
surrounding country and he growled deeply, "By God, old Colonel, I'm a'going ter do it!" And he waded out into the angry
waters and began to swim.

But in the settlements of East Texas, Ned soon learned that
his lot in the West was not different than before.

In the small town of Live Oak, the young ex-slave found employment helping a blacksmith who had been kicked by a horse
while shoeing. The man was not unkind, furnishing Ned with
good food and a clean warm stall with two army blankets for
bed. It was the best Ned had seen since Appomattox. In the few
days he began to let down his guard.

Before the end of the first week the grateful youth found himself able to smile again without fear. He could walk out on the
streets without looking behind at every step. If he still chose to
step off the narrow walks to let a white man pass, or had to bow
and give way and bare his head to the womenfolk and not speak
to them, then this was cheap and reasonable price for the only
full belly and dry bed a man had known since the Arkansas
beginnings.

Perhaps, Ned thought, lying one night in his stall amid the
fragrance of prairie hay, listening to the lash of the rain on the
tight roof overhead, just perhaps, now, there was something to
this idea of being a free man, even black.

The next evening, while delivering a newly shod mare to a
customer of the town, Ned came upon a band of young settlement toughs in full cry after a small halfbreed urchin. The pursuers were older, about Ned's age; and their quarry, darting past
Ned at the opening of an alleyway between buildings, ran with
walled eyes and gasping mouth which the former slave understood as he understood the baying of hounds, the whistle and
patter of buckshot in the brush, the ricochet of rifle bullet off
trunk or stump or split-rail fence. The boy was terrified, and in
some danger of his life. As Ned drew back to let the bullies pass,
the urchin discovered that the alleyway was a cul-de-sac. He tried
to hide in a tangle of discarded trash at alley's end, but the town
youths at once began to overturn and kick away the refuse, hoot-
ing and yelping like curs at a rathole. As the halfbreed boy

would leap from one covert to the next, the remaining toughs would stone him and strike at him with brickbat, barrel stave and bare hand.

Out on the main street Ned Huddleston tied the mare to a nearby hitchrail. He did it without hesitating. He had been where that dark-skinned little boy now skittered ratlike and squealing. He knew what the ragged waif felt, how his heart hammered and his throat closed, and he knew that he could not let another smaller and weaker human creature suffer such terror alone.

Ragged, bone-thin, a brown scarecrow who would frighten no one who did not peer carefully into those deep-set, haunted eyes, Ned glided down the alleyway and through the circle of whooping town louts. The first the tormentors knew of him, he was simply there, facing them, the bloody urchin pushed protectively behind his braced legs.

Suddenly there was an ugly stillness. During it Ned prayed they would back off, would let him take the small boy and get out of there. But Church Hibbard was the leader. He was a big boy, muscled like a pitbull, and his father owned the saloon and the livery stable and was Mr. Somebody in Live Oak. Church wasn't about to back off. He reached down for a bigger rock.

"What's the child done, Mr. Church?" Ned asked. He knew young Hibbard's name, knew who he was. He forced his grin and the softness of the words. "Likely it ain't nothing to stone him no more over. Wouldn't you say, suh?"

Here the small boy tried to say something to his defender, but he spoke in Spanish and Ned did not understand enough of that Texas second tongue to comprehend. "Be still, tad," he whispered, patting the tousled head.

"Church," sneered one of the pack, "you going to let that uppity tarbaby put off on you like this?"

"Yeah," chimed a compatriot, hefting his stave. "That damned breed kid stole that bread off your old man's free lunch in the saloon, didn't he? What you going to tell your old man? That the kid whupt you? Or you cowtowed to some biggity nigger boy don't weigh enough to scale-tip a sick cat?"

Ned had been paid that afternoon. He had in his pocket his wages for five days. It was one Yankee greenback dollar, all he had in the world, and the most useable money he had ever been given for any reason. But he took out the precious wad of paper, and handed it toward Church Hibbard.

"Taken it, Mr. Church," he said. "She'll pay for the bread, won't she, suh?"

Church sniggered, then snatched the dollar bill.

"Lookit here, boys!" he crowed. "The richest nigger in the whole damned state of Texas. He's offering one Yankee dollar in paper for this thieving little *cholo*. I hear any more bids? One dollar once, one dollar twice, one dollar—"

Ned had quietly taken the halfbreed urchin's hand and was dragging him up the side of the nearest building, trying to ease away while the town boys guffawed at Church's auction. But Ned was too late. Attracted by the merriment, three passers-by were coming down the alley. These were grown men. Town leaders. Citizens of substance. To demonstrate it, they barred the way to Ned and the halfbreed boy, the good clean smell of redeye whiskey redolent upon their breaths.

Facing them, Ned had to turn his back to Church Hibbard and the others. Again the bad silence thickened. Ned could feel the youths behind him move. He could hear them closing in. Suddenly he knew that he was in very great peril in that darkening alleyway in Live Oak, Texas.

"Evening, suh," he said pleasantly to the nearest man, and in the instant leaped and struck him a raking blow with his elbow across his nose and cheekbones, knocking him, bleeding, back into his fellows. Ned fell to the dirt, rolling in under one of the other men, his long legs lashing; the second man went jarringly to the ground, his feet swept from under him. The third man swung a clumsy reaching blow at Ned on the ground and the Negro came up inside of the arm's length and brought his skull against the man's chin with a ringing crack that split the Texan's mouth and sharded four of his front teeth. Before any of the trio or the startled youths could react, Ned seized the small halfbreed boy, sped up the alley, and vaulted with the lad to the bare back of the newly shod mare. Spinning the animal, he drove her out of Live Oak into the gathering night of the brushlands.

A mile out of town he halted the mare and got down, holding her while he settled the rescued child of the *monte* on her back and fashioned a crude rein of the tie-rope. He handed this to the boy, smiled up at him, gave his leg a reassuring pat. "Don't snatch no more of that there barroom bakery goods," he advised the hunched rider. "We uns cain't afford it." Then he slapped the mare on the haunch, sending her on down the road, the halfbreed youth clinging to her.

When the thud of the hooves told him the two were safely away, Ned fled into the night toward a stream he knew ran like a new moon south of the town. In the bottomlands he found what he wanted, marshy ground thinly filmed with water where neither dog could track nor human eye seek out. Going through this swampland for another mile, he found a sluggish side channel with another familiar thing he had hoped to find—a muskrat house showing above the stagnant water. Submerging, he swam under water and came up beneath the trapped air of the mud-and-stick dwelling. He was bitten five times as the alarmed residents scurried to vacate, but he knew these wounds were a small wage for what he sought to save—his life.

He was right. Within the hour the yelp of dog pack and the flash of lantern and the calling back and forth of the manhunters began. Dogs and men beat along the creek brush, splashed the swamp, swarmed back to the road. Curses filled the darkness, watch fires were set, pickets established.

With first flush of daylight the hunt was renewed, but Ned had by this time made a tiny hole in the mud roof of the muskrat nest and inserted a small hollow stem of cattail, through which he breathed while the townfolk devoted the morning to nigger hunting in the south-bend flats of Snakeowl Creek.

By midday all but the smallest boys had gone home; the mare had been found loose on the prairie and it was assumed the "murderous nigra" was well into the next county south, so Ned could make a bigger hole letting in some precious sun and entire lungsful of clean air. That night he left the swamp and dog-trotted due west until daylight, holing up in a coyote den in a drywash bank the whole day, emerging again with dusk to resume his flight. By the third dawn he had covered a distance greater than one hundred miles, and he felt he was safe.

The long run westward had been no blind journey. In Live Oak he had heard of the life and the land out there—a big land, a different land, with another breed of people. He had heard that the timber thinned and disappeared out there, the grass grew thick and tawny, and ran in waves like the Gulf below

Mobile, smooth and lifting and endless out to where the sky shut it off. That was a livestock land out there; cattle and horses, not hogs, nor sheep, nor goats, were the commerce of those upswept prairies and clear-watered streams. A man who knew stock would be welcomed out there, be paid for what he could do, not what he looked like, or how mean his clothes were. It didn't even matter how dark his hide was, to hear it told in the blacksmith's shop. There were sure enough some nigger cowboys out there past Fort Worth; everybody knew that.

The talk of cattle and horses had fired Ned Huddleston's mind. He had already decided that when he had saved an enormity of wages, as much as five Yankee dollars with luck, he would bend his path out there toward wide sky and restless clouds. Men who loved livestock, whose whole lives were spent with animals, such men could not be small.

Maybe it was just a little farther across the river than Live Oak that old Colonel had been talking about.

Maybe when a man got far enough west he would find it. Maybe Fort Worth was where that freedom land began.

# 7.

It was May now, ordinarily a beautiful time of sun and light breeze in that country of hill and plain, thicket and grassland, homestead and open range. But on the morning Ned drew near Fort Worth a cold and driving rain slanted from the north. The wanderer had slept with only a cover of weed and creek brush the past night, had eaten nothing but such bitter spring buds and berries as the young season afforded. Indeed, so far separated were the settled places for the latter part of his journey that even for a thief as bold and skilled as himself the capture of the straying pullet, the theft of flour, beans or other real food from the isolated houses or their outbuildings had been a near impossibility. He had lived only because his hill country wisdom permitted him to fashion fishhook, line and lure from the threads of his own garments, or to design rabbit, gopher or water-rat snares from braided longgrasses and bottom creepers. On this fare of uncooked small game and raw spring greens he had maintained traveling strength, but no more. Now, crouching in the lea of some hillside scrub, he studied the passing wagon ruts of the Fort Worth stage road below, knowing he had come as far as he could on spirit and hunting skills alone.

Somewhere on these outlands, beyond the city's reach, he would have to search out the loneliest dwelling he could find which still gave promise of the things he must have. No driven, vagrant Negro could dream of entering or even approaching a large settlement. He had heard that there were almost two thousand folks in Fort Worth. Old Johan Niendorff, the blacksmith in Live Oak, had informed him that in the whole state of Texas there were only five cities with more than two thousand folks in them, so a man had to believe that Fort Worth would be something, and that a freed slave had better come into it wearing decent clothes, and having shoes on his feet and six or four bits of hard money in his pockets. Otherwise he was going to get himself grabbed by the first deputy sheriff or hard-eyed merchant who saw him, and carted off to the town hoosegow, where he could try to tell the marshall how it was that a six-foot black boy from the old states could get so far west looking so desperate without having robbed or killed or stolen from half a dozen places along the line.

And Ned knew what that would mean.

The thin youth "savvied" well lawmen and telegraph keys and wanted flyers. The last year of the war and the first seven weeks of the peace had taught him that if he didn't look clean and have a parcel of hand-luggage of some kind, with at least some small coins for lodging and meals—well, no use glooming over that. It was enough to realize that the law in Live Oak had had plenty of time to let the law in Fort Worth hear about the bad nigger, Ned Huddleston. Ned's one defense was to look like a quality colored man. That way he might last long enough in Fort Worth to discover where those stock ranches were further west, and how best a man might set out to look for work on one of them.

As he huddled in the rain trying to make some plan, the stage

coming from Dallas slopped past. It lurched over the ford at
Fossu Creek, then was gone around the far bend, southwesterly,
toward the city. Ned nodded, wiping the rain from his eyes,
spitting it from his mouth.

The precise directions of streams, the angles of roads, the lay of
surrounding land, these things were never trivial to the forager—
no more so than the schedules of stagelines or, back where they
ran, of railroad trains. Where the fox went in, he must know how
to flee back out and away. Especially if he were a black fox,
with hounds and buckshot pellets and rifle balls to dodge. If a
man forgot a creek crossing or road fork he could be led to grim
pastures, not green. And so Ned nodded and spat out the rain
and got up from his haunches and started down the hill toward
the dim track of a ranch trail he had just noted, which led away
from the main stage road into the trackless brush beyond the
Fossu Crossing.

# *8.*

Ned followed the wagon ruts of the ranch track away from the
stage road, hurrying through the misting rain. He came to where
the trail went up and over the ridge beyond Fossu Crossing, and
he went on deeper into the brush, slinking like a brown wolf to
the murky crest of the next rise. Below, he saw the homestead.
The faint line of wagon wheel marks ended there, three miles
from the stage road. Ned's dark eyes swept the tiny valley which
sheltered the landowner's few bottomland acres, his wood lot,
fenced corral, the snug cabin, rough-board outbuildings. This
was a good, if threadbare place. Care was shown in the way the
furrows of the creek-bottom field were plowed, the neat repair
of fences and of cabin's woodshake roof, the orderly arrangement
of the dug well, the woman's clotheslines, back-stoop washtubs,
the entire thrifty, hard-worked place.

Ned lay on his stomach on the ridge, looking for the man of the place. He began to get nervous when he did not see him. It was pretty quiet down there.

Then Ned heard something. It was a familiar sound: in the suddenly quiet lulling of the wind, he could distinguish the rhythmic thud and bite and thump of someone digging. He located the sound as coming from past the cabin, hidden from him by that structure.

Ned could see no dog, nor was there a sign of movement of wild bird which would indicate the man might be working in the creek timber out of sight, nor was there sound of ax, harness chain, snort of horse, anything to locate another worker than the digger beyond the cabin.

Gambles in their sum made up the tablestakes of life, a fact well admitted by Ned Huddleston. He left the ridge, went straight across the clearing to the cabin, drifting with the speed and ease of a smoke puff. Shadowing along the front wall of the place, he came to the growth of weedy flowers, edged by creek stones, which ornamented the unpainted boards of the front corner. Flattening himself against the wall, he peered around the corner. Starting to pull back instantly, he stopped, held by the sight which met his narrowed glance. He straightened after a long moment and stepped silently into the open.

The woman did not see him. Neither did the yellow-haired child, nor the ragged small-breed mongrel which the child held in her arms, and upon whose burr-caught, shaggy coat her tears fell. The woman did not cry. Likely she had already done that. Now she dug the wet heavy ground outlining the oblong hole which alone told the watching stranger his ear had not deceived him. That was a grave the woman was trying to grub out, and now Ned knew where the man was, and why that clearing and its pretty bottom acres lay so drippingly still that late May morning. *Thunk, thud; thunk, thud;* how many graves in wet heavy earth had Ned Huddleston heard being dug? A hundred, a thousand? The good Lord alone would remember. Ned didn't want to. He went toward the woman and the little girl and the mongrel dog, stopping far enough for them to still be undiscovered.

"Missus," said the Negro youth softly.

The woman straightened, and he could read fear in every tensing line of her. The child turned full around, unthinkingly, with a child's trusting quickness. The dog, seeing the dark-faced scarecrow, thin and stark against the winnowing rain, uttered one squall of defiant terror and vanished under the cabin's raised-sill flooring.

"Missus," repeated Ned quietly, "please don't be afeered. I wouldn't harm no human creature what needs he'p. Honest to Jesus, lady."

He came to the graveside. The child darted to her mother. The woman turned slowly, sheltering the child. Ned halted an arm's length away from them. The gallant dog, steeled by the emergency, charged headlong from beneath the cabin. Ned put his thumbs in his ears, bent to the ground, his brown face nearly on a level with the courageous mongrel's. Fluttering his long fingers, the ex-slave emitted an explosively perfect imitation of an enraged tomcat, complete with hissing spit, into the astounded cur's face. The animal screeched wildly, reversed itself in mid-attack, again disappeared beneath the cabin floor.

The little girl laughed outright.

The weary mother smiled for the first time in forty-eight hours. Ned straightened. Gently he took the shovel from her.

"Missus," he murmured, "I done this a hunderd thousand times. You go along and get your man ready. He's in there, I reckon."

He nodded toward the house, and the woman returned his nod. She stood a moment, watching him.

Ned was not a reassuring thing to see. He was literally in rags. He had no shoes. Thorn cuts and grass rot and water fester disfigured his feet. Every bone in his body was visible. His hair, unshorn since Appomattox, grew wildly away from his head, rain plastered, mud caked, shoulder long. It was straight hair, but it was thick and black and coarse, maning his bony skull with an unbelievably ferocious look. Ned knew this. He had seen himself in every clear-watered stream of the journey. And he could see the woman growing pale.

"Lady," he told her, "I am Ned Huddleston. I am a free man. Please leave me he'p you. You and the little one."

The woman shook her head, afraid, confused.

"I know how I look, Missus," Ned said. "But I seen only hard times since the war. I was raised decent; I've knowed better; my folks was quality."

"Mama," said the girl, squinting up at Ned, "I'll watch him for you. You go along in, like he said."

"Hush," said the mother. "Be still, Belinda!"

Her voice rose, and Ned smiled and reached out his hand toward the little girl. After a moment of shyness, she smiled back and put her small hand in his gaunt pink palm.

"Suffer the little child to lead you, Missus," Ned said, and seized the shovel hard, and began to dig.

"Lordy, Mama," said the little girl. "Lookit that mud fly!"

The mother nodded and turned for the house. Times came when people had to trust one another. Even lone white widows and savage-looking tramp Negro men.

In the house, she glanced back secretively from the lone window of the bedroom alcove. Belinda was laughing and chattering noisily as a redwing reedbird. The young stranger was bending the haft of the shovel, flinging the dirt, and at his feet, helping him dig, was Hannibal, the ragged mongrel.

The woman uttered a dry, racking sob. She sat down on the bed beside her dead husband and began to cry for the first time in the two days of loneliness and fright.

# 9.

Thetch was the neighbor's name. He lived over the ridge from the widow's place, and Ned could tell the next day, when Thetch drove up in his ramshackle buckboard, that the widow more than disliked the man, she feared him. As he watched from the horse shed where he had slept the night, and where the widow had asked him to hide when she spotted Thetch's rig, Ned decided that he didn't care for the neighbor either.

It was a bright morning, clearing after the hard rains. Everything sparkled with sun and water drops. Ned, refreshed by the warm dry night's rest and by the supper and breakfast fed him by the grateful woman, had believed things were turning his way. But now there was the narrow-eyed man on the seat of the buckboard, small-talking the uneasy widow while his ferret's glance ran over the place. And Ned could tell by the way that Thetch kept darting his eyes from the new grave to the new widow that there would be trouble. Thetch was that kind of scrub-stud. A bachelor because he had neither the earning ability nor the strength of spirit to keep a woman, he would prowl the mates of other men like a stray dog. Ned had known his kind, dark-skinned and light. Thetch was already thinking of how to come at that poor woman. He said so with every new-sneaked look at her, and between his words he was leering at her over there by the back stoop.

Presently, though, the neighbor clucked to his team of mustangs. Evidently his hints for a cup of coffee, as well as his sanctimonious offers to see to the plowing of the bottom field, get in the stovewood, round up the milch cow, had been politely declined. Also, the widow appeared to have successfully covered up the fact that she had had help with burying her husband. For in all the time Thetch stalled at the back stoop he never once looked toward the horse shed—the only place other than the cabin where a man might possibly be waiting under cover for the neighbor to leave.

It was Belinda, with blue eyes and happy smile, who, as Thetch gathered the reins, could not suppress the secret. She had been cautioned by her mother to say nothing to the neighbor of the new "hand." But Belinda was only four.

"Mister Thetch," she said, "we got a new friend. His name is Ned, and he can dig better than a badger."

"Oh?" said Thetch, eying the mother and letting the reins go slack. "Ned, eh? There's no Ned around here."

"A boy, just a boy on the drift," said the woman. "Came along yesterday. Helped us bury Tom."

"Where's he now?"

"Gone along I suppose. I fed him, told him he could sleep the night in the shed. I got lots to do, Mr. Thetch."

"Sure you have." Thetch just said it and kept watching her.

He reached under the seat of the buckboard. His hand reappeared wrapped about the breech of a sawed-off 12-gauge shotgun. "Boy," he called, without moving to look toward the horse shed, "come on out here."

Ned knew it was no more use then, and he came from the shed to the back stoop and stood where Thetch could see him. The neighbor's pale eyes flicked to the widow.

"A *nigger* boy," he said, and said it in a way, and with a look, that left the widow no decent answer.

"Mr. Thetch," she said, flushing deeply, "you get off my land and you stay off of it."

"Sure, sure I will," nodded Thetch. He swung the shotgun to cover Ned. "And I'll just take this nigger boy of yours along with me. Get in, boy."

Ned shook his head. "I ain't going with you, Mister," he said. "You going to shoot me, you do it right here."

"Why, boy," grinned Thetch, "whatever are you talking about? I was only meaning to give you a lift on into town, seeings you'd lost your way from the main road, and all."

"I may have lost my way," replied Ned evenly, "but I ain't lost my mind, Mister. I ain't a'going with you."

"Oh," said Thetch in that soft bad way he had. "A smart nigger, eh?"

"No, suh," insisted Ned soberly. "Just not crazy."

Thetch nodded and cocked both barrels of the shotgun. But the widow moved into his line of fire, her gaunt face set hard. She was pretty in a faded way, and Ned guessed she was even young. There was still a certain grace and vigor when she moved. But homesteading lost years and youth faster than any life but foraging. The woman was determined, however, even if very much afraid, and Ned understood that was what men called bravery in war. What it was in a woman he didn't know, but it made his heart beat and his pride rise.

"Mr. Thetch," she said, "if you don't leave my land, I am going to the sheriff in Fort Worth and swear out a warrant for your arrest."

Thetch was interested. "Oh?" he said. "And what for?"

"For molesting a woman, Mr. Thetch; a good woman, and a lone-dwelling widow of a good man, one day past the burying."

"Missus," said Ned, "please don't push for me. I will get along right now. I'll just cut acrost the field into the bresh. No trouble, please now, Missus. I owes you."

"No," said the woman, unflinching. "It's Mr. Thetch that's going. And right now. And he knows it."

Thetch did indeed know it.

The times and temper of the frontier did not take kindly to the bothering of decent women—especially widows or others who lived alone.

"You've took me wrong," he said. "Women always take me wrong."

"Maybe that's because you are wrong," said the woman.

Thetch nodded, turned to stare at Ned. "Nigger boy," he said, "you better be gone when I come back. I mean to see no harm comes to this good lady and her tot. I don't like you hanging around. You're too growed. Get scarce whiles you've the chance. Ma'am," he said, touching his hat brim, "I'll drop by when you're feeling better. Good day to you."

The widow did not answer him, only stood watching as the buckboard climbed the ridge.

"That's a bad man, Missus," said Ned in the stillness. "He'll be back. Ain't you no kin in the town?"

The woman seemed puzzled. "Kin?" she murmured.

"Yes'm, kin," answered Ned earnestly. "You know, folks you can go and stay with for a spell. Or maybe who can come out and stay with you."

"Oh," she said. "No, we haven't anybody."

Belinda, too long ignored, reached for the ex-slave's calloused, clawlike hand. She smiled up at him, her eyes deep with the reflected blue of the rain-washed sky.

"We got Ned, mama," she said to the prairie woman.

"Child, child," said Ned softly, and pressed fiercely her small pink hand in his.

The woman, too, was affected. But she knew, as Ned knew, that the Negro youth could not stay now. It was not that she heeded the mean, wicked minds of others like neighbor Thetch, but Thetch would spread the word of a rag-tag colored drifter in the area, and that could bring nothing but suspicion and trouble to this bone-thin, gentle and deep-voiced Negro boy who said he was sixteen, yet in whose eyes and face were the marks of a hundred years and more. She did not want harm to come to the half-starved wanderer who had appeared in the hour of her need, and whom she had trusted because of Belinda's smile and hand-clasp of acceptance. So she nodded now to Ned, and their eyes met, and Ned murmured, "Bless you, Missus," and they understood one another and also what was owing and what was not.

It ended with Ned setting out for Fort Worth in clean work clothes and decent shoes which had been the husband's. Also he bore with him four dollars in silver coins, an insistence of the widow's, and a small strap trunk of fresh socks and underdrawers to furnish that "quality" so needed for his journey.

He even was given the loan as far as town of the husband's stock pony, the animal and its furnishings to be left at the Mercantile Livery in Fort Worth. It was as high as Ned Huddleston had been on the ladder of good luck.

# 10.

Had there ever been a day like this one? The youthful horseman thought there might have been, maybe, back in the years when he had run the rocky Ozark hills wild as any razorback weanling. But in the times he remembered no sun had shone as warm as this one, no breeze smelled as sweet, no bird song compared with that now bursting from meadow and thicket beside the Fort Worth road. Jesus God, thought Ned, and yesterday morning at this time he was shaking in the rain like a distempered dog, looking down on this same road planning to rob or break in in order just to stay alive and get on west where the work was.

He looked down at himself astride Tom Shucart's good horse and stout calf-roper's saddle. Didn't those buckhide workshoes shine almost like white man's dance-pump leather? Didn't that silver money jingle nice? Wasn't Old Ned Huddleston something to see that day?

Or was he? A shadow crossed the youth's face. It was only a morning's ride into the city, but Ned suddenly was overtaken by the instincts of his trade. Something was wrong. He began thinking about the sheriff and wandering Negroes and maybe about trouble spread ahead of him by Thetch. In the end he pulled the brown gelding off the stage road's ruts and camped in some rocky brush atop a ridge north of town. Here he spent the day watching the road for any sign of Thetch or a group of riders heading toward Fossu Creek that might be a posse sent to check up on a roaming ex-slave.

But in all of the long day he saw nothing suspicious.

The next morning he felt better after a night's sleep on the ridge—he always felt better for a stay out under the stars—and saddling the gelding, he rode on down to the stage road. Within the hour he was jogging down the main street of Fort Worth looking sharp-out for the Mercantile Livery. He never found it. Instead, when he turned into a hitchrail near the center of town to inquire about the stable's location, he found himself surrounded by three heavily armed deputy sheriffs and a crowd of citizens.

All too late he saw Thetch in the forefront of the group backing the officers.

Ned knew something was wrong, but he could not flee, and would not if he could. Those deputies would gun him down right there. He knew that from the snatches of the crowd's talk he heard and the sound of Thetch's mean voice knifing through the growing uproar.

"Don't try nothing," one of the deputies warned. "Get off that stole horse easy and slow."

Ned got down. "Ain't no stole hoss, suh," he said. "The Missus out to the Fossu Creek place loaned him to me to get inter town with. I'm supposed ter leave him at some livery called the Mercantile."

"Sure," said the second deputy. "The Missus gave you them clothes of Tom Shucart's, too, I reckon—and that suitcase."

"Them are Tom's shoes he's awearing!" declared one of the citizens, pointing suddenly. "Tom bought them from me only last month."

"You ought to know, Mr. Ames," nodded the third deputy. "Nigger, don't move no more."

[ 31 ]

Ned had been stepping around nervously, badly frightened, looking for a place to run and seeing nothing but the closing trap of sunburned faces around him.

He put his hands up over his head without being told.

"That's him," said Thetch, with strident certainty. "The same as I described him to you. Poor, poor Mrs. Shucart—"

"Yeah!" shouted one of the men. "What are we waiting for? He's got Tom's horse, his clothes, his shoes, his grip; and there's that poor widdy woman alaying in her own blood and—"

"God Amighty!" breathed Ned. "You saying something's done happened to the Missus? You meaning I done something to her?"

"Get a rope!" yelled someone in the back.

"Hell," said a raw-boned giant getting down from a freight wagon parked nearby, "he'd ought to be hoss-whupt fust." The main group fell away to let the teamster in. He coiled a ten-foot blacksnake whip with split-end Mexican poppers and then lashed it too quickly for the eye to follow, snaring Ned's feet and pulling him down into the gutter. In the instant the teamster was growling like an animal and cutting him with the rawhide thong. Two of the deputies, looking over the crowd, saw a tall man come striding up the boardwalk. At once they moved in on the teamster and drove him back from the fallen Negro.

The third deputy made a play of waving the crowd back with his shotgun. "Morning, Sheriff," he greeted the tall man. "Here's your renegade nigger. He rode right into town cool as grass dew. Thetch says it's him for certain." The sheriff looked down at Ned, then around at the growing crowd, paying no heed to the deputy.

"Who whipped this boy?" he said into the hush which had fallen. "I want the man who whipped this boy," he repeated. "Right now."

The huge teamster sneered and stepped forward. "You got him, Sheriff," he grated. "What you aim to do with him?"

"Get a rope, get a rope!" insisted a high voice from the rear. "Hell, we ain't trying no nigger-whipper here. That poor woman's dead and worse! What do you say, boys?"

There was a scattered shout and the surge of the crowd returned, closing on the sheriff.

The latter wore a frock coat. From beneath it there appeared a long-barreled United States Army Colt. The weapon flashed in

the morning sun, its blued-steel barrel bouncing off the forehead
of the hulking teamster. The man fell like a topped pine, slowly
and with a visible rebound, into the gutter beside Ned Huddleston. "Bring him along," the sheriff said to the deputies. "And
break up this crowd. Thetch," he ordered, "come down to the
jail." He reached for Ned's hand and helped the youth to his
feet. "You all right, boy?" he asked, and when Ned nodded that
he was, he said to him, low-voiced, "All right, move right on
ahead of me and don't drag your feet. Nobody'll harm you."

Nor did anyone. The people of that town knew their sheriff,
just as they knew his deputies. Ned was brought safely to the
jail and lodged in a cell. Thetch, questioned by the sheriff, told a
story to chill any vagrant Negro's blood: the widow Shucart had
been found by Thetch only that past dawn, beaten bloody and
her clothing torn off. It was her night clothing, and the "nigger
boy" that Thetch had warned to leave before he returned was
gone. The widow was unconscious, likely dying, if not already
dead. The little girl had slept through the assault, could tell
nothing of its dark secret. But what more proof could be wanting? There was the nigger with Shucart's horse and all. And
there was the widow all-over blood, her night things hoisted and
ripped and, well, God, it made a man sick even to talk about
it.

It made Ned sick, also—sick to his soul. The Negro youth
knew how it had to have happened. He could see the evil Thetch
returning to that quiet house in the valley in the dark of the pre-
dawn. He could almost say what smothering and throat-barring
and violating had been done; the only thing he could not see was
how the poor woman was left alive.

When Thetch had concluded his report of the crime, the sheriff went into another room seeking records and handbills of
wanted Negroes in Texas. Thetch, watching through the partly
opened door, saw he was thus occupied. He arose and glided to
the bars of Ned's cell and said in his thick voice, "I told you I'd
be back, nigger boy," and that was all. When the sherff returned, Thetch was again seated by his desk, innocent as
skimmed milk. But Ned Huddleston's dark eyes never left his
narrow wicked face. And when Thetch was told he might go, the
gaunt Negro youth called softly to him, "Mr. Thetch, I'll be back,
too."

Thetch laughed and made a foul remark, but he went out quickly and Ned knew he had frightened him. He had meant to.

Before that moment Ned was almost beaten. He had given up. There was nothing important about trying to fight his black man's luck. The noose waited for Squire Huddleston's boy, whether from a court of law or by those people on the street yelping for the rope. What more heart or spirit could he show? What was his life worth anyway? He had been beaten, shot at, whipped and stomped a hundred times. There just came a time when a man stopped running and stood and waited for the dogs to catch up.

Hearing Thetch's story to the sheriff had brought Ned to bay; it had bled him out. But Thetch had made the mistake of his life in sneaking to the bars of Ned's cell and crowing that he had come back to the widow's place. Ned knew then that his instinct concerning the cold-eyed neighbor had been true. And, knowing this, he had his reason *not* to die.

# *11.*

As a forager Ned had learned that the greatest article of war in man's armory was the knife. Like the Indian of the American plains or his own black ancestor of the African veldt, the ex-slave understood that no man must allow himself to be taken in the field without a trusted blade.

In this way, although he was patently unarmed when captured, the same weapon was on his person that he had carried from First Manassas to Petersburg and beyond. It had not been found in the jail search because, hours before, in the camp on the starlit ridge, Ned had dismantled it. He had unscrewed its odd brass haft-cap and hung it on a frayed string about his neck where all good whites could see that it represented nothing more sinister than the sort of voodoo trash the "nigras" were forever fashioning to ward off evil or attract good. The incredibly thin blade and its tempered haft-tang—the work of Villalobos in Old Spain, stolen from a dead Union colonel of cavalry in the powder smoke of Bull Run—he had secreted in the heavy sole of his shoe, slitting the leather the long way and inserting the blade from the arch to the toe, easily possible due to the size of Tom Shucart's feet. The leather washers which had formed the haft itself had been slipped off the tang and crammed into the toes of the shoes. It was the sort of survival art that only war can sharpen in a man, and Ned had been four years sharpened.

The Villalobos blade was thus reassembled only minutes after the darkness of night had come to the cellblock. The other item of Ned's desperate scheme required much more time, and time was what the gaunt youth had least of.

As yet there was no yowling torchlight mob in front of the jail demanding the rights of the honest residents to the black devil's life. But worried townsmen of some remaining decency had come in an unbroken if furtive stream to warn the sheriff that such a mob was collecting at a dozen saloons. The prisoner had also heard that little Belinda Shucart was safe in town with the wife of the Mercantile Livery's owner. At the news, the thin youth's lips moved thankfully.

Watching constantly for the deputy from the outer office, Ned's dark fingers fastened the strips of his clean underdrawers into a braided noose. When he knew, by ear—which could "see" better than most eyes—that the deputy was momentarily alone, he fastened the makeshift cord to the bars of his high cell window and hung himself with a muffled sound of strangulation only loud and convincing enough to bring the deputy running. The latter, seeing only that his prisoner had hung himself and thinking of the citizens' fury at being so cheated, did precisely what he had been ordered not to do under any circumstances—he entered the prisoner's cell.

When he laid hands to Ned's bony form to free it from the noose, he found suddenly that the noose was about his own neck and so tightened that he could not utter even a gasp for help. Then came the point of a gleaming Spanish knife held to his lower belly with the soft words, "You maken a sound, white man, and I cut you open to your eyeteeth." The deputy could only nod weakly, and Ned let him suck one sobbing breath of life back into his tortured lungs. With that, he struck the man with the bone of his forearm beneath the base of the skull. The deputy slumped and fell unconscious.

Ned took the fellow's gun, cartridge belt, boots, spotted calfskin vest, and wide Texas hat. Donning the articles, he bound and gagged the deputy, rolled him face-down in the cell's lone bunk, and threw the gray jail blanket over him. Locking the cell behind him, he went into the outer office and peered out from an edge of the drawn window shade. The night traffic was light. Suppertime was just past; and with the twilight lingering, not yet full dark. Before the jail, head drooping, hipshot, hopefully full of oats and not watered of recent, stood the deputy's saddled steeldust mare.

Ned's dark eye gleamed when he saw the animal. She was a blood horse. She would run.

Drawing the deputy's big hat low in front, Ned waited for the walk immediately in front of the jail to be clear. When it was, he stepped out into the yellow light of the street lamp, walked directly to the steeldust, swung to her back, and turned her out into the rutted mud of the street. He did not put her to the lope, or even the trot. She had a swift singlefoot and he let her take that gait southward, away from Fort Worth and from the Fossu Creek country where tragedy had stalked the farm of Tom Shucart.

If, once free of the lights of the city, the steeldust mare was heeled about to circle back to the brushy ridges of the Fossu Crossing, no man ever discovered. But in the cold morning light of the day following Ned's historic lone breakout from the Fort Worth jail, Thetch's team of mustangs was found grazing in harness along the stage road near the ford. Thetch was in the driver's seat, his throat cut ear to ear.

# 12.

Ned, with the fox's cunning, kept to the main track. It was
night and he had a start. They could not track him until daylight, and then they would have their problems: they were just
white lawmen and he was Ned Huddleston. He could see them
quartering all that sageland southwest of town trying to cut a
trackline that wasn't there. The morning, anyway, would be frit-
tered away before somebody would think to check the stage road
itself. By that time, Ned would indeed be into the brush, but far,
far away. The posse could ride its whang-leather ponies down
to their hockjoints, and likely would; they still weren't going to
head Ned Huddleston. Not if the steeldust mare stayed sound
and her rider kept his wits about him and slept light.

The instincts of both the hunter and the hunted had been
refined in him by the cruel years of war, and they would not
betray him now. "Keep west, keep west," the voice inside him
kept repeating. "Ride out, ride out," it said. And he nodded and
held the mare steady and stayed with the stage road through the
silent starlight hours.

Ned Huddleston, fleeing south and westward for his life, could
not have imagined the true nature of the haven he sought. He
could not possibly know that he was heading for what the
Texans and their Mexican fellows called *Comancheria,* the land
of the "Enemy People." There was no way he might have understood the real bounds of that vast uplift of semi-arid grassland:
the Red River on the north, Rio Pecos to the west, ramparts of
Fort Worth to the east, headwaters of the Nueces and forks of the
Colorado on the south. Nor could he at that time have named a
single one of the seven main Comanche tribal families occupying
the vast *llano* toward which his natural impulses now drove him.
Yamparika, Kotsoteka, Kwahadi, Tanima, Tenawa Nokoni and
Peneteka would have sounded to him like juju talk. He was

simply a frightened creature running in the darkness away from danger.

That Fort Worth was the major outpost of the middle prairies was information as alien to Ned as to some denizen of the moon. He only felt that beyond Fort Worth began what the native Comanches called *pohoi*, "the wild sage." He only felt that out there the wind was king, the wild horse ran free, some other man than the white man made the laws. And feeling these truths, he *knew* that westward lay the land where a man might disappear—providing he could escape into it.

So, well before first light streaked the east he veered the mare into the trackless tawny sea of the buffalo grass, away from the traveled road, up into a lonely cluster of rocks where nothing larger than a coyote might approach unseen; there, weary, he made camp.

He was satisfied, certain that it was a good beginning. One more ride like the one just made and he would be west enough from Fort Worth.

# 13.

But Ned had miscalculated. He had told himself that no white lawman was going to track Ned Huddleston through the night. He was right, and he was near-dead wrong; no white man did track him through the night: it was a Lipan Apache named Limp Nose who led the Fort Worth posse under the glow of a "Comanche" moon to the foot of the fugitive's rocky lair.

When the whistling snorts and whinnies of the steeldust mare awakened Ned, the morning sky was still the clear green of dawn pinkened only faintly in the east. But if Ned had much to learn of Texas posses and Apache trailers, he knew all there was to know of horses. The mare's edgy whickering spoke to him in a language which he knew better than English. She was smelling other horses. And where there were other horses at that hour, in such a lonely place so far from the main stage road, there would be men on those other horses. And those men would not be friends.

Ned pulled the deputy's Henry Carbine from his blanket; snaking to an opening in the surrounding boulders he peered below.

He saw at the glance that he was surrounded. A posseman was posted, rifle barrel aglint in the coming sunlight, to close off every avenue of possible descent from the rise where Ned now crouched—with the one exception of a hogback ridge which ran from his vantage toward what he now realized was the stage road he thought he had left so far behind the night before. And that hogback was not passable to a horse. The posse, bred and born in horse country, understood the meaning of that—and so did Ned. A man afoot in horse country is a man dead.

Ned Huddleston wondered bitterly whether the posse had only been running down that cursed stage road on blind chance, and by even blinder chance had stumbled across his trackline leaving that road. And had that road, looping so sharply back upon itself past where Ned had left it, thus brought the posse, as it did its own treacherous course, to within a few hundred yards of Ned's fortress?

These painful questions were no sooner asked than denied. Off beyond the circle of rock and jack oak-sheltered riflemen, just exactly out of long-aiming range, a group of possemen were building a breakfast fire at the picket line of the posse's horses. In that group Ned's keen eye at once pounced upon the tall middle-aged sheriff who had saved him from the Fort Worth gutter, and next to him stood a man who seemed so small that Ned at first believed him to be a boy. But as the rising sun's light stabbed into the picket-line camp and fell upon the dwarfed figure, Ned knew that neither blindfolded luck nor the loopings of the stage road had betrayed him. That little man was not a white man and not a lawman. He was a red Indian; a native scout who could run a trail like a wolf, by sight or scent, by day or dark, and now Ned knew where he was and where he was apt to be before the long day was done.

[39]

Where he was, was trapped; where he was apt to be, come sundown, was shot to pieces, or strung up from the nearest cottonwood.

Ned poked the short blued-steel snout of the deputy's saddle-gun out of the opening in the boulders. Come on, he thought, come on. By God, we will see who dies the hardest. The sun must have winked from the slight movement of the weapon's barrel, for immediately he could see the Indian gesture to the sheriff and point up toward him. Even at the considerable distance, he felt as though the tiny red man were staring him straight in the eye. Ned didn't like that. For some reason it made him more uneasy than the sheriff and all of his men.

But now the sheriff was getting on his mount and riding toward the slope. He rode right on through the ring of his riflemen, halting only when he was far enough up the slope to be heard by anyone hiding at its crest.

"Huddleston," he called, "surrender and you will be taken back for fair trial. That's my word to you."

Ned could have killed him with a squeeze of the trigger. The thought stood in his mind, but he brushed it away. The tall lawman had been fair to him. He had not once called him nigger, he had not roughed him either by hand or tongue; he had only done his job. He could not help it if it was a bad job, or if circumstances made him believe that he was chasing a bad colored man.

"Sheriff, you was decent to me," he called back. "So don't come up here. You stay back. You let them nigger-whippers come up here. I thank you, Sheriff, and that's my last word on it, suh."

It was his last word, too. All efforts to engage him further were in vain. Finally, the sheriff told him that the Widow Shucart was somewhat better. The doctor had said she would likely live now, and could talk before long. If Ned's story had been straight and the widow would back it up, then he had nothing to worry about. The sheriff himself guaranteed dropping the other charges, such as Ned's assault on the deputy. It certainly was a gamble, but it was a sight better one than if Ned chose to turn it down and stay up there in the rocks.

However, there was only an echoing silence from the ridge in answer to the lawman's proposal. What passed in Ned Huddleston's mind in those moments he was never to confide. Did he know of some other charge of which the honest sheriff was not yet aware? Something that would cut the heart from all the lawman's well-intentioned guarantees? Or was it simply that his faith in the white community was too shattered to permit him to make a good judgment of the amnesty offer?

Whichever it was, Ned hesitated and was lost. The sheriff turned back through his rifle lines, ordering the siege to begin. As the posse fire commenced and the hidden riflemen scuttled and ducked from cover to cover, advancing their stations up toward the cornered Negro youth, Ned clenched his teeth and cheeked his own weapon.

"Come on, come on!" he repeated fiercely.

But he said it like he was praying it, and it was not clear whether he was courting or defying death.

But the possemen were convinced very quickly. Within twenty minutes, two of them had been shot by the dark marksman above, three others cut and scraped by flying rock chips and wood splinters from near-misses of what appeared to be deliberate head shots. The wounded men were bleeding profusely but not mortally. Ned had made his point. In the heat of high noon, the sheriff ordered the men back into safer cover. A strategy meeting was called at the picket line and a decision was made to simply hold the fugitive up there until lack of water drove him down. There was no hurry. The posse had all the time in the world, and all the water it needed flowed in the tree-bordered Brazos not a mile off. Near to hand was plenty of jack oak shade, a prairie full of mesquite roots and cow chips for fire fuel. The question was purely one of how fast the doomed man would dry out.

"In this heat," said the tall sheriff, "two days."

On his blazing hilltop Ned agreed to the estimate. He had no shade save the sundial shadows of the boulders themselves. And worse, in the last fusillade of rifle bullets sent upward by the frustrated posse, a whining ricochet had struck the steeldust mare below her left ear, killing her instantly. Before that, Ned had been able, far back in his mind, to think about the last ditch of the doomed—the flying dash at full gallop down the slope when darkness fell, riding the hundred-to-one hope that the answering

[41]

fire of the possemen would miraculously miss his mount and himself, letting them through to run for the river—and that one more day on the trail toward the west and freedom.

Now the trim and gentle animal lay lifeless in the sun, her flanks already green with the crust of blowflies. With her lay Ned's hopes. He was afoot, surrounded, with no water, and almost out of ammunition. A mile away was a river full of water, and a blessing of cool green shade. And beyond that river was a land where a man might roam and hide forever. One mile. Three minutes on a good horse, less than that on a racer like the steeldust mare. It nearly made him put the muzzle of the Colt to his own head. That would stop the thirst, and bring the cool water and the bosky trees so easy, so fast. It would be so simple. But Ned had one more question to ask, one more answer to wait on.

"Lord Gawd," he said aloud, and looking upward, "is you still with me?"

When he lowered his glance, it fell upon the distant dust-thread of the stage road. A column of red-dirt haze was moving toward him from the east across the cut in the rocks of his ridge, which let the road pass on to the river. And suddenly Ned knew that he was not forsaken.

He blinked away the sweat-sting from his eyes, crinkled his gaunt face to its first grin since Fort Worth.

"Lord," he said, "you surely do put wild things in the mind of this here heathen child."

# 14.

A pair of turkey buzzards were already wheeling above the ridge, drawn by the dead horse. As though to further Ned's cause, they ceased their preliminary sweeping of the ridge itself to settle in the familiar swinging circle directly over the fugitive's hideout.

"Amen, amen," muttered Ned, noting the dark birds, and went swiftly to work.

He knew from sun flashing off the lenses that the posse had at least one set of field glasses, and that one of the possemen was posted at all times to scan the ridge with the glasses. Moreover, there was that runted Indian who could evidently see better without glasses than his white companions could with them. It followed that Ned must be extremely smart. "Old black fox," he said to himself, "you got to beat a redbone Injun hound, plus a pack of Texas hunters what can ride and shoot plumb deadly. Providing you learned your work in the war, though, they'll find they ain't running no spring-whelped cub."

It was Ned's habit to talk to himself. Since the death of Snakehead at Second Manassas, he had not had a friend, black or white—had not dared, nor cared to have one. "Friends," Snakehead had told him, "is something you is better off without, happen you is a nigger." In the lean years since, Ned had remembered that gloomy advice, but he was not the same in heart as Snakehead.

Ned had it inside of him to admit it was warm when the sun was out. The war had only built a high wall around his native impulse to befriend. So if simple survival demanded he ride or creep or walk alone, he did the next best thing; he became his own friend, and learned to talk all the while to Ned Huddleston, especially when in bad trouble, as now.

In this same safe circle of friends, he included God, earth, sky, rock, river, any inanimate object that was around, and always, of course, the animals, birds and fishes, who would not betray him either.

So he talked to the buzzards, the dead mare, the oncoming stagecoach, the road, the river, whatever his restless eye fell upon during the desperate minutes to follow; and as he talked, his hands and lean body moved with an art and skill guided by one idea, one determination—to go free.

From pulled tussocks of the tough bunchgrass growing in the ridge's spine, he made a dummy. Upon the base of grass and torn blanket, he put his shirt and the deputy's spotted vest and tall white hat. He needed only the upper body of his grass-filled Ned Huddleston, and that he molded to lie as though crouched behind the dead mare with the muzzle of the saddlegun pointing down at the distant picket line of the posse. One moment the figure was not there, the next it was. And that was the chancy part of it. How long would those possemen wait, once they saw their man lying still behind the mare? Ned knew that they would sight from below only a narrow boulder-notch view of his bait. But it was enough for them to find and to study for motion. How quickly *would* they find it, and how long would they delay before understanding the silent circle of the buzzards and coming up through the rocks to get the flyblown body of their bad nigger? This was a question Ned could not wait to answer.

He grinned at the dummy, and said, "I got me a stage to catch, going west."

And he had. Naked but for workboots and trousers, Ned wriggled, slid and scuttled his way down the bouldered crest of the ridge, straight toward the vertical cut of the stage road. The Lipan Apache trailer, Limp Nose, saw him halfway along the route and, next instant, he was picked up in the field glass of the posse lookout. The gamble was not one of deception now. It was Ned's estimate of his own speed down the ridge, against the incoming pace of the coach. Both lines of motion must meet at the gap. If Ned was one gasp late, the coach would pass by, and he would be caught at the edge of the drop-off with no possible chance to regain the higher rocks. Half-naked, thick-throated with thirst, unarmed save for an almost empty Colt's revolver, he could leap to the hardpan of the road and break a leg or let the posse, already mounting behind him, run him down through the brush on foot like a crippled coyote. The end would be the same—a bullet in the back or through the head.

But his guess was good, and he did not miss his ticket westward. He was there when the stage was there; in his leap downward fifteen feet to the swaying topside luggage rack of the Concord he broke no limbs, but only some baggage of the passengers within. Before either shotgun rider or driver could react to the heavy thump of his landing behind them, he had struck the first on the back of the head with the Colt's barrel, slumping him unconscious in his seat; he then jammed the weapon's muzzle into the astonished driver's spine.

"Keep 'em loping like you got them, suh," said Ned Huddleston. "Only a little bit more so. We is running late."

The stager lashed up his teams. He was not paid to argue with highwaymen. Nor did his western caution of the breed encourage him to take any liberties with a specimen who would jump fifteen feet from the rocks of Brazos Gap just to get a free ride across the river.

"You just paid your fare," he said. "You can pull that cannon out of my kidneys any time you care to."

Ned eased the muzzle away. "Don't look back," he said.

"I ain't the curious kind," answered the driver, and shook up his teams again.

As they rolled, Ned stripped the other rider of his coat and hat, donning them quickly himself. The exit of the gap was still a hundred yards ahead when he kicked the guard's unconscious body off into a passing brush clump and slid into his vacated seat, the shotgun cocked and ready in his dark hands.

"What's this here job pay?" he said to the driver.

The latter looked at him for the first time, and shook his head. "Company don't hire no niggers," he said.

"Pshaw!" said Ned. "You noticed."

The driver glanced at him quickly. It was on his tongue to say something about smart niggers, but he did not; and he was glad when one of the passengers stuck his head out of the coach window to inquire what had thumped the roof and what in the name of God was going on up there, what with bodies falling off into the roadside scrub, posses riding up through the dust of the rear, and the coach's own four-horse hitch hitting out so fast for the river.

Ned leaned over the side and knuckled his brow respectfully, like any well-taught colored man.

"Good morning, suh," he said. "Fine day. Turned off a mite warm, though. You mind pulling your head back inside, suh, fore's I blows it off?"

The man was not a westerner and did not catch the flat sound of danger in the Negro youth's pleasant greeting. But he was gun-shy, and back into the window went his flushed face. "Thank you, suh," waved Ned. Then, quickly to the driver. "Slack off on your teams. Posse's took the bait."

Glancing back over his shoulder into the shadows of the gap, the driver saw the possemen loom up through the dust of the coach and halt about midway of the cut. This would place them about where the escaping prisoner would have come out if following the crest of the ridge. Ned, also looking back now, noted that some of the men were dismounting to beat out the scrub and rubble growth at the bases of the cut on both sides of the stage road. The tall sheriff directed this group. The remainder of the men rode on through the gap. For a nasty moment, Ned could not be sure what the orders for this bunch might be. Then, with a vast sigh, he saw that they were all doubling back up the near side of the ridge where they thought he might be hiding. In the same moment, he saw the tiny figure of the Lipan tracker loping down the decline of the ridge toward the edge of the cut. Ah! Ned thought, the little red runt had guessed him wrong; he had figured Old Ned would stay up top, that, being a black man, he would lack the innards to jump for the road, and would cower up there and surrender, begging.

Ned looked ahead to the river. Halfway left to go. Maybe two, three minutes at the speed they were making now. Then, the ford proving bedrock and smooth, as it appeared from the approaches, another minute or so to the far side, and two more to the bend of the road out of sight past the bottom trees. Five minutes, and the posse constantly falling behind. With every jingle of the trace-chains, every bobble of the whiffletrees. It was good doings, man; just about a miracle.

On the far side of the Brazos, past the trees, he had the stage halted. The driver, working at Ned's orders, cut the horses free of the harness and tied the three mounts in a line behind the horse Ned had selected to ride first relay upon.

The new shotgun rider meanwhile had requested the passengers to empty out their valuables and stuff them into a leather messenger's bag. The pouch was then slung to Ned's horse, and he was ready.

The picture of him pausing for the final moment, legs braced in the dust of the stage road as he strode out to see around the bend toward the crossing, was one the passengers remembered well.

Cross-belted low on his bony hips were the Colts of both driver and shotgun rider. In his left hand he carried the driver's Spencer carbine, its cartridge belt looped over one wide shoulder. He was breathing hard and hoarsely, for he still had had no water. The whites of his eyes showed wildly in their stabbing search of the ford, and the far side. His hair, which the Widow

Shucart had barbered for him with her dead husband's horse shears, was still long, and hung from his head in lank shags and tangles. His mouth sagged open, like a rabid dog's. Dried spittle flecked lips and chin. And the passengers, even when he turned his back to them, made no move.

In the stillness, all could hear the drumroll of the posse's hoofbeats coming up to the Brazos. The colored youth had only minutes to get away, yet when he returned from the bend and swung up on the lead horse of the string of four, he had time for a strange gesture which marked him all the miles of his outcast's odyssey.

Unfastening the leather messenger's pouch, he let it slide to the ground. In it was money, a lot of money, and the gold and diamond rings and watches which were more treasure than Ned Huddleston might ever dream to possess. But Ned did not want that kind of treasure, or any kind, from folks who had helped him.

As the pouch hit the ground he spurred the lead horse off. When the posse hammered up, he and the four mounts were already black dots against the red of the road and the glare of the westering sun. The tall sheriff watched after him a long, museful moment, then nodded his gray head.

"That about skins it out," he said. "Let's go home."

It was a forceful argument. A four-horse relay ridden by an animal master like the escaped Negro badman was not going to be run down that day, or the next week. The posse repaired the coach harness and placed some of their mounts into it, and passengers, possemen and stage driver started back over the Brazos and eastward along the Fort Worth road.

It was not until a rest halt some miles along that the Lipan tracker Limp Nose was missed.

"He'll show up," said the sheriff. "He's due five dollars for his work, and he'd murder his own mother for two bits. Let's get along."

"Mount up, boys," ordered his first deputy.

As the cavalcade continued strung out along the road, its riders could still see behind them the upthrust of the ridge marking the crossing of the Brazos. The first deputy, riding with the tall sheriff, looked back at the rocky crest, now dark against the sinking sun.

"Funny thing about that Injun," he said to the sheriff.

"How funny?"

"Well, back yonder at the ford he asked me if he could have the grub sack. You know, just to borrow it for a spell."

"That's uproarious, sure enough," said the dour sheriff.

"Naw, naw, that ain't what I mean. There wasn't any grub left in it; we'd cleaned it out back at noon-dinner on the picket line."

"He wanted an empty grub sack?" A slight frown creased the sheriff's weathered face.

"Yeah, ain't that funny?"

The sheriff gave the deputy a slow headshake. "Not if you know that Indian," he said.

"How so? It's still an empty grub sack, ain't it?"

The sheriff shook his head again. "It won't be," he said, "when he brings it back."

# 15.

As the day drew on, Ned began to search for a place to sleep. He had long since left the stage road, cutting across the prairies by way of recent cow or ancient buffalo trails, keeping along the high ground but off the ridgetops where he would be silhouetted. He had found water in a spring branch and drunk his fill cautiously, since no fox runs well with a belly of sloshing liquid. He had even shot a summer cottontail and broiled it over a small fire, made with mesquite twigs as dry as bone dust, which sent aloft no more smoke than a good cigar or pipe. Now ahead loomed a suitable elevation for the night's hole-up. It was the highlands of a drywash tipping northward to the Brazos drainage. As he climbed, he found dense brush, good jack oak timber, heavy sweet grass and a panoramic vista of his backtrail. There was, indeed, but one thing wrong with that lovely silent place;

looking back on the sweeping view of his trackline, perhaps four, or five miles down, a mounted figure toiled toward Ned's high nest.

The Negro youth watched the crawling dot for twenty minutes to be absolutely certain of its destination, its sure intent. The figure did not hesitate, did not turn aside. And Ned knew that this was no wandering cowboy, no chance rider going toward the sunset. This rider was following Ned Huddleston.

Ned checked the sky. Already it was going twilight green. The long early summer dusk would stay another hour, likely more, plenty of time to bring the mounted figure up to any camp made here. Ned weighed the advantages of making a run: he was fresh and strong, and he had four horses. But would that guarantee that another twilight at another camp would not show the same rider coming on? That dot moved like it was wound up with a clock key, crawling, crawling, crawling. It didn't seem to Ned that it would run down, or tick out.

"We'll stay," he said quietly to the waiting horses, and led them on up into the little overlook meadow he had selected for his first freedom camp.

# 16.

Ned lay on the flat slab of the rock overhang. Beneath his shelf lay the camp he had arranged for the man who should now be climbing from below along his trail. The fire was banked and sending up enough smoke to draw in half the Comanches east of the Pecos. His horses were staked out to graze in a normal manner. His bed spot was made under some spreading scrub growth to give shelter from night dew and wind. From where Ned crouched, he could just see his own new boots sticking out toward that banked fire, the toes turned out and upward the way a man on his back would turn them. To get to that bed spot and find out that those workboots had no black-and-pink feet inside of them, a man would have to pass beneath Ned's waiting place.

But the trouble was that no one appeared from below. It was night now. The silence stretched on eerily, but there was still no sign of a visitor. Ned had strained for a horseshoe clink against pebble, a stub of unshod hoof, a slipping of foot, a squeak of saddle-girth or scrape of leather, anything to tell of the passage of man and horse upward to his lair. Nothing. There had been no sound for the entire time Ned had crouched on the rock. He had seen the man come into the two-mile distant opening of the blufflands just as the last twilight failed, and seen him enter the upward-trending cleft of the trail, then lost sight of him because of the outward bulge of the bluffs above the prairie land below. But he had not been able to make out the identity of the figure so far off and in the very late light. So it had been wait and wait and wait—an hour now, for the simple climbing of a trail which Ned had ridden in half that span.

He thought of leaving the rock; of hollering into the night that he was a friend, and that any man who traveled that land was his friend. Come up, he heard himself inviting the unseen guest. I ain't going to harm you. All I want is to get along, to go free. You're welcome, whoever you are. Speak up, sing out, you're safe with Old Ned.

But he had seen men in the war. He knew that to give up to nerves like that was what weeded out the ones which would go home from the ones who would stay forever in the field.

He stayed on the rock.

The wind started up. He had stripped naked to use his pants to stuff into the workboots and to make sure his body pressed on that sun-warmed rock would not make a sound if he moved it even slightly while waiting. Now he began to shake with cold. A man's mind could torture him in a night watch like this. It was easy to think that minutes were half hours. Yet Ned was certain that yet another full hour passed before he saw it.

He never did hear it.

It was just that suddenly, between burning eyeblinks, there was a darker patch of the night standing in the throat of the blackness at the mouth of the trail's entrance to the tiny overlook meadow camp.

The animal fibers that were so incredibly tuned in Ned were

what warned him. It really was not even that he saw that darker darkness. He felt something over there. And so he began to watch it, and *then* he saw it move.

It came into the meadow's knee-deep carpet in two or three gliding steps; then it halted. Ned could see the form now, black against the gray of the bluffside. Its head turned slowly. It made the quarter-moon circle of the area beyond the banked fire which was the only place in the grassy camp a man might be sleeping under cover. Ned saw the head stop and hold steady on a line with those workboots. Then he saw the form bend and drift, making no sound over the grass, skirting the fire to get around to the bedding place without making a silhouette. And then Ned's dark lips lifted over his white teeth, and the cording muscles of his lean body gathered like springsteel. For Ned had been a few years cured in this art of the night; his reckoning of the stalk tallied dead-on—the intruder passed directly beneath the flat shelf of rock, and halted again.

He stood now between the glow of the fire and the line of Ned's vision. In his right hand was the bared knife, dull-gleaming. In his left hand he held an empty grub sack, suspended just over the grasstops. Ned felt his heart bump and the breath grow tight in his pinching nostrils. *The Indian.* It was the wizened native posse tracker. It was the little man with the mummy's wrinkled face and long black hair, his hide burned by sun and wind to the color of smoked leather, as dark, nearly, as Ned's. And he was watching Ned's empty workboots and pants' legs with a naked knife in his hand.

The Indian heard the scrape of Ned's pounce from the rock above, but he was not as quick as the Negro boy, nor nearly as strong. Ned attacked as a lion might, aiming for the nape of the neck, striking his foe a terrible blow with smashing hand between the shoulder blades.

The stroke should have separated the small man's spine, killing or paralyzing him. It did neither.

It blacked his mind for a few moments, long enough for Ned to pick him up by his lank hair and drag him to the fire for examination, but then he was stirring and muttering in Apache and shaking his head and complaining in broken English that his skull was packed with exploding lights and vast pains, and why was it that a harmless and peaceful man of the country could not

[51]

come to the fire of a dark-skinned friend without being attacked and knocked down in the manner of a newborn buffalo calf by a sore-breasted grizzly?

Of course Ned was not taken in by this muddled disclaimer, but he did appreciate it. It was artful enough to pique his curiosity.

This little fellow was clearly a brother forager. He was half Ned's size but much the same color, and it might be, after all, that he had a story to tell. In any event Ned had him now, like an injured but undamaged mouse, there to play with or to finish off. He went over to where one of the stage horses was staling in the dusty grass, the tiny stranger in his grasp. Holding the tracker beneath the animal, he was rewarded with some gasps and sputterings which indicated a return of clearer thought on the part of the reviving Apache; when he realized the source of his restorant, he cried out suggesting a peace talk in which he guaranteed to do most of the speaking, and very quickly and with utterly straight tongue, if granted the moment's parole.

"Go on ahead," Ned invited. "You mighten as well die with a cleaned out mind."

In view of this hardly veiled threat he was surprised enough when the Apache candidly admitted that he had come to bring Ned's head back to the Fort Worth sheriff in the posse's empty grub sack.

This was purely a business matter, the withered Indian explained. There was nothing personal to it. He, Limp Nose, was a highly paid specialist, and the white man would give him a certain amount of money for certain heads of certain badmen, no questions asked. All that Limp Nose had to do was return the head to the sheriff's office and he would be paid. The usual method of transportation was a sack, since this got around the curiosity of passers-by along the trail. Any sack would do. Indeed, it was a pity to bloody-up a fine grub sack like this one, with the sheriff's brand imprinted upon it in official ink.

Ned nodded his sympathy and understanding.

"What you figure to get for a head like mine?" he asked. "Course I know it ain't wuth what a white man's head would bring. But just supposing you was to have brung it back to the sheriff in good shape, with no holes in it, or nothing?"

"Five dollars," said the little Lipan with pardonable pride.

"Jings," said Ned softly. "That's a mort for a nigger."

The Indian didn't seem to comprehend this statement, but he went on to say that as an Apache, he must repay a life for a life. It was a law of his people, as old as the rocks were old. His hand was now in Ned's forever. The powerful black youth had just spared him when he could have killed him. "You give Injun him life," he said sonorously, "Injun give you your life. *Wagh!* Me, you, blood brother. Fight always same side."

Ned was not altogether easy with this five-minute switch of allegiances, but the Lipan sped on to ensnare the lonely colored youth with visions of life on the western plains. In the end he convinced Ned that there was a practical future for them both "on west."

There was, he explained, so long as Ned was determined to raise livestock, a white man's system in that "farther along" country called calf-sharing. This meant that the rancher who needed help with his range cows but could find none, or could not pay for help with money, would get men to work his stock by giving them one of every four calves they caught and branded for the owner. Limp Nose represented himself, further, as knowing just such a needful and generous rancher, only two more rides toward the sun. If Ned wished, they could declare themselves partners, and Limp Nose would lead the way to the new riches tomorrow.

This idea filled Ned's mind, and he was no longer on guard.

Suddenly, the Indian declared he could no longer keep his eyes open, and suggested bed immediately.

Ned agreed reluctantly. But long, long after Limp Nose was snoring thunderously, the Negro youth lay wide-eyed, staring at the stars and thinking about the wonderful chance to go straight and make a decent way for himself as offered by a little Indian man who had come to take his life, and instead had given him a new life.

It was thus that he was alert when the snores of Limp Nose eased away, and the small and crouching shadow came gliding to Ned's couch of brush. Ned still could not believe it, yet he saw the burnish of the blade in the starlight. He tripped the Apache with a blow of his long leg at the other's ankles, seized the murderous dwarf, and swung him into the wall of the bluff which lay behind his bed spot. The impact broke the Indian's lower vertebrae like a string of shells, left him writhing on the ground with the aimless looping and humping of a runover snake.

"You was some friend," murmured Ned down into the glittering, pain-crazed eyes. "I'll be a better one to you."

# *17.*

Far west of Brazos Crossing the driver of the eastbound stage hauled in his teams with sudden curses. The animals stood quivering, flaring their nostrils at the stake driven in the very middle of the Fort Worth road. For the veteran stager it was not the stake, but its ominous burden, which drew his eye. Shortly, as he stomped up to the barrier, his nose was also drawn. The stink of that sack in the summer sun was overpowering. The driver knew that smell. And he knew the signature of the green blowflies which clouded-up from the sack at his approach.

But the lifting away of the fly crust also permitted him to see another signature upon that sodden bag—PROPERTY OF FORT WORTH JAIL—and without opening the sack he slung it outside the coach where its terrible scent would not sicken the paying passengers, and whipping up the spooky teams, he sent them on the gallop past that sunlit empty place. When, at eight o'clock that following night, his run rolled to a halt in front of the Fort Worth sheriff's office, no attendant or deputy could be influenced to open the sack, for the story of Limp Nose's grim mission had been told about in the department, and the sheriff had left strict orders that he be called when and if the borrowed grub sack were brought in.

The sheriff was summoned from his hotel up the street, his dinner cigar and double bourbon being interrupted by the message. When he arrived at the jail, he was brief, blunt.

"Don't bring it in here," he said. "Fetch a lamp out yonder on the boardwalk."

His deputies moved reluctantly, one bringing the bulls-eye lantern from the cellblock, one carrying the putrid sack at arm's length from the rear of the stage.

A crowd of loungers who were attracted by the morbid bait, was barked back by the irritated sheriff. Another sharp command brought the second deputy to loosen the drawstring of the grub sack, while his comrade aimed the light of the bulls-eye on the boardwalk before the jail.

The severed head of Limp Nose spilled out of the sack into the glare of the lantern's coal-oil eye.

The crowd made its expected sound, half horror, half delight. The sheriff and his first deputy looked up and exchanged a silent glance. The tall officer took the toe of his boot and pushed the head back into the stiff mouth of the grub sack. Leaning, he righted the sack with the head in it. With his free hand he brought from his pocket a roll of greenback bills. With practiced thumb he sheaved off five single bills, wadded them together, dropped them in the sack with the head.

"Five," he said. "The hard way."

He handed the sack to his first deputy, and stalked back up the street to his cigar and his bourbon whiskey.

# 18.

Living off the country, Ned made his way westward into the outer *llano*. He followed a shadowy trail, avoiding all settlements, all settlers. Occasionally he saw the Comanches far off, but they either did not see him or did not want his four mediocre harness plugs and coarse black scalplock, so similar to their own. He found his first great herds of buffalo and marveled that the gargantuan beasts could exist in such number near cities where thousands dwelled. He saw, too, the antelope and white-tail deer in herds and, lastly, the moving distant clouds of grace and beauty which were the wild mustang bands. His heart never ceased its high beat, from each daylight to each dark, in that wondrous land. He knew now that here was his home and here was that freedom that had been promised him by Squire Huddleston "across the river." It had, in truth, been across many rivers, but his old master had not lied to him. There was freedom for men who hunted it hard enough.

Yet he was still looking for one thing: the herds of longhorned cattle whose breeders and owners were in need of help.

Ned hadn't seen a head of domestic horned stock, other than the infrequent homesteader's milk cows, since leaving the middle pastures of the Brazos. Despite his suspicion that the treacherous Limp Nose had deceived him again, he continued on west. Soon there were no more houses, no more small settlements, no more milk cows, no dogs to run out and bark when their noses caught from afar the alien scent of the passing dark rider and his four-horse string.

The antelope steaks were good, the deer tenderloins fat and juicy, the water clear and swift, the grass succulent and sweet-cured in the arid sunlight. Ned fleshed out and so did his *remuda* of stolen mounts. But presently a man began to worry how far west was West. It was growing just a little too lonely out there, and he wondered if he had come too far to nowhere.

Then in the third week he met a friendly band of Comancheros, the nomadic halfbreed Mexican and Comanche buffalo hunters and traders who roamed the Southwest, summer to summer, in their picaresque gypsy caravans. These jolly people were delighted with Ned. The Negro youth danced and sang and played the *guitara* for them like any *hidalgo* of the pure blood. Ned believed he had found a home at last. The Comancheros for their parts were so grateful they filled him brimful of *aguardiente*, a native liquor in potency midway between green corn whiskey and uncut carbolic acid, and never charged him a penny for the treat. Rather, they took from him his four horses and his Spencer carbine and his two Colt revolvers, with all the ammunition. But to be fair they left him with his real weapon, the Spanish Toledo knife, together with some straight advice from

the *jefe,* or chief, of the band: if he were to find the work he
longed for, he must go south and south and south. The Texans
with the cows were much farther down toward Old Mexico. Ten
pony rides at least. Long rides. And plenty of Tanima and
Tenawa and Penateka Comanches roving the plains along the
way. But then, *hijo!* It was better than where he was wandering
when the Comancheros found him; right squarely in the middle
of the Kwahadi country! Yes, go south, *Negrito.* In a hurry. Peta
Nokono, the Kwahadi chief was a warrior given to taking hair
first, then talking. *Ai, Chihuahua!* What great luck for their
comrade "Nedito" that they had found him in time. With this
advice, his halfbreed hosts departed. As he watched them out of
sight, Ned had good cause to question again the quality of
friendships in this new land. Here he was with no horse, no gun,
no bullet, and three hundred miles from the settlements of the
white man. And the Comancheros called *that* great luck? He
shook his head and looked around at the debris of the nomad
encampment.

He was ankle deep in fire ashes, horse and mule droppings,
piles of dumped buffalo innards, drifts of gnawed humpribs and
sucked-clean marrowbones. The stench was impressive to a man
still queasy from strong drink. Ned held his breath, seeking to
hold down his gorge with it.

Perhaps if he took a longer view of his problem, things would
appear better. He forced his unsteady vision to focus farther out,
but the vistas beyond the offal of the nomad encampment proved
no cure.

The earth seemed to stretch ten hundred miles in every direction. Nowhere within the limit of the bloodshot eye did an elevation stand higher than a prairie-dog mound against the far horizons. If living creature stirred out there, Ned could not detect
the motion. Not even a hawk wheeled within that vast blue bowl
of soundless sky.

Unknown to Ned, his wanderings had taken him steadily
north of west. He stood now nursing his qualmish stomach and
throbbing head in the very center of the true *Llano Estacado,* the
awesomely empty "staked plains" of the Texas Panhandle, that
strange tableland which frightened the mind by its very flatness
since, once deeply enough into it, no landmark of retreat could
be marked. A man caught afoot in its middle was like a fly

immured wingless in the warp of a monster carpet—Ned could not see over that carpet's nearest pile, so could not imagine to move by any pathway to reach its closest ending.

And Ned Huddleston, surveying this buffalo-grass world without boundaries, tried to be brave. Tottering over to a nearby cutbank he sat down and addressed himself to the surrounding void: "Well," he said, "Anyways, you is free, Nedito."

The cotton-mouthed croaking of his own voice startled him. "Did I say that?" he asked. Then, as he always would in adversity, he laughed at himself. But when the *aguardiente* pain in his head started up by that laugh had eased, the echoing loneliness crowded in once more about him.

"Hoo, Lordie, Ned," he murmured, shivering. "What you going to do with all this freedom?"

# 19.

The decision came to Ned as a matter of professional pride. The Comancheros had beaten him at his own game, but they hadn't done it honorably. There was no art, and no thieves' integrity, in getting a man dead drunk and cleaning him out while he was at the disadvantage of their vile *gardente*. So, very shortly, Ned set out along the broad trail left by the nomads.

That night, having rubbed himself all day on the trail with the droppings of the band's various animals, he stole into the sleeping compound of the new camp without drawing so much as a sniff from the village curs. Like a black wraith he drifted to the chief's wagons.

Rolling up a spare blanket he put Gomez's hat upon its furled end—Gomez being the *jefe* of the band—and into the "breast" of this effigy he plunged the chief's own knife, which he had lifted from its scabbard attached to the bulging waistline of the snoring leader. Pausing only to retrieve his precious Spencer and its ammunition belt, which Gomez had also appropriated to himself, Ned ghosted toward the nearby picket of fine mounts chosen for tomorrow's running of the buffalo.

From this haltered array he selected, untied and led successfully out of the sleeping camp Entero, the first love of fat Gomez, and past question one of the great horses Ned Huddleston had seen in his life.

Entero, whose name meant "the whole thing," "the pure article," "all of it," was a dappled-gray stallion whose short back, dished foreface, trim quarters and flowing, high-rooted tail bespoke the blood of Arab and Turkoman beginnings through the proud studs of the Conquistadores.

He was a Kehilan, a drinker of the wind, and although Ned had no knowledge of the Arabian origins of this animal he had known the horse to be an unusual one on first sighting. As for the horse, whether he sensed in Ned some ancient African kinship, or if it were only the Negro youth's superb hand and touch, he went with Ned eagerly. Man and horse seemed to have been waiting for one another; it was not a theft, really, but an elopement.

When, next sunrise, Gomez missed his knife and his gun and his dappled-gray stallion, in that order, his first loud declaration was for instant and unending pursuit of the thief.

He pledged bawlingly to that cause his life, his fortune and his sacred honor. Then his pure-blood Comanche wife brought him to sit down in the shade of the buffalo-hide fly propped out from his first wagon, there to contemplate, with all its nuances, the prospect of his own knife buried in the heart of his own blanket furled in effigy beneath his own sombrero.

"How much do you want to pay," the Indian woman asked him, "to get that horse back?"

What Gomez answered to that Indian bluntness proved important to Ned Huddleston—there developed no dustcloud of Comanchero pursuit upon the ex-slave's backtrail. By the second morning away, mounted and moving southward on the airy back of Entero, Ned was ready to accept this good news. He drew a deep breath of relief, touched the gray horse lightly at the flank. "*EEeee-yaahHH-hooOOOOO!*" he shouted the Rebel yell at the empty sunshine of the glorious morning, and off he and the great horse flew—over the nearest rise of the prairie into the arms of a Kwahadi war party returning from the settlements and attracted to change course by the alien echoes of the Confederate war cry.

"Hoo, hoo!" said Ned lamely, after halting the gray in a sliding shower of red Texas dirt and green mesquite beans. "Could you good gen'mens tell a poor nigger boy where is the nearest cow ranch needing a free hand?"

The Comanches looked at him. Only the wind stirred the feathers of their headdresses.

They were a copper-skinned people, large-headed, broad-faced, thick-bodied, short. If they were not ugly to look at, Ned decided they would do until something true-ugly showed up.

"Morning, suh!" he grinned at the leader. "Sure is a tolerable fine day. Yes suh!"

The Comanche chief spoke some words in his guttural tongue to the brave whose painted war pony stood beside his own. The brave nodded and rode forward on his pony to confront Ned. By some past fortune, the man had learned a quite understandable broken English. But this discovery that he could communicate with the feathered horsemen returned only fleeting hope to Ned's breast. The linguist, who introduced himself as Pin Oak Jack, meticulously explained that there was no question that Ned would be killed, but the chief first wanted to know where he had gotten that gray horse.

Since this request came punctuated with a series of steel clinks of rifle hammers being cocked, Ned decided to make a quick and clean breast of the entire affair. He thought that he was buying only that time he could take to tell of his adventure with the Comancheros of Gomez. Yet, as he went fearfully along, with Pin Oak Jack translating, he saw grins and nods breaking out among the windburned listeners. By the time he had reached the details of his entrance into the sleeping camp to spirit out the horse and gun and cartridge belt, he had drawn even a round of deep-grunted approvals which sounded like *"Wagh, wagh!"*

When he then concluded with the device of the effigy of Gomez stabbed with its own knife and left beside the sleeping Comanchero to discourage him from meaningful pursuit, the chief of the war party pushed his pony forward and put out his right hand, like a white man. With clear friendly intent he proclaimed in Comanche, *"Puha, puha!"* which, Pin Oak Jack explained, meant that Ned's personal medicine was extremely potent.

Trying hopefully for a plainer translation, the young Negro was told that he was now a blood friend of the Kwahadi chief, Peta Nocono, providing he did not now hesitate too long in accepting that famed chieftain's offered hand.

Ned let out a whoop, siezed Peta's hand and shook it with a good will that very nearly unhorsed the Comanche.

And that for the moment was gratefully that. The Indians dismounted and made a breakfast fire. They had not eaten in twenty-four hours, due to the hard pursuit of the Texas Rangers, who had hung onto the Comanche trail a hundred miles longer than usual. They had killed a buffalo calf just before hearing Ned's whoop; they now roasted the meat while Pin Oak Jack told their new friend of the perils of settlement raiding, and its very poor pay when the luck went bad, as it had done on their own present journey.

These remarks, interlarded with general comment on the wild life of the Comanche and mouthfuls of the fat young calf meat, soon had Ned deciding that all red men were not like the Lipan tracker, and that these Komantcias were all right. Indeed, when the invitation to join Peta Nocono's band was offered Ned by Pin Oak Jack, he began to seriously consider it.

Pin Oak Jack then excused himself, went to his pony and took from his saddlehorn a war bag reminding Ned uneasily of the grub sack of Limp Nose. But he was sure there were no heads in that sack, for it clearly lacked the necessary weight. He was correct.

Pin Oak Jack spread a blanket and then dumped the contents of the war bag on it and spread the articles out to air and dry in the sun. They were of various lengths and sizes, and conditions of cure, but they were all fresh within the week. Three small children, Ned thought, and five grownups. Not human heads of course; only human scalps: white folks' scalps, all eight of them.

When Pin Oak Jim came back, Ned spoke from the heart. His journey, he said, had been a long one. To quit it now would be to admit that his *puha* was weak. He must, he lamented, continue his quest to find the cattle herds of the south. It was his purpose, he lied nobly, to fall upon those herds as the wolf might, taking every animal possible to build himself a vast herd which no white man might ever equal. Surely his Comanche brothers could understand that. It was his own way of making war on the palefaced devils. *Wagh!*

Pin Oak Jack told the Negro youth that he was crazy, but that if he would rather herd cows than run buffalo, his Comanche friends would honor his poor demented mind. Let each go his own way, each fight his own war.

*"Ehaitsma,"* added the Comanche chief, Peta Nocono, putting his hand on Ned's shoulder. He spoke feelingly in his Indian tongue, prompting Ned to ask Pin Oak Jack for his meaning.

The squat brave grinned and spat a shard of cracked marrow-bone into the ground at his feet. "Him mean you hell of man for just boy," he said.

Ned thanked them, and waited at the fire spot while they mounted and rode away. When they were far off he waved to them and thought they turned to wave back. He was never sure. They had given him blankets, a beautiful soft-tanned calf robe, buffalo meat and *ehaitsma,* their word for "close friend who is only a boy." But they were Comanches, and he still felt the chill of that first silence and stirring of warfeathers as they sat on their spotted ponies watching him. After they were gone he left the camp quickly, giving Entero his head; he did not look back again to wave toward his meeting place with the Komantcias, called by all the other Indians, the dread "Tshaoh," the Enemy People.

Ned Huddleston could neither read nor write; but he knew that freedom was not spelled with eight scalps drying in the summer sun.

# 20.

Ten days later Ned found the South Texas cattle country. New herds were being built up out past the populated frontier, and men were pushing their stock out onto the prairies from the catclaw and savannah pastures of the Big Thicket country over toward the Gulf Coast.

At every one of the lonely ranch houses he found decent treatment. He was welcome to feed and water his horse and himself and to stay for one night's sleep. After that it was move on, no help needed, times are tight and sorry, boy.

Texas beef was a drug upon the state. Bred up virtually undisturbed during the war years when the Yankee gunboats prevented delivery across the Mississippi into the South, and the Union troops stopped any movement north, the Big Thicket herds had mushroomed into the enormous glut of Texan longhorns which Ned now encountered. They spilled out of the lower basins of the Nueces, Guadeloupe, San Antonio, Colorado, Brazos and Trinity—and they still had no accessible market.

The Negro rider found also that most of the larger owners were transplanted southerners. Even those who were civil to him saw him as "boy," and not because of his youth.

Moreover, his unaccountably fine horse, new repeating Spencer carbine, and his beautiful buffalo robe drew suspicion. It was not the "outfit" of a cowboy, nor did its obvious value encourage the owners to trust Ned's request for mean-hard cow work. Negro badmen might be scarce in the Southwest but they were not unknown. This tall boy with the war-scarred face and deep, soft voice was not what he said he was.

The greetings became shorter, the invitations to light down fewer. Here and there a woman was kind and gave him food. Children loved his happy nature and outlandish tales of the great war. Some older men who had lost young sons in the struggle and who still kept the thirteen-star flag of the Confederacy in their cabins above the fireplaces, showed compassion for his wartime service and its hardships.

But in truth there was no work; or there was none until the blessed day which brought the dispirited wanderer to the austere but understanding doorstep of Mr. Jash Oakes.

Oakes was no southerner; he was a fair man. An abolitionist from the non-slave state of Kansas, he kept his prewar history to himself in case it might incite his less enlightened neighbors, but he was very big for Negro rights in his heart, and always had been.

"You'll find respect here," he told Ned. "You'll be treated the same as any other. I believe in the rights of all men to be free. To me, you're not a black man, and I'm not a white man. We're just two men, fair and square and equal."

Ned could not absorb all of this at one time, particularly since he had only asked for a job.

But Oakes also gave him that job. He was a very poor man, he said, having only a few cows which he managed to herd himself. He could not honestly pay any man a dime for helping him, because he didn't honestly have a dime for such pay. But he did have an idea.

Soon—surely by the next spring—there would be a rich and ready market for horses. Words and rumors of hope were flying everywhere, from the *brasada* of the Gulf to the *llano* of the western rivers. A market without end existed in the Union North, because meat was expensive up there. In Texas it was worth six dollars for a whole four-year-old steer, grassfat and weighing maybe half a ton. Delivered up North, that same steer would bring as much as forty dollars. The thing was to set the trails and get the drives moving for those northern markets, and then Texas would see more money in cattle than any sane man dreamed. Now those trails were being set and would be ready before the next spring. All the cattle Ned had skirted around and ridden through in his many days of work searching would be gathering into trail herds for the big push north. And, just there, came the shrewd idea of Jash Oakes.

Some claimed there were half a million head of cattle, yet how many saddle-broke cowhorses were there to move that half-million head up all those trails to all those Yankee markets? Ahah! You bet. Not halfways enough. Why, come the next new grass and that great '66 drive, a man could get whatever he asked for a good horse, well broke.

"Glory!" Ned cried, dark eyes shining. "Ain't that somewhat!"

Mr. Jash Oakes allowed that it was. Now, he said, if Ned were to devote his plainly remarkable way with horses to catching and breaking for cow work the wild mustangs that swarmed the prairies a little out, Oakes would stake him to all the outfit required for the venture. They would split whatever Ned might catch one-and-three of every four, just like the calf sharers did, only they would turn the split squarely about. Ned would get the three, Mr. Jash Oakes would take the one.

That was hard to believe. Ned had never heard of any share-cropping where the owner took the short end. But Mr. Oakes convinced him that Ned's was the greater part of the risk and talent, and that he therefore deserved the lion's part of the killing.

"When the count's made," he concluded feelingly, "you won't be stuck with no livestock, neither, son. I'll give you a paper right here at the ranch, which you can cash at any bank in this part of Texas. That way you'll be free to go on and make whatever you can of your life from the start that paper will give you. I'm privileged to do it for you, Ned Huddleston, so don't say another word of thanks. It's me that you've made happy, lad, and you that us whitefolks owes a decent chance to. Now get to your planning, 'pardner.'"

Ned made his plans with a happiness he had not known since Siloam Ridge and the old slavery days in Arkansas. He was out-fitted, went into the hazy plains and for twenty hours a day for three months he "mustanged," learning as he worked. With summer gone and the September value of broken saddlebroncs beginning to climb as Oakes had prophesied, Ned returned to the ranch with fifty-seven head of the finest *mesteño* horses the surrounding ranchers had ever seen; and every solitary head was hand-gentle and saddle-steady, with not a spur-slash nor quirt-burn among the lot. It was an incredible gather, worth real money, and Oakes kept his word.

With the last head safely penned in the home corral, he produced the paper he had promised Ned in payment for his share. It was a "wanted" flyer from Fort Worth. The picture above the caption, which read $500 DEAD OR ALIVE, was a crude woodcut of what might be any Negro male. But the name that went with the woodcut was spelled NED HUDDLESTON and Ned understood very well what his name looked like in print, even though he could not write it himself.

"How long you had the paper, Mr. Oakes?" he asked quietly.

"Long before I had you," answered the Kansan, just as quietly. "Now take it and get along. You're getting your chance."

"Gitalong," said Ned. "That's a funny word from you."

"Don't laugh over it too hard, boy."

That face behind the advice was as rock-cold as any he had

[65]

seen, Ned decided. And suddenly he knew that south Texas had just closed in on Ned Huddleston.

"No suh, I won't," he said; and he got Entero from the horse shed and went riding very fast away from that place and from Mr. Jash Oakes, who respected black men and believed in their rights to be free.

21.

Ned rode until nearly sundown. He kept Entero on the lope and went skirting every sign of ranch house, wagon road or cattle trail. He did not suppose that the Fort Worth flyer Jash Oakes had would be the only one out there on the *llano*. It was by the sheerest luck that some other rancher than Oakes had not spotted Ned. In that way, he admitted honestly, the abolitionist had indeed given him "his chance." Now he knew what he was: an outlaw. Maybe underneath what looked to be only a mean and small trick that was what Mr. Jash Oakes had been bound to tell him.

One thing sure, Ned Huddleston was getting to be a man of no small value. Add the five hundred dollars on the wanted bill to the fifty-seven broke horses at even thirty-five dollars a head, and you had yourself a going bid of a mort more money than a man could figure on his fingers. For a boy who had originally been worth four dollars and fifty bars of hog-lye soap, Old Ned had come a far piece up the line.

"Hoo, hoss," he said to Entero. "We mighten as well laugh about it; ain't nobody going to weep over a rich nigger like me."

The gray stallion whickered and bobbed his head, jingling the bits chains. Ned returned the nod, believing it to have been in direct answer to his statement. "Yonder ridge," he said to the horse, "is where we'll sleep. River loops it on three sides, so we got a view ain't nobody going to creep up on us past. A good place, hoss, for two like us what ain't go no other friends."

When they had forded the stream and climbed the rise, Ned discovered two things at the top. He and Entero were not alone in that prairie sunset, nor were they the only pair to have an eye for that river-moated high ground. Spurring a laboring horse in from the plain toward the north flank of the rise came a desperate rider, and behind the rider swirled a dust cloud of a kind known all too frighteningly to Ned Huddleston: *posse!*

Ned's deep voice tensed with the muscles of his face.

"Come on, come on!" he heard himself fiercely urging the hunted man. And when the gray stallion whinnied in response to the words, Ned clapped a hand over the belling nostrils and whispered, *"ho-shuh!"*—he had learned the Indian calming-sound from the Comancheros. Entero at once fell still, and Ned quickly swung him down off the skyline. Returning to the crest on foot, he was in time to see that the fugitive below was not going to "come on," not going to make it even to the river.

Five riders had emerged from the posse dust cloud. They were firing now, not at the fugitive but at his horse. The third or fourth of their rifle cracks knocked the animal sprawling. Its rider managed to leap away from it as it went down, but he was limping badly, an ankle turned during the jump. Before he could more than start for the riverbank, the five men had raced up and surrounded him and were down off of their horses, rifles leveled.

It was then Ned realized that the wanted man was unarmed. And, more than that, that he had been previously wounded in the chase. The clear sunlight of the late day let Ned see things as through a polished glass. The panting victim's shirt was glued to his body by both old and new blood. He could not bear his weight on the injured ankle. Yet he stood at the river's bank and waited for his captors with a pride and a bearing which Ned Huddleston recognized.

This was a man like himself. He was surely not one of the possemen's breed, not one of their hound-pack kind. Almost in the instant, the thought's accuracy was borne out by a hard Texas voice from across the stream.

"All right, Mex, you've rode out your last stole horse this side of the Rio Grande. You got any greaser prayers you aim to get said, you'd best start criss-crossing yourself."

"*Nada de eso*," answered the other. "It's no affair of God's. I won't bring him into it. Be damned, all of you. *Gringos!* I spit on your mothers' memories!"

He did spit, too, nearly hitting one of the riflemen.

"Get the rope," said the man to his fellows.

Ned had heard those words before. They made a communion, as did the doomed man's hard pride, with the young Negro's compassion. But in the end, it was not this empathy which decided Ned. It was an even greater bond. The voice of the cornered one, for all its defiance, was not the voice of a man. This was a boy about to die; a boy no older than Ned Huddleston.

Two men came with the rope, while three guarded the youth with their guns. They dragged him to a nearby cottonwood and flung the rope up over a sturdy bough above. The noose end was put about the boy's neck, the free end tied to a saddlehorn. No man sat in that saddle. None of the five cared to be the one who did it, the exact one.

When all was ready, two men still held their rifles in the ribs of the captive. The other three men stooped and gathered handfuls of river gravel.

"All right?" gritted one of them to the others.

But his answer did not come from any his comrades, and the gravel which would have "jumped" the riderless horse and "made a good Mexican" of the prisoner was never flung.

Ned's two shots came so close together and with such jolting effect that the posse was stunned. The first shot struck the right-side rifleguard in the shoulder, knocking him in a flying cartwheel away from the noosed youth. The second shot hit the left-side guard in the hip, twisting him to earth with a bursting scream of pain. The other three possemen, recovering from the surprise, forgot everything but survival and dove for cover. In the same moment, the captive was freeing himself of the noose, but not letting go of the rope. Instead, he hobbled along its line to the waiting saddled horse which, prairie-trained, stood like a rock to the tautness of the lariat. The three possemen had not yet come back up from their plunges into nearby haven of rock and brush, when the prisoner was galloping the "hanging horse" into the ford of the river. By the time the three had recovered sufficiently to lever-off aimed shots at the escaping quarry, only pure luck could have guided their lead to lethal purpose.

And luck was through with them. The Mexican boy got away around the slope of the high ground, going south. He was met on the far side by an excited Negro youth of his own age, and the two splashed over the south loop of the river, away through the gathering prairie dusk toward the distant Rio Grande, running free, running wild, for Old Mexico and another life.

# 22.

Terresa, who had no other known name, was a willowy boy, neither so tall nor so powerful as Ned, and had the features of a poet. He also had the style. His speech was fluent and full of reaching phrases, and he seemed to have that southern manner revered by Ned as "quality." Terresa was quality. From first meeting he and the nomad Negro youth found *simpatico*. It was as though, Terresa said, fortune had brought forth a delivery of true *gemelos,* of true twins, in their pairing.

It was in this close spirit that the boys fled southwestward across the Pedernales, the Blanco, Hondo, Frio and Nueces to the Big River.

It was as well that some affinity girded them, for the members of the shot-up posse, Terresa belatedly revealed, were not mere *hombres del monte,* but Texas Rangers. This group, the Mexican youngster warned, were the Comanches of the *Americano* settlements. They rode the best horses, had the best weapons, and never gave up.

Indeed the Rangers, picking up their track below the Anacacho Mountains in the far corner of Uvalde County, ran them all the way across the Kinney roughlands. At their first strike for the Rio Grande, an alerted second force of the "gentlemen in the

white hats" very nearly cut them off from ever reaching Terresa's motherland. A hot fire was exchanged and their escape
upstream was due only to the Mexican youth's superb knowledge
of the local terrain and to Ned's great skill in shooting down
three of the pursuing mounts in the course of the wild fox-and-
hounds chase through the Quemado badlands of the Rio Grande.

Ned, who at first learning of the Rangers had not quite appreciated the Mexican youth's *respeto* for his would-be-executioners,
now comprehended the feeling entirely.

"Hoo-ee!" he said to Terresa, when at last they had made the
crossing into Villa Acuna on the Mexican side and were safe.
"Them rascals plays for permanent."

"They do," agreed Terresa. "Their favorite dance is the airy
trot an *hombre* does at the end of a rope. And they are certain
death for Mexicans and horse thieves, as any Mexican or any
horse thief can surely attest."

"Hmmmn," said Ned. "How them Rangers feels abouten niggers?"

"Niggers?" Terresa repeated.

"Yeah," Ned grinned. "Black boys like me."

"Ah," said Terresa softly, "I see. *Negritos.*"

"*Sí!*" Ned laughed, pleased with his expanding Spanish.

"Well," said Terresa, touching spur lightly to his stolen
mount, "you will learn soon enough the answer to your question.
It is in the nature of our future."

"I reckon I got to believe you, *hombre*," Ned declared.

"You had better believe me," nodded Terresa quickly.

"Oh?" Ned had caught the quickness.

"For a surety, *amigo mio.*"

Both youths were riding easy, leaving Villa Acuna, cantering
out upon the wide free plain of Old Coahuila. The sun was good
on their backs still dripping water from the Rio Grande. For
Ned, at least, fear of the Rangers had been left at the Texas
border. But Terresa knew better.

"You see, comrade," he continued, "being a Mexican and a
horse thief is the manner by which I make my living. So our
future will guarantee that you see the Rangers again."

"*Our* future?"

"But of course! Don't you want to be a horse thief with me,
Nedito?"

Frowning honestly, Ned looked back toward Villa Acuna and the Rio Grande. "I don't know," he said. "How them Rangers feel abouten *nigger* hoss thiefs?"

"*Hijo!*" laughed Terresa. "Follow me and find out!"

Ned followed him then, and for the next six months, until winter was gone and spring not far behind. Coahuila knew them well, and Chihuahua. They were not strangers in Nueva Leon, Zacatecas or Durango. Once they were in Sonora, even, and once in Sinaloa. And many, many times they traded back and forth across the Rio Grande, into Texas.

Their business was stealing horses: horses stolen in Mexico were driven into Texas to be sold; horses stolen in Texas were sold in Mexico; and even horses stolen on one side of the river and sold on the other side, were restolen on that side and driven back to the original side for the final profit. It was a chancy game but they were the masters of it.

That winter in Old Mexico was spring in January for Ned Huddleston. Terresa had charm and he was charmed, and not only with horses.

"Terresa, Terresa!" the brown-skinned girls sighed, while their mothers sniggered and looked the other way and the kiss was stolen, or the rose, or the blush, or the entire bloom of the tender flower, who cared? Not Terresa.

"Come, *hijo!*" he would cry to Ned. "It is late and the river is low, and old Santiago's mares will grow old before this maid believes it when we say *adios!*"

And away they would ride, gathering the mares, or the geldings, or the mixed herd, striking at the *haciendas* of Gomez or Santiago or Moreles or Hipólito Sanchez, *ai, que tal!* the pity of it all. Weep for the poor rich men, the fat swine with the *pesos* and the *peones!* Cry for them in the heart, *compadre!* And gather up their herds for the long run to the Rio Grande, *Santos!* what difference?

Ned could not resist this madness. It had been too long since boyhood, too many years had disappeared in hardness and cruelty and war. Now here was another youth, his own age, who laughed at life and swore it was for spending, not hoarding, not saving. One must see the other side of the river while there was time, and take his maid and his money and his gambles with the gun all in the same good grace.

[71]

Why work? Did wise men ever toil for hire?

*Jesus Maria!* Out there was wind and sun and the fresh rain in the rider's face. Always there were more horses and some other market for their sale. In between there were the lonely coyote-crying camps on the *llano,* the long passes and winding trails of the *montanas,* the high sweet scent of pine, the smells of wood-smoke, brewing coffee, saddle blankets drying by the fire, and always the good horse between the legs and another far ride, and fast.

The life was what Ned had dreamed it might be up in the southwest country of the mustang and the Comanche where he had searched for the freedom he found here.

There was even a certain shy and decent senorita of a small town near Acuna. This gentle child, Dolores, had looked with favor on the tall and brawny Ned, and he, no Lochinvar like Terresa, had blushed when he asked her hand of the black-robed *padre,* whose ward she was. To his vast astonishment the priest had blessed the match and said he would speak to the girl. Let Ned return with a dowry of some proper kind, and it was all done save the speaking of the words and sprinkling of the Holy Water.

It was, in fact, this romantic situation which brought Terresa to his most gallant inspiration: if Nedito must bring suitable evidence of his real worth to the bride, then let the tribute be gathered properly. For some time now the *rurales* and *federales* of the Mexican states of Coahuila and Sonora had been following a bit too closely the business raids of Ned and Terresa; a mistake might mean the end, the airy dance for both. They decided they would take a certain large herd of high quality over the Big River to Del Rio, where a buyer they both knew was waiting. The prize would be very great, and Ned could send for the girl and go to live with her where the Gulf waves washed the pebbled beaches of Campeche and such a thing as a horse thief had never been hung, nor, *quita!* even heard of.

Ned, completely swept away with visions of family life with Dolores and Terresa's wild tales of the balmy shores, fell happily in with the scheme.

The gather, planned in last detail, was executed with Terresa's flair and madman's courage. The beautiful herd of blooded stock was gotten safely away from the savannahs of its Mexican pasture and driven by paths and water holes known only to Ned and Terresa and the desert coyote, across the Rio Grande to the holding place on the American side—Dry Devils Fork, above Del Rio.

This was in April, the seventh month of Ned's exile.

It was also the spring of 1866, the time that Jash Oakes had foretold that the great herds would be gathered for the trail-drives to the Yankee markets.

Ned's thoughts could not help but return to the memory of the Kansan's prophecy, and he grew restive. For some reason he felt this last journey to Texas was full of fate and fortune. There was something in the darkness of the spring night, something which warned as well as beckoned, something which made him vastly uneasy.

"Terresa," he said, low-voiced, and after a long wait for the Texas buyer. *"Vamonos,* let's get out of here, *amigo.* This place is hoo-dooed."

"You're yearning for that girl!" the Mexican boy laughed.

"No," denied Ned. "I got the feeling, *hombre.* Let's drift."

"What? Without our money? Just leave the horses here?"

"It's juju," said Ned. "Niggers has got it. Mexicans ain't. You coming?"

"Never!" said the other. "Not without my money."

Ned moved closer in the night. He put his hand to his companion's arm, fingers tightening. "Terresa," he said, "don't auger with the juju, never. Come on now. Leastways, leave us go up in the brush a bit and watch to see what comes to our fire with that buyer from Del Rio."

Terresa sobered. He did not laugh now. He was familiar with Ned's juju powers. The tall Negro youth saw things and heard things of which ordinary men were not aware. Too many times his eerie instincts had saved them from traps where no other weapon could have defended them. The Mexican boy nodded, dropped his voice.

"All right, *hombre,*" he said. "But understand that I do this thing for you and not for Terresa."

"Yeah," answered Ned tersely. "I do it for Ned and not Terresa, too. Move out slow, like as if nothing was spooking nobody. I'm going to make some loud talk about finding a bed spot. You make some more about going down to the spring for cook water.

Grab the bucket; gimme the blanket. Slow, slow. Keep talking, *hombre*."

They left the fire. Terresa was whistling a Coahuila tune, Ned was mumbling to himself, foolish "nigger-talk," that a listening white man would have expected. There was no sound anywhere of visitors. But the horses were beginning to move, to bring up heads, still chewing mouthfuls of grass, to flick ears and to flare nostrils—sensing just the first faint rustle of something alien.

Clear of the firelight, Ned ran to where he had Entero picketed in the scrub beside Terresa's black Sonora racer. Terresa was there a moment later, having doubled back up from the spring. "Nothing yet," he told Ned. "I could see the fire as I came by. Maria! but it's quiet."

"Take the hosses," said Ned. "Go up the Dry Devil a quarter mile and wait. Happen I don't show, or you hear shots, take out."

"*Hombre!* You can't do it."

"I got to do it," said Ned. "I got to know."

Terresa gripped his hand, took the reins of the horses. There was no point in arguing with the Negro youth. He had his own strange way of doing things, and he would do it if he said he had to. "*Hasta luego,*" said Terresa, and was gone through the blackness with the two mounts.

Ned did not answer him. He was already gliding through that same blackness, back toward the dim red glow of the fire spot where the horse buyer from Del Rio had told them to wait for him.

# 23.

There was a pile of outcrop rocks just above the meeting place on Dry Devils Fork. It was the only elevation in the land at this point, rising some thirty feet above the fire. A favorite campsite and rendezvous of the highline riders, it was familiar to the Rangers who came that way in dusty chase of the rustlers and horse thieves who swarmed the border pastures immediately after the War between the States. Nor was its location any mystery to Cap Pottle, the fat "wet horse" buyer of Del Rio.

As Ned now shadowed up the rear of the rise and came bellying out in the tall grass of its top, this last fact was established chillingly. The horse buyer was just riding up. He was the halfbreed son of a Coahuilan mother, who had christened him Capitano and imparted to him some of the Spanish-Indian sensitivities. He stopped his horse well out from the fire. "Terresito?" he called. "Nedito? It is I, cousin Capitano."

An ember popping in the abandoned fire replied with tiny loudness.

"Hola," said Cap, cupping his fat hands. "A donde estan, hermanos?"

A dust-devil drafting up from the arroyo spun the ashes of the fire spot lonesomely.

Hesitating, the halfbreed decided to take the grazing horse herd as proof that all was well and assume its owlhoot owners to be momentarily absent on some ordinary business of animal care. He came toward the fire, dropping his mounts' reins, pouring himself a cup of coffee from the black pot simmering in its coals.

But he did not drink the coffee. He held the steaming cup only long enough to be certain, in the stillness, that neither of his "brothers" were indeed near. Then he went swiftly back to the

[75]

edge of a cutbank fifty feet from the fire. Straining intently, Ned could hear the exchange of voices then following.

And as Capitano and his Judas-pack hidden below the cutbank conferred, Ned could see the fire-gleam striking the blued metal of rifle barrels.

"Listen," said a Texas voice, "don't get cute with us, *amigo*. You're not going back to Del Rio nor no place excepting back to yonder fire. And you just set tight right there until your customers come back. Now beat it."

Ned's spine tingled. He knew that sand-dry voice. It belonged to Captain Emmett Forbes, and Captain Emmett Forbes belonged to the Texas Rangers. He was the same *jefe* of the White Hats who had nearly trapped Terresa and himself against the Rio Grande in the Quemado badlands, and who had since vowed to bring them both to Texas justice.

"But, *Capitan!*" the halfbreed buyer objected. "I will be precisely in the middle!"

"You put yourself there," rasped the Ranger. "It wasn't me that barefoot *padre* from Acuna come over the Rio to see. He didn't bring that dumpy Mex girl to my place, with her story about this here stolen horse-herd dowry Huddleston was fixing to bring her. Nor it wasn't me that promised them the five-hundred-dollar reward for the nigger. That was you, *hombre*."

"But, *Capitan*, what could I do? The *padre* knew of the reward. He had the cursed poster rolled up inside his holy cassock. I am innocent. I only told you what my young cousin Dolores told the priest, and the priest told me. With such knowledge, could any honest man do less than I have done?"

"Oh, I doubt it," said the Ranger captain. "But for honest men like you, *hombre*, we'd be out of business."

That was the end of it. Fat Pottle came scuttling, pale and uneasy, back to the fireside. He picked up his coffee cup once again and made loud sounds of sipping from it, exclaiming in border Spanish over the discourtesy of his hosts in letting him cool his heels while they were up to *Dios* alone knew what.

In his bunchgrass covert Ned did not smile. He could hear the Rangers moving out from the cutbank. Some were going to the left, some to the right. They would be circling to flank the fire. It was time, and more than time, that Ned left the rise and ran for the arroyo.

But he had waited too long, and been too intent upon hearing the evidence delivered against Dolores.

The Rangers had gotten beyond his retreat path before he could take it. He heard their whispered calls in the darkness, and suddenly could not tell if they were a dozen or a hundred men. He thought for an angry instant of shooting Capitano Pottle through the head, but he knew in the same instant that the fat halfbreed had been the least of his betrayers. Now if that friendly *padre* from the flyspeck village below Acuna were down there by that fire!

No, thought Ned, it wouldn't be any different with the priest than with the cowardly horse buyer. They were only men, just as Ned was a man. They hadn't held him in their arms. They hadn't whispered to him in the dark. They hadn't sworn to wait for him where the roses of the mission chapel grew over the old adobe wall.

"Come on, black boy," he told himself. "It ain't no wedding band that's set to strangle you; you got a ring of Rangers to bust loose from."

But again the fraction's pause had done its damage. Anger was still in him, robbing his dark limbs of skill. His crouching movement dislodged a loose rock. It went over the side of the rise above the fire, building in its wake a rattling spill of smaller chips and surface float. Its slide had not even halted below, before the bellow of the Ranger rifles was exploding other dirt and flying chips of rock into the face of the trapped man above.

# 24.

Two bullets raked Ned. One burned across the bunched bicep of his left arm, the other channeled his thigh. Neither wound was crippling, but they caused great pain and warned that he must be gone from there or die. The enemy was too numerous and even random shooting was bound to strike him again and again.

If not, if luck let him live to see the sunrise, then it would be the rope. For once the light came there would be no chance of leaving the rise. Now, for perhaps a few minutes, he might win free of the Ranger trap by a straightaway dash for the arroyo.

He started to his feet and was met by a hail of Ranger fire which literally blasted him back into the grass. He lay with the sweat eating like acid into his eyes. He did not know if he had been hit again, and it did not matter.

He was not going out on foot through that ring of steel.

If he had Entero with him there in the dark, he might drive the horse through by pure speed. But on foot he could not move fast enough. He would be heard and seen far too quickly, and for far too long. Well, good-bye, Ned. Anyway, Terresa had made it free. That much you had done, black boy. You had saved your friend.

And Terresa would remember him. He would tell the good people of Coahuila about Old Ned. It wouldn't be like he hadn't lived at all. Somewhere down there in one of those adobe churches with their mission bells and dusty little graveyards, out beyond the *padre's* garden, a stone would say *Ned* on it.

"Nigger," Ned suddenly warned himself, "you don't stop funeralizing yourse'f, you going to start up weeping before the casket come by."

He had no sooner uttered the thought when he heard the sudden wild yammer of a coyote out toward the arroyo. Ned didn't think. He threw back his head and ki-yi-ed back, yappy and crazy, the way the brushwolf did. There was an answering yip, and then the hammer of horses' hooves driving in from the arroyo.

As the incoming rider cut straight for the rise, the Rangers held fire for fear of hitting their own men on the far side of the circle about Ned Huddleston. Moreover Captain Forbes hoarsely yelled into the night to wait for the madman to join the nigger up there on the landmark outcrop, and then fire.

But, like Ned, Forbes had made the tactical blunder of underrating a Mexican fighting man. Terresa brought Entero beside his own black racer wildly flying to the crest of the rise, and Ned, whom no Comanche could outride, rose from his cover like a black puma and struck with one great leap for the back of the straining gray stallion. His fingers found the flowing mane and twined into it with the grip of death. The gray did not break stride except as slowed by the last lunge upward to the outcrop's summit, and this fleeting hesitation was enough. Ned was up and astride him, even as Terresa released Entero's reins and leaped the black on over the cascading drop to the fire's side below. And, after them, the gray plunged downward in the shadow of the black's path, with his own dark master lying along his neck, fiercely talking him onward into the sailing leap over the cutbank beyond the fire.

During the brief seconds of Terresa's rescue dash, wild Ranger lead richochetted the night. It was a human reaction to the unbelievable course of the outlaws jumping their mounts down the thirty-foot decline, through the scattering ashes and firebrands of the campsite, away over the cutbank into the outer prairie. No man could lay a calm set of sights under such conditions.

Then Captain Forbes' hard voice was calling out for all the shooting to slack off.

"Gather up!" he ordered grimly. "We been prim-rosed."

At the fire, they rebuilt the flame, heaping it high. By the light of the kindled blaze they saw, on rock and hard dirt below the outcrop, what they had hoped to see—the spotting of a blood trail—and they knew that they could wait for morning, losing little.

There was not one line of bleeding, but two. It might be horse blood, but the better possibility was that both outlaws had been hit, one of them evidently hard-hit. Forbes' men had run these two before and knew they would hold together. Neither would leave the other to save himself, and the one that was trying to help his stricken comrade would be found where the wounded man was found.

"Put the coffee on," said Forbes, rising from his examination of the sign. He rubbed the fresh blood between thumb and fingertips, wiped it on his leather chaps. "It won't be noon before the bad-hit one is down."

# 25.

The Ranger captain was wrong; it was not noon but nearing nightfall of the next day when Terresa could ride no more. Ned had hoped to gain another darkness. Under cover of night he might have found some haven in which to hide his wounded comrade. Then with both horses, he could have gone on and likely outdistanced the Rangers to circle back wide and bring some help to Terresa. There were plenty of Mexican people living in the Texas *brasada,* and if Ned could find such a family Terresa would have all of human aid possible. He and the Mexican boy had agreed on the plan. They had gutted-on the whole terrible afternoon with Ned holding Terresa in the saddle, both gasping, *"siga, siga,* go on, go on," and *"otra noche, otra noche,* another night, another night."

But they were not going to get that other night.

Casting ahead, Ned saw the river, green against the red and yellow of the *llano.* It was nearer than the Rangers. They must reach it, for Terresa needed the drink he had been groaning for the past hours. The fever of his wound was destroying him.

*"Poco mas,"* Ned whispered fiercely to his semi-conscious companion. "Yonder's water."

"And trees?" asked Terresa, no longer able even to see clearly.

*"Si,"* answered Ned, standing in the stirrups to stare ahead, *"muchas arboles, amigo.* And better than that, we got a split channel with a brush clump island! Hang on!"

Terresa's hands locked on the horn of his saddle. His head moved weakly. *"Esta muy lejos?"* he asked.

"No, not very far."

The Mexican boy grinned wanly. *"Tengo prisa,"* he said.

*"You're* in a hurry!" croaked Ned, hoarse with thirst. "What you think I'm doing? Riding this hoss backward?"

"*Mas aprisa, por favor,*" panted his fellow-rider, and the pale smile was gone.

"We're going as fast as we can go," said Ned. "Keep a strangleholdt on that horn and pray it's fast enough."

Terresa nodded in reply, and must have prayed as well. For the flight was swift enough and, with the first Ranger shots lobbing high-arched into the trail dirt all about them, they came to the river and got over its south channel onto the island. Their pursuers, coming up, wheeled back for cover as Ned blasted them with his saddlegun. Judging the denseness of the island's cover and the desperation of the men they were chasing, and weighing both against the wound of Terresa and the nearness of day's end, Forbes ordered his men to cease firing.

"Bonham," he said to his lieutenant, "take half the men and cross over. Build a watch fire over there. We'll do the same on this side." He turned to the hard-faced dusty riders waiting behind them. "She ends right here, boys," he told them. "They'll never lay a trackline away from that island."

Lieutenant Bonham looked at the river above and below. He peered at the sunset silence of the island's impenetrable thicket. Then he shook his head uncertainly.

"I don't know," he said. "With that damn nigger, I wouldn't bet you ten cents Confederate. I ain't convinced he can't fly."

The comment drew a sunburned grin or two, but the men were tired. They crossed over the river at the ford below the island and took up their stations on the north bank. On the south bank, the others settled in. The twilight was brief, for the spring was young yet, and the weather cloudy with that same threat of rain which had darkened the escape from Dry Devils Fork. But the men sided with Forbes, and reckoned young Frank Bonham was showing a trace of nerve wear. Nothing human was going to get off that island.

Lieutenant Bonham proved obdurate. "Niggers," he allowed, "ain't hardly human." There was general quiet agreement to this proposal, and the men went about the preparation of their suppers and the picketing of their horses. Yet, if the substance of Bonham's statement were fanciful, its sum was not. On the island Ned Huddleston had not quit, and within the hour young Ranger Bonham was made a prophet without honor.

# 26.

Not long after the watch fires had been laid, Ned, who had cleansed and bound Terresa's wound as best he might, noted a commotion in the south-bank camp. A rancher's chuck wagon, of the canvas-covered, possum-bellied variety which spearheaded trail-driven cattle herds, had drawn up at the ford below the island.

Straining eye and ear, Ned quickly understood that this wagon was in front of a big bunch of cows on the drive. The wagon's driver, who was as well the camp cook, was telling the Rangers that he was going on as far as he might that night because of the threatening storm. A wet prairie did not impede the herd or its guardians, but it was hell for a heavy chuck wagon to get over. Now the cows would not be along until midnight or so, but they would be along. A big storm would bring up the river into its willows, and the trail boss had decided to drive on through the night on the chance of beating the high water at this particular crossing.

Neither the Rangers nor Ned could see any holes in the cook's argument. With a warning to get on across and clear out *muy pronto,* the chuck wagon was waved on.

The cook claimed he wanted to check his teams' harness before going in the water, however, and the start across was delayed. In that delay Ned saw the hand of Providence. "Praise be!" he said softly, and raced back to where Terresa lay resting. The Mexican boy, poet's face or no, managed a splendid Spanish curse and a bravely gestured sign of assent.

"It's crazy in the head, like you are, *hermano,*" he said. "But we have no other plan, and I would rather die in our own way, than by the rope they coil for us."

Ned stripped their two horses of saddles and bridles and untied them. Neither man would leave his beloved mount bound

[ 82 ]

and waiting. Entero and the black must have the same chance to go free as Ned and Terresa.

Ned then carried his Mexican comrade to the foot of the island and lowered him into the passing current. "Hold hard to my belt," he told the other, slipping into the dark waters beside him. "I'll cling to the brush till it's time." Terresa nodded, and the two lay on the current below the overhanging scrub.

"*Maria!*" whispered the wounded boy. "What in the name of the Holy Father is that dung-headed *cocinero* doing?"

"Easy, easy," ordered Ned. "Yonder he goes, getting up on the seatbox, now."

The cook lashed up his teams. The heavy chuck wagon rumbled down to the ford and out into the shallows.

"Now!" said Ned, and let go of the brush clump.

He and Terresa each drew in the deepest breath his lungs would encompass. Submerged, they bobbed along the rocky bottom of the stream. Its ten-mile current carried them true as arrows to their target. When the chuck wagon reached mid-channel and was slowed while the teams plunged and lurched to pass its deeper waters, Ned and Terresa surfaced hard against the sagging possum belly of the vehicle.

"Hoo, Jesus, hold tight!" whispered Ned into the Mexican's ear, and Terresa held like grim death to the edge of the belly. Ned, quick as a black otter, dove beneath the belly to come to its downstream side, his progress and his purpose overlaid handsomely by the curses and shouts of the driver, and by the lungings and splashings of his laboring teams.

The possum belly was a big canvas tarp of bull buffalo or steer hide attached beneath the chuck wagon in the manner of an oposum's pouch, to carry firewood from camp to camp on the frequently treeless plains of the *llano*. From this portable woodpile Ned now clawed out the necessary hole for Terresa and himself. Returning to the upstream side, he lifted his wounded comrade into the emptied-out sling and piled in atop his slender body.

The floating on downstream of the discarded firewood, being hidden by the wagon's top from both Ranger and driver views, was not noticed. By the time the latter had the wagon out of the heavy current, the stream was clear. At the same moment, the liberated horses of the outlaws, realizing their masters were gone, chose to swim for it on their own, heading perversely for Captain Forbes' side of the stream. Here they provided some additional brief diversion before escaping into the outer prairie. On his side, young Bonham never thought to challenge the chuck wagon, but merely ordered his men to join those of Forbes in building higher the watch fires of both banks.

Plainly those damned horse thieves were up to something. And, by God, whatever it was, they weren't going to put it over on the Texas Rangers.

The chuck wagon rumbled on. Its creaking wheels and dripping possum belly left a thinning trail of water away from the island channel crossing. Overhead, the storm muttered and threatened but did not break. The miles toiled slowly past. No pursuit came from the crossing, and Terresa dozed fitfully, the fever rising in him again. Ned forced himself to stay awake, praying and watching. Sometime before dawn, in the very blackest part of the night, he saw it, far off over the plain: Just a wink and a gleam of light, of yellow lamplight. With the lamplight Ned's foxlike hearing picked up the distant bleating of goats.

He awakened Terresa and together they rolled out of the possum belly into a heavy grass beside the trail. When the wagon had gone, creaking and complaining through the inky dark, Ned took Terresa in his arms and made for the distant beacon.

His eyesight and hearing had not lied to him. The light was from a hovel's lamp, lit for the pre-dawn milking of the baaing nannies; and he found, as he had known he must when he heard the goats, a lonely Mexican herder's home, and with it, that sanctuary he had dreamed for Terresa.

For himself there was no haven. He went on that same night, halting only long enough to be given food, a blanket and a great warming draft of *gardente*. The man, Amelio Chavez, got him away in the gray dawn, hidden in a burro cart full of mustang hides. The hides were going to the house of Hipólito Zangara, the saddlemaker, fifteen miles north by east. At Hipólito's he slept the day, starting on that next night.

The brown-skinned sons of the *monte* could help no more. They were poor *descamisados* of the American side. Between them they had no decent horse or no gun that would fire. All they could give, they did give: the clothing of a Texas Mexican and the soft-voiced gentle bidding of *"Vaya con Dios."*

[84]

If Ned did indeed go with God, or whether he made it by Huddleston guts and horse thief cunning, the legend does not tell. But the bare bones of the folklore show through the sands of time, nonetheless. So much is known: In that April of 1866, with the first great tides of the trail herds heading north, Ned Huddleston came to Red River and, crossing over, disappeared from Texas forever.

# 27.

For five years Ned Huddleston wandered the northern ranges. Now and again he worked at ranches, mostly breaking horses, and tales of his uncanny ability to gentle and train a kinky bronco spread from the Indian Nations to Montana. Unfortunately, Ned's other skill with horseflesh ran by report even more swiftly ahead of him, and thus he was two times jailed for stealing horses, and two times he broke jail to go free. He was run by uncounted angry ranchers and posses of roundup crews, but never caught. Yet, like the lobo wolf which hunts too long and too hard in one country, Ned began to sense that a change of preserves was indicated.

The spring of 1870 found him in Wyoming trapping mustangs. It was a lonely life but wild and free. In all his wanderings he had not taken another friend or sought another woman, nor had he made company with the Indians. He had learned about these things.

For a comrade, who could replace Terresa? For a mate, what female would not do what Dolores had done? As for being a squawman—by far the most attractive life for a free Negro on the Great Plains—well, he had not forgotten the Comancheros and the Comanches and those eight drying hanks of whitefolks' hair on the blanket of Pin Oak Jack.

Ned might not owe the white man much but pain, yet he had

not seen Indian hair taken by whites, and he felt more at home with the "pale faces." Indians were crazy. Since Ned tended a bit in the same direction, he reasoned that two cracked heads were not better than one sound skull. Healthier for him, he concluded, was his course of lone-wolfing. It gave him a lot of time to plan for his future, and it gave the ranchers and settlers of Colorado Territory and the Oklahoma Indian Nations time to forget their plans for his past. Lonesome he might be, but not *that* lonesome.

So he stayed out on the plains.

Later that summer, however, weary of talking to the wind and to his wild horses, and with the smell of an early autumn in the mile-high Wyoming air, he met a fellow hat-waver on the trail out of the mustang pastures.

"Waving the hat" was simple outlaw courtesy of the road. If a man riding alone in that vast land saw another rider coming his way, and if for purposes of vanity or security he did not want that other rider coming close enough to see his features or the markings of his horse—not close enough to identify either in court—then that man stood in his stirrups and waved his hat. The second man, if of sound mind and half-smart, would wave back and ride as wide around the loner as the land permitted.

But on this occasion the other rider, rather than waving his hat when Ned signaled for the swingout, drew his pistol and fired it five times up in the air and waved a clay jug of whiskey.

Ned could taste that liquor. He hadn't had a drop since the new grass came.

Well, how much could a drink cost him out there where he was? If the other rider proved nosey, Ned could always steal his horse and let him walk into Laramie or Rock Springs with his information about seeing the Negro badman Ned Huddleston.

When he and the transgressor had ridden up to one another, however, no such drastic hostilities were required. Ned had a packhorse full of fresh antelope steaks, bacon, beans, coffee, sugar, even white flour and saleratus baking powder. The newcomer, a positive giant of a Mexican from the South Pass mining camps, was virtually starving for a decent meal, being totally lost and trying to keep his spirits bright and his belly pacified by sipping from the principal burden of his own pack animal: two carefully padded panniers full of trade quality

Taos Lightning, the frontier rot-gut supreme.

A deal was soon and happily, arrived at; camp was made in a stand of bullpine nearby and Ned, nearly as great a cook as a horse thief, prepared a prairie feast. Broiled antelope, sugared coffee, saleratus biscuits and bacon-grease butter, ah! what sweet repast, and noble, particularly washed down with native skull-buster whiskey and topped off by some of the Mexican's beautiful black Sonora cheroots.

The huge fellow—his name, he said, was Pablo Herrera—proved more than a purveyor of drink and smoke, however. The consignment of whiskey was owned by his brother, he told Ned. The brother was of the name of José Herrera, called Mexican Joe by the *gringos* up here in this cursed cold north country. Joe used the whiskey in trade with the Indians. Such commerce was risky, of course; but men who could understand the Indian sign language and were not afraid of feathers and paint were much in demand in brother Joe's business. Now if good new friend Nedito would care to ride on into South Pass with Pablo, there was every chance that gainful employment might be the result.

Ned had no moral sentiments against selling whiskey to the Indians. He would sell anything to anyone who needed it and had the money to pay, and he explained to his Mexican brother that his morals were those of a white man, that one must not be misled by his dark hide. To this, the giant Pablo nodded.

"You remind me of my young cousin who likewise works for José," he said. "You will like our cousin. He is a man of much experience and rare judgment."

"Good," said Ned. "I got me a pretty rare judgment of my own. About as rare as they come, I reckon."

"It is a deed, then?" asked Pablo.

Ned put out his hand and they shook in earnest.

"It is a deed, *amigo,*" he said.

In South Pass there was an unexpected bonus. The young cousin of Pablo and Mexican Joe Herrera proved not so young. Indeed, he was of the same age as Ned Huddleston, and of course he was Terresa.

Both friends wept at the reunion. Neither had imagined to see the other in this life, particularly under such ideal arrangements. *"Hijo!"* laughed Terresa, unabashed by his tears. "Did I not tell you that together we would grow rich? Now you will see!"

Ned blinked and brushed at his eyes. "I'm done rich a'ready," he said. "Ain't I found you again?"

Introduced to the *jefe* of the clan, Ned found Mexican Joe to be a man determined to make good by his own initiative in the dog-eat-dog arena of free enterprise. He had no complaint with the American system of every man for himself and, through the commercial advantage of his reputation as "the premier knife fighter of the plains," experienced little trouble from competition.

Joe was not only big and tough and mean; he was smart and hard-working. A member of his official "family" did not get paid for loafing. As a mining camp, South Pass was on the boom. Joe had been there two years and had not wasted his time. He had interests in a faro parlor and ran a private high-stakes game of his own for miners who had "struck it" but did not care for the labor of toting it to Denver. Taking up with the camp's queen-lady of cash virtue, he soon had control of the prostitution trade, as well as of the lady's heart. By day, when other gamblers and procurers slept, Mexican Joe was out upon the hinterland rustling cattle for the butcher trade in the mines, and somewhere between his busy nights and the shining hours of sunlight he found time to supervise brother Pablo's "whiskey route" among the local Wind River Shoshone. All of this industry was not lost upon Ned. When no more beef was needed to be rustled from the herds of the neighboring friendly ranchers, no ambitious competitor in the prostitution trade required a few knife cuts to teach caution, and the Wind River whiskey deliveries were caught up, Ned was put immediately to swamping out the sawdust in the gambling tent, or polishing up the spitoons in the bordello.

These menial chores impressed Ned only with Mexican Joe's thrifty wisdom, and the Negro outlaw complained to no one. The fact that Herrera would trust the new member to relieve either Pablo or Terresa at their whiskey-selling or cattle-rustling chores, yet reserve to Ned alone the janitorial work, was an interesting bigotry. In a less robust community, or one with more time to worry about such discriminations, Ned might have suffered irreparable trauma. As it was, when the profits for any particular venture were divided, the Negro "cousin" received exactly the same split as the Mexican, and so did not care whether it came from cuspidor burnishing or brand burning, so long as it was equal.

But if Ned were content with Mexican Joe's leadership and with the social order of South Pass, the responsible pillars of the camp were not. "That damn Mexican," they decided, "has got to go. If he ain't run out of town before the snow flies, he'll run us out with the spring thaw."

They began by alienating Joe's red light lady friend. Acting upon the best legal advice of the camp's totally crooked judge, she cleaned out Joe's entire and considerable fortune in stored dust and nuggets, and took off in dead of night for destinations unknown save to the "legal committee," which had sanctioned the theft.

The committee next sought to subvert a member of the Herrera gang to perform the remaining necessity, the "removal" of Mexican Joe himself.

Happily for big Joe, they chose the wrong man.

"José," Ned reported laconically, "I done been offered the chance to butcher you out, but the pay wasn't right."

He paused to let the Mexican vent his Spanish temper in marvelous profanity, then let him have the other side of the blade, twisting it a bit with his wry grin.

"Now that ain't the whole of it, *jefe*," he said. "They done hired theirse'ves another nigger to do the job and, iffen you will pardon the suggestion, *Patron*, it look like they done got you coming and going and halfways between. *Que tal!*"

"What is that, you black horse thief?" raged Joe *"You* would dare suggest *anything* to Herrera!"

Ned shrugged, no longer grinning. "Ain't trying to suggest nothing, Josélito. Just saying what they told me and undoubted told the other nigger; onliest one can lose is you or the nigger. Nigger kill you, fine. You kill the nigger, fine. One way you is dead, and the other way you is deader."

"What? What is that you are saying?"

"I is saying nothing," replied Ned, "but I is telling you something; you get in that knife fight with that nigger and you kills him, you going to swing for it."

Herrera paled, seeing the committee's trap. But he was a man who would fight a bear. No puny *gringo* pack of vigilantes was going to stampede him out of South Pass. He sought out the hired assassin and, in a folklore knife fight which spilled in and out of two log taverns and a canvas bawdy house, left the poor fellow expiring appropriately in the gutter before the unpainted emporium which bore the legend *TAXIDERMY AND MORTUARIUM* above its sun-bleached lintel.

This could well have been the end for all of them, for the committee seized Joe before he got his breath back from the chase. But Ned had gathered Terresa and Pablo, and while the committeemen argued about where they should lynch their former competitor, the Negro led his comrades in a daylight dash up the boardwalk on flying horseflesh. There was, of course, a spare and saddled mount for the prisoner.

The crowd, swarming about the captive, eager to exercise its citizenship, was not ready to be taken in the rear by four horses on the full fly. There was, moreover, a local ordinance against riding horses on the sidewalks of South Pass. Probably a dozen public-spirited drunks were knocked to the ground by the charge. Another two or three dozen were stomped upon by the wild-eyed mustangs. The committee retired hurriedly to caucus, and Mexican Joe was lifted to his horse, still trussed for the airy trot. Away went the rescuers led by black Ned Huddleston, whom the South Passers knew as Tan Mex, both from his association with the Herreras and his relatively "Latin brown" complexion.

As a gesture of good will, and as a signature to actions of his own planning, Tan Mex did not leave South Pass without warning its citizens of the risks of pursuit.

Shaking loose the noose from about Joe's bronzed neck, he turned his horse about and charged back up Main Street, building a fine round calf-roping loop on the way. He was in time to deftly "heel" the chairman of the committee, as that fearless leader dodged desperately to reach cover.

Reversing his mount once more, the Negro rustler put the spurs in deep. The horse hit out on a digging gallop, and the chairman followed. Since there had been a good summer shower that same morning, the street was just muddy enough to prevent any serious loss of hide. But when, five hundred yards outside town, Ned turned his fat calf loose and galloped on south with the Herreras and Terresa, the point had been dragged into the head of His Honor. There was no posse dispatched from South Pass.

# 28.

Brown's Hole, or Brown's Park, as later called, lay in the extreme northwestern corner of the Colorado territory. Its northern fringes pushed into Wyoming, its western flanks encroached upon Utah. Its geography, together with its utter remoteness and semi-arid climate of light snowfall and moderate temperature, made "the Hole" the favored wintering ground of the outlaws. Almost literally a "hole," this giant fortress in the mother stone of the O-wi-yu-kuts Plateau was bisected by the Green River. The Green, a major artery of the Colorado, entered the outlaw redoubt through the sheer portals of Red Canyon on the north, looped eastward thirty-five miles over the floor of the park, and disappeared with frightening suddenness through the cliff-girt cataract of the Canyon of Lodore.

Due south the hideout valley was cut off from the outside by the impenetrable mass of Diamond Mountain, broken by the Crouse Creek and Sears Canyon trails.

To the north was the equally immense rampart of Cold Spring Mountain, presenting another nearly total wall. To the west lay naked badlands where no water ran, while eastward was the valley's one reasonable entrance. Here, Vermilion Creek split the heart of the Limestone Divide to empty into the Green two miles upstream of the fearsome portals of Lodore. Bordering the creek ran the sole and narrow rut by which wheeled vehicles might gain entrance to the Hole, and it was by this Vermilion Creek wagon road that Mexican Joe Herrera, Pablo and Terresa came in the late summer of 1870—some accounts say 1868—with their Negro guide, Ned Huddleston.

When, in his wanderings since crossing Red River, Ned had learned of the Hole, he never revealed. When queried uneasily whether his earlier explorations of the area could help their present "business," the Negro partner said he could think of three very fine outlets for their mainline branches of merchandise. In order of importance these were (1) a local band of Yampatika Utes who could outdrink any Shoshone tribe, (2) a constant and growing need for replacement horses by the emigrant wagon traffic which ran nearby the Hole on the way to the California Cutoff, and (3) a steady demand for eating-beef by the same emigrant trade.

Ned pointed out that these latter travelers should also be in the market for the beautiful Ute buckskins, moccasins, beadwork, saddlebags and braided halters of the Yampatikas which the Herreras would take in pay for their redeye whiskey deliveries. Moreover, said Ned, and most important, the Hole was a place where cattle herds in wholesale numbers might be hidden until top market conditions developed. There was little or no winter die-up inside the mountain walls of this wonderland park of the Rockies. God had made it for his lost lambs like themselves, and if those strayed sheep couldn't make it pay off, then Ned Huddleston didn't know pinto beans about the bandit business.

It developed that the ex-slave's intelligence report was well above bean level. The gang saw very little hard money at first, but they won an immediate wealth in the matter of safety from the pursuit and persecution by the honest cattle ranchers or lawmen outside Brown's Hole. Within the refuge, the Yampatikas, once they had tried the quality of the Herrera rotgut, behaved in a friendly and neighborly manner. The other scattered non-Indian residents could offer nothing of serious opposition to the tightly knit Herrera organization. Mexican Joe soon owned the secret basin. True to Ned's prediction, the cattle rustling and horse-thieving trade flourished and the whiskey sales to the Utes soared. Black man, Mexican, renegade white, red pagan Indian, lived cheek-by-jowl; if not whelming over with brother love, at least each knew fraternity enough to survive without notable bloodshed.

Yet it was neither this outlaw camaraderie nor the good business upon which it fed which gradually gave Ned a simple understanding of himself and his place in the complex of bad men and brute conditions of existence which was Brown's Hole in the late 1870's.

"You know what we is here?" he asked Terresa one day.

They were paused atop a scarp of Diamond Mountain, resting

their horses after a hard climb to reach the Hole with a stolen Utah herd. Terresa, surveying the bleak browns of the winter-killed foliage below, and shivering in the October wind, shook his handsome head.

"I know what *I* am here, *amigo*," he replied. "I am cold and lonely and homesick. I want to go back to Coahuila and get warm!"

"No," Ned said. "I don't mean that. Ain't nobody miss that warm South sun and them cotton-cloud Mexico skies more nor Old Ned. But we is something here that we wasn't never down yonder to Mexico, or Texas, or even back home where I come from."

"You will need to name it, my twin," said Terresa, cursing the cold. "For I cannot see anything here except dead leaves and dark snow clouds and another long winter in this Christ-fore-saken northland."

"It don't matter," said Ned, teeth chattering. "Dead leaves, brown grass, blue-cold snow all around, it ain't nothing. It ain't nothing and it don't matter. *We is free here.*"

"Free?" Terresa laughed. "Free to what? Freeze to death? Die of loneliness? Or of wanting a woman? Or simply for want of someone who can write his own name, or has been to Mexico City, or is *not* wanted for murder, to talk to? *Quita!* You must be crazy."

He spurred his horse back toward the slowing band of stolen cattle, speeding the animals into the canyon trail downward to Brown's Hole. Ned looked after him a moment, his dark eyes clouded with thought.

"Yeah," he said softly to his horse. "Crazy to be free, maybe." And he touched the animal with his quirt and went on down the canyon hazing the drag of the Utah steers.

# 29.

Ned was not dismayed by the sensitive Terresa's failure to see the Hole as he saw it. He continued to think that he was a free man within the starkly beautiful confines of the mountain park, and to so conduct himself. In the beginning nothing denied his dream.

He lived through the winter with the other members of the Mexican community on Dummy Bottoms of Vermilion Creek, the good-natured co-equal of any cattle rustler, horse thief or murderer among his coffee-colored peers. He refused no assignment that Mexican Joe awarded him. In the division of the spotty loot from the first jobs, he drew his cut without complaint. As business improved with the advent of spring, he even had a few hard dollars in his frayed jeans, as well as a contented belly filled with *frijoles, chili* and *carne* and corn *tortillas*. But it was those very *tortillas* which initiated the trouble.

Joe Herrera and the others, about a dozen men now, shared a common *Latino* bond. To them the corn that made the *tortilla* was a matter of commerce at least as important as stealing cows or horses, or selling trade whiskey.

The supply of shelled corn had been purchased or traded mainly from the emigrant wagon trains, but those people usually did not even have enough grain for their own journey, so the supply was ragged and unreliable.

As Ned knew from his janitorial employment in South Pass, Mexican Joe let no member of the gang languish, and drove himself harder than any. It was thus no surprise to the ex-slave when Joe became inspired to grow his own corn.

The trouble came in the details. Ned had become known to the denizens of the Hole as Tan Mex, his South Pass alias. This did not displease him, as it gave him a Mexican identity, a welcome respite from the pleasures of being a free Negro. Because the appellation was applied most widely by the white members of the community, it held a double attraction, since Ned, in his simple way, thought that the whites actually believed him to be, well, at least partly of the Spanish strain.

The "white community" of Brown's Hole in that second year consisted of scattered unimportant outlaws like Hank Golden and Tip Gault and some forgotten squatters who ran a few dozen or a hundred head of cows hoping to aid the natural increase by stealing from their rustler neighbors, who in turn shared the ambition in reverse. If not honest, these white men were at least cattlemen. They not only stole but they tended their herds, and the result was that some four thousand head ranged the Hole in the late sixties and early seventies. Since their Mexican brothers preferred beef eating to cattle herding, some friction obtained. The Latin attitude was that, with all those cattle running free in the basin, why worry about raising your own? It was not a commercially sound enterprise, and Joe, always with the keen business eye for profit, disdained it. But it was the tortillas, in the end, not the matter of cattle rustling, which brought the climax.

One day Juan José Herrera, provoked by the undependable supply of corn, issued his most incredible command: "Clear the creek-bottom flats of the rabbit brush; Herrera will grow his own *grano!* Come, grub out every root. Level the land. Haul the earth and the stone and erect the dam across the *riachuelo* of the Vermilion. *Mas pronto, mas pronto!* Everybody work."

And everyone did work, for the alternative was to consult with the ten-inch sheath knife of Mexican Joe; an order once issued was to be obeyed, no exceptions, no excuses. But Tan Mex, complete with his new dignity and aware at last that he was somebody, declined.

The agrarian vistas open to a Herrera were invisible to Tan Mex. The excitement of raising the level of Vermilion Creek to create a head of irrigation water for the dusty flats now asnarl with rabbit brush, greasewood, bullsage and buckthorn, stirred no kindred spark in the dark breast of the one-time forager.

"I seen enough of chopping brush and grubbing with a cotton hoe before I was ten years old. Go 'way far off and lay down in a quiet corner, José. Tan Mex don't aim to work the field for no man no more—he's free."

By what odd logic Ned would bridle at fieldwork and grin at

emptying spitoons was his own secret. But Mexican Joe was no more interested in the Negro rider's psyche than Tan Mex was in Joe's home-grown *tortilla* project. There was a very bad moment of silence between the two, into which young Terresa hurriedly projected himself.

"Cousin," he said to Herrera, "let me talk to my old friend. He does not understand the poverty and heartbreak of your own life. I will explain it to him."

Mexican Joe drew his ten-inch blade. From his shirt pocket he extracted a whetstone. Very deliberately he began drawing the weapon's steel back and forth over the abrasive sharpener. It was a gritty, eloquent sound.

"Very well," he told Terresa. "Meanwhile, I shall prepare my own argument."

Terresa took Tan Mex aside. He talked hard to him. Herrera, he said, had worked like a dog when he first came to the North. Freighting by ox-wagon from Granger to the South Pass gold fields, he earned the stake with which he began. With the stake he brought to South Pass that same *gringo* lady love who was later to reign as the queen-bee of the camp, and to fleece Joe of his last Yankee dollar. This betrayal had made Terresa's older cousin a fierce fellow. After that he trusted no one, and all must do as he told them or face his knife.

For a man with a poet's supposed eloquence, Terresa fell short under stress.

"Listen, *hombre*," said Ned, when the tale was told, "iffen me and you was to team together, like in the old days down to Coahulia, we could whup the lot of them. I will handle your cousin Joe; you jest keep them other *paisanos* off'n my back."

They were standing in a small growth of scrub perhaps thirty feet from the waiting gang and its hard-eyed *jefe*. Terresa, for the first time in Ned's memory, showed anxiety. There was a paleness to his fine features which heredity had not put there.

"*Por Dios!*" he whispered. "Are you indeed mad, Nedito? You cannot go against him with the knife. No man may do that and survive. Did we not see him against that other *Negrito* in South Pass?"

"Is you afraid, Terresa?"

"Never!" came the instant denial. "How dare you?"

"Then I ain't stupid," nodded Ned. "I ain't intending to come at him with no knife." He stooped and picked up from the creekside flotsam a drift stick, hard and knobby and heavy as a Ute war club. Hefting the cudgel, he nodded again. "You keep 'em off my back, like I said," he ordered, and went out of the thicket without waiting for Terresa's agreement.

Facing Mexican Joe, Ned bobbed his dark head for the third and final time. "Here," he said. "Let's see you hone that there *cuchillo* of yourn on this." Before the gang's chieftain could so much as lift his upper lip to snarl his disdain of such meager armament, Ned had struck him a terrible blow across both shins. Mexican Joe went to earth with a screech of pain.

So unbelievably fast was his opponent, however, that the *jefe's* body had not yet reached the ground when the cudgel slashed in again, this time cracking the wrist of the knife hand. A second scream ruptured the first.

Tan Mex stooped without notable haste and retrieved the dropped blade. Running a pink-balled, black thumb along the razored edge, he shook his head. "Wouldn't harm warm butter," he announced. Then, tossing the weapon in front of Mexican Joe, still panting in pain upon the creek bank, he said, sounding honestly sad, "*Jefe,* I reckon I have tore my shirt with you; how come you to make me do it?"

Herrera was on his feet now, helped up by giant Pablo and Terresa. Thinking Terresa had been behind him all the while, Ned felt a tingle of uneasiness. Hadn't his handsome "twin" understood the arrangement? Well, that was Ned's fault. He ought to have been sure before leaving the brush clump. It didn't matter, though. All was well that wound up with nobody killed, and he and the friend of his Coahuila days not even scratched, *gracias a Dios.*

Mexican Joe, breathing with difficulty, did not agree. Glaring at the Negro outlaw with the eyes of a wounded animal, he swore that he would dismember Tan Mex, black joint by black joint, upon the next encounter. The *Negrito* horse thief would be wise indeed to understand the threat in its context of Mexican Joe's unquestioned bravery. And should he select to be somewhere far south of Brown's Hole by next daylight, that too would show a high order of native intellect.

Terresa, staying at Herrera's side, made a final passioned plea for Nedito to listen and believe. He must leave the Hole and must do so because not ony the *jefe* but every member of the Mexican encampment would be bound by "Spanish honor" to avenge their leader's disgrace.

To this, Ned shrugged and replied to his friend with great confidence. "Well, come on, *hombre,* what do we care? You been wanting to head home since way last fall, anyhow. Now you got company."

"No, no!" said Terresa, clearly alarmed. "You do not understand, my twin. These are *my* people."

Ned stood there thinking as hard as he knew how to think. "What does that mean?" he said at last.

Terresa was not comfortable, but he was no coward. "It means that *I* stay here," he answered. "You go alone."

Ned understood it then. Terresa was afraid to go with him, and it took courage even to tell that to Ned. But it would have taken more courage—and more than just courage—to have told him nothing, just to have come across that circle of silence and taken his stand by Ned's side. That would have answered everything.

Terresa, wild, high-riding, gallant Terresa, who would risk his life for his Negro friend against the Texas Rangers at Dry Devils Fork, would do nothing for that same friend against these people he called his own.

Ned realized sadly that Terresa had not changed; it was Tan Mex who had tried to change, and who now knew why he had failed.

He backed away from the Mexicans, holding his driftwood club warily. He was going to go, if they would let him, but not without his good-bye to Terresa.

"No, old friend," Ned told the pale youth, "it ain't that they're your people, *hombre;* it's that they ain't mine."

With the words he disappeared into the bottom brush and from the history of the Herrera gang.

# 30.

Ned was not unhappy as he left the Hole. Only the odd matter of Terresa's desertion disturbed him. Since he would never understand that strange behavior, except as he had named it—a matter of the Mexicans denying him the kinship he had sought—the Negro wanderer did not dwell upon his banishment.

Saddling his stout bay trail horse, he placed his outfit upon the bony back of Jeff Davis, a piebald packmule which he had more adopted than stolen, and together the three comrades set forth southward.

It was almost summer and the air was warm and heady with the scent of pine. The streams sang from the runoff of the dwindling snowpack, and grass sprang yellow-green from every bed of moist soil. Each ambush of rocky crevice, or gnarled root, waylaid the trail with bursts of flower fire; Indian paintbrush of red, orange and white, lupines of blue, larkspur of darker blue, yellow buttercup and glacier lily, harebell, crocus and a dozen more sprayed the mountain greenery at Ned's feet. As far toward any compass point as his delighted eye might reach, there was nothing but beauty, bounty and birds singing.

"Hoo, boys!" he said to the gelding and the mule. "We ain't rich, you say? Got nothing in this world, and nobody what wants us? We's busted, broke-flat and been disowed? Down on the luck? Dealt dirty? Done wrong by again?" He straightened, filling his broad chest with the piney air. "Lord, God," he said, "listen to this mountain talk!"

He halted the animals, sweeping a long arm across the timbered flats.

"You hear that jay a'rasping yonder? You catch that rock-pig a'whistling sharp and shrill? That hawk a'wheeling up there? That crow in yonder pine? You know what they're chirping about, what this here old green mountain be trying to say to us?

"Old mountain, he say, 'Why, hello there, Ned! Where you been all this time? I been a'waiting here for you and where you been? Off somewheres yonder rooting with them other pigs along them creek bottoms, that's where. Stealing critters that ain't yours. Lapping up all that wolf-pizen Injun whiskey. Cussing the white man. Scandalizing the Lord. Putting up with all them others, that little old Mex gal, them Texan Rangers, that there half-pint 'Pache tried to lop off your head, them hoss-thieving Comancheros, them scalp-stripping Comanche braves, the whole lot of them. Hoo, Ned, you been wronger than sin; I been your onliest friend all the while, me and them birds and animals. Turn loose your stock; you're here, you're home, boy. Root down. It ain't no place else in all the world for you, but me and them. Never was, Ned, never was . . .' "

His voice trailed off, the wind sighed away stirring the pines, and he nodded mutteringly, "That's right, old mountain, that's right. I finally hear you straight."

The brown gelding cocked his ears and whickered. The pinto mule stretched its rubbery neck and brayed hoarsely.

Ned shook his head happily. "Ain't no use to auger it," he said. "We're staying."

He had been loafing down into the White River country, figuring to bear east below Yellow Jacket Pass, south again to Tennessee Pass and over it into the new Colorado diggings. There he believed he might be profitably employed hunting meat during summer and fall for the booming but isolated gold camps.

Now work could wait. He had a splendid outfit and there was no point in turning honest before he had to. Sure, living with outlaws and thieves just naturally brought a man down. Maybe most of the poor fellows he had met along the way hadn't learned better, but Ned had. He had been raised decent, even if he hadn't thought about it for five or six years, and if he put his mind and muscles to it, a man knew that he could hoist himself back up to where he had started from. That mountain had really been telling him to light down and think about things —take the time there, where it was all beautiful and quiet and the air smelled good, to get his brains untangled. Then, when he was all straightened out, he could follow his spirit wherever it led him, knowing it wouldn't lead him into any more places like Brown's Hole.

"Hoo, boys!" he cried to his animals, feeling uplifted. "Lookit up in them aspen where the crick tumbles off that little bench—that's prime wood, water, grass and wind-shelter."

He turned the brown gelding into the slope, climbing toward the bench. The spotted mule followed with professional approval, recognizing the easy life as quickly as its master. He stretched his ropy tail stiffly out behind him, elevated his hairy muzzle, made the silent mountainside shudder with the rusty *scrreee-haww, scrreee-haww* of his brass-lunged agreement with Ned's decision.

There was, indeed, but one detail of trouble in this agreement of the mule's and his master's instincts. Someone else had shared them.

Jeff Davis's bray was answered by a kindred *scrreee-haww* from above, and when the ascending trio topped the slope trail, they saw before them a lone tipi of a familiar design.

"*Shoshone,*" Ned said to the horse and the mule. "Walk soft and maybe we won't get shot."

They did not get shot, finding instead a grateful welcome. The occupants of the camp were a Shoshone squaw and her five-year-old halfbreed daughter. The woman was short and wide, with a flat head and very big and homely face, calling herself a name which sounded to Ned like "Tickup." The little girl was tiny, fine of feature, shy and sweet. Her name, pronounced in the guttural tongue of the ugly mother, came out "Mincy." Ned was never sure afterward of those names. He tried "hiccup" and "wickiup" and like words on the woman, and "mincemeat," "Mindy," and "Missy" for the child's name. But the upshot was still Tickup and Mincy, and so Ned remembered them that way, and that is the way they remain in the legend.

Tickup, it seemed, was the property of one Croad, a squawman described by the woman as a habitual beater of females, most especially of small children. She and Mincy had been trying to escape him, but he was too vigilant and too jealous.

Ned, eying the bony-headed, duck-bottomed Shoshone woman, nodded in outward kindness to this vanity, but inwardly wondered at the quality of white man who might guard this dusky gem from theft or yearning. His ability to communicate with Tickup, however, was limited. Her English and his Shoshone, even abetted by their mutual mastery of sign language, did not impart to Ned a suitable description of the absent Croad.

He learned that the brutal squawman was a white prospector, "a yellow-dirt digger," as the woman said in Indian terms, and that he either was or was not the father of the little girl, Mincy. When Ned tried to clarify this matter, the squaw got "vapory on him," and "sort of drifted off, smokey-like."

He was left with the impression, through this evasiveness, that Mincy had been sired most likely "several white gold hunters back," but that her father had indeed been a white man could not be doubted. The shy tot never drew those delicate, fine-cut features from any heathen redskin; most surely her daddy was a southern gentleman. She was quality; Ned knew the marks. He had been brought up on them and there was something about that southern blood that bred on. Once raised to appreciate its fine lines, a man could recognize them anywhere.

This self-induced certainty about Mincy's bloodline only added to the resentment against Croad which the story of the poor mistreated Shoshone woman was building in the breast of Ned Huddleston.

The idea of making a virtual slave of an ignorant Indian lady and, then, actually *beating* that fine little baby girl roused all the anger in Ned. Why, by God, if it was the last thing he ever got done in that life, he was going to stand up to that rascal Croad. He would give him what for when he showed up from the hunt the squaw said he'd gone on, and then he would sieze Tickup and Mincy away from him and bear them off to safety. He would do it even if he had to help her and her little girl clean on back up into the Idaho country, where the squaw claimed her tribe lived.

"Listen," he said to the Shoshone woman with words and handsigns, "you and the little one stay in the tipi when he comes. Old Ned will take care of everything. *Wagh!*"

Since *wagh* was a universal plains and mountain Indian word taken from the charging grunt of the grizzly bear, the woman was convinced she had found a champion who would at last free her from the vicious Croad. She made signs of gratitude and agreement, took the little girl and went into the tipi.

Ned, somewhat surprised by the speed of her obedience, looked behind himself.

Croad was there. He was there and he was big and he was mean and he was something else: *Southern.*

"Well, nigger," the big man drawled, "you'd best get ready to crawl. You've put your black foot in the wrong door this time. Start whimpering, boy."

Croad had gotten between Ned and his horse. The Negro rider's Winchester was in its saddle scabbard, while the white man's rifle was in his hands. But Croad was not going to use the gun, not on this visitor. He went, instead, to Ned's horse, his pale eyes never leaving Ned. From the high horn of the outlaw's Mexican saddle hung a braided rawhide quirt which the southerner took down. Placing his rifle against a boulder, he flexed the quirt in his two hands and moved unhurriedly in on Ned.

The latter stood as if tranced by some juju of his past against which his tested courage and fighting skill were powerless. Yet if the white man was big, so was Ned Huddleston: he measured six feet and two inches in that twenty-second year of his life. He weighed, the legend was to say, "a hard two hundred pounds," with a thirty-two-inch waist and a forty-six-inch chest. But still he stood there and let Croad quirt him again and again across the face and shoulders. When he broke, it was to drop to his hands and knees, not to strike back, and Croad left him there disdaining even to look back at him.

Ned stayed down. He was still there when the Shoshone squaw came out of the tipi at Croad's order. The woman waddled over and stared down at him. There was an expression on her face of complete blankness. Bobbing her head she hawked noisily and spat upon the crouching Negro.

"*Wagh!*" she said, and walked away.

But Mincy, the little girl, came up slowly to Ned, holding something in her hand hidden from the squaw. Ned did not want to look at her, and he wished she had not seen him there. It hurt him more than the quirt cuts to have the tiny child come and stand like that, watching him the shameful way he was.

He moved on hands and knees away from Mincy, getting over to the nearby rocks. He sat there, his back pressed up against the cool stone, head down, avoiding the child, the mother, Croad, even the camp itself. But Mincy followed after him, and when the squaw and Croad were busy with breaking camp, she put her small hand on the bleeding black shoulder, patting Ned softly, slowly, with little taps of tenderness.

The beaten outlaw raised his welted face. Mincy was crying. Great silent tears, eloquent in the sun, rolled from wide eyes which Ned now saw were dark blue as the mountain larkspur. "Honeychile, honeychile," said Ned, whispering as he took the pudgy fingers in his hands, gingerly as he would some fragile wayside flower. "Don't you do that, please."

Ned bent his head and kissed the tiny fingertips.

Mincy held forth to him the object she had shielded from her mother's view. It was a little rag-and-rawhide "medicine doll" of the kind given each Indian girl at birth, usually by the maternal grandmother. To the Indians, the miniature figure represented the child itself, and no person could take it from its owner. It was an Indian girl's closest possession and was never given away.

Ned looked at the limp and soiled treasure offered without words or explanation, and because he understood the language of the young, he made no attempt to reply; he just took the doll and put it inside his frayed and whip-cut hunting shirt beside that other priceless gift carried there since Second Manassas, the water-erased letter of Colonel Huddleston.

# 31.

For reasons of his own Croad moved on. He and the Shoshone woman and the little halfbreed girl departed while Ned still sat among the nearby rocks.

They did not bother Ned's outfit, but when the woman began to pry into the burden on the spotted packmule, Croad stopped her. "We ain't thieves," he said. "We ain't like him."

In that moment, Ned imagined the squawman had beaten him

for the same reasons Ned had not fought him off. It was as natural for Croad to take a quirt to a thieving nigger as to a wet dog or anything else he didn't want in his house; and it was just as natural for the nigger to do precisely what Croad had ordered him to do: crawl and whimper.

"Someday—" Ned muttered, as the renegade white man and his little family started toward the slope trail to descend from the bench. But he knew he was not talking to Croad; he was talking to Ned. He shook his head, the movement making him wince with pain. He didn't even hate Croad. Ned had watched him pack up the little camp, and Croad had shown a will to help the Shoshone woman with the work. He also carefully put Mincy into place atop the old mule's packload, even giving the child a pat on the leg and what appeared at the distance to be a quick, tight smile. And when Mincy cried out that she had forgotten some trinket at the campsite and began to dismount, it was not Croad but Tickup who ran over and struck the child full in the face. Ned could hear that blow clear over in the rocks, and he could feel it.

"Injuns!" he gritted between set teeth.

He watched the shabby cavalcade disappear. The last to go over the crest was the rat-tailed packmule. Mincy turned, as the animal lurched downward from view, and Ned believed that she waved good-bye to him. But maybe not. It was a steep trail downward over there, and most likely she had only thrown up a small arm to keep her balance.

"Good-bye anyhow, honey," Ned called softly, and waved to the empty sunshine where the little girl had been.

After a while, Ned got to his feet and caught up his grazing animals. He went away from that place without looking back. Love had been there, and ugliness. It was a place to ride away from and to forget. But there was one thing he would remember, when he had forgotten a hundred Croads or brute-animal Indian squaws; he would remember that little sad-faced halfbreed girl— he would always remember Mincy.

# 32.

Again Ned's trail grows dim. There are blind and unbelievable stretches in it. The best that may be made of the four years until the fateful summer of 1875 is a compound of hazy fact and perfervid folklore. Yet the tale is not without nomad logic.

Ned went on from High Creek Bench to the Colorado diggings, where he spent the summer hunting for the gold camps. He lived apart from his brothers, white and red, as well as Mexican. The local Ute bands called the lone Negro huntsman "Brown Fox," and fox he proved; fox enough to know that, summer on the wane, winter was coming and that, at those altitudes, no man stayed the season outside the shelter of the settled camps.

It was in the first days of September that he left the high country. If he meant to winter south, then return with the migrant wildfowl, he did not say. Half a dozen tales hung behind him along the southward track.

He was going back to the Staked Plains to live with the Comanches or the Comancheros.

He had heard an Indian rumor that his great horse Entero had been seen heading a band of mustang mares down on the panhandle *llano,* and he intended to find out if the horse were indeed Entero.

It was also said that he yearned for the dark-eyed maids of Old Mexico, his experience with Dolores to the contrary; and that he planned to settle in Coahuila and raise horses and halfbreed babies.

It was known that he burned with revenge against Jash Oakes, and some believed he swore he would turn himself in to the sheriff at Forth Worth and ask for the mercy of the law. Others claimed he had vowed to determine the fates of the two Rangers he had wounded in saving Terresa from the noose, and would make amends to them, or to their families.

The stories shared a common thread: that Ned Huddleston had forsaken the outlaw life and taken an oath to ride the straight trail.

Well, perhaps. . . .

"I first met him," said George Baggs, a New Mexico trail driver, "way out past Tascosa at the headwater crossing of the main Canadian. I was moving a herd of nine hundred head north from over in the Tucumcari country, the season getting late and all signs pointing to a bad early winter.

"Ordinarily the water would be low that time of year, but the river was into the willows, swimming water bank to bank.

"While we were trying to shove the herd in, up rides a bunch of draggle-tailed Texas Rangers asking had we seen a colored man in the area. Said they'd been running this Huddleston fellow for five, six years, had recently heard he was back in Texas and gone on the hunt for him. They had only two days ago cut his trail and jumped him out of the Comanche camp of Pin Oak Jack down on the Frio Draw stretch of the Rio Blanco. The captain of the bunch, a mackeral-jawed mean one named Forbes, allowed they had chased the colored fellow right up to our herd and would just push their ponies through our cows and take a good look to be sure their badman wasn't laid up underneath none of those New Mexico steers.

"Well, we allowed that the first Ranger choused up our stock before we got them crossed over the stream in good order was going to get laid up under that herd for certain. They could see we meant it, and they stood off and we got our cattle over that high water.

"I thought no more about them or the colored man, for those were my own cattle and I could smell the snow in the wind. We drove only a short ways from the river, and bedded. The rain slacked, we got a fire going, the coffee set to boil and the steaks to burn. Pretty soon, up out of the blind prairie looms this big black man, soaking wet and streaked every inch with river mud. He looked like a drownded ghost, and the boys rose up off their haunches like a herd going to run.

"We naturally knew this was the colored fellow the Rangers were running. But we weren't precisely cheering for the eyes of Texas right then. Moreover, the poor devil said he was going

[ 107 ]

north and would make a hand as good as any on the drive. While we were hunkered there thinking it over, the colored man spoke up, quiet and polite, but kind of proud, too.

" 'Suh,' he said to me, 'I is got to tell you I is the man them Rangers wanted. I was laying right in amongst yonder steers, not thirty foot from where you was having it out with Cap'n Forbes.'

"Well, now, right here you can bet we all went to looking at one another again. The idea that a dismounted man, any color, can mix in with a big river-spooked mill of longhorn range cattle, then lay up under their bellies and never set off those cattle to running, or at least to moving wild away from that man on foot to show the Rangers where to start looking for him—well, by God, it just ain't any ordinary man can do that.

" 'Go on ahead,' I said to the colored man, watching him close. 'Tell us what elst you done then?'

" 'Well, suh,' he grinned, 'I just cotch me aholdt of two big steers I seen was trailmates. I squoze myself in betwixt them and they squoze me right back trying to stay together. So pretty quick long we come down to the river square past the Rangers. I drop from betwixt my steers and grab onto their two tails and they took me inter that water slick as a pair of brockle-face otters.

" 'Never had to swim a stroke, suh. Just held underwater and was towed over by cow-power.'

"That was the drift of his story, and when he'd finished it the boys voted unanimous to take the colored man along. That's how come the Baggs herd got into Brown's Hole instead of being froze solid outside in that Blue Hell winter of seventy-one.

"Far as I know, or ever heard, it can be laid to Ned Huddleston that the first actual herd of trail cattle found the Hole to use for wintering-through."

Whatever truth there was in this account of Ned Huddleston credited to the New Mexico stockman, the facts are these:

George Baggs did bring into Brown's Hole just ahead of the first hard snowfly of the winter of 1871-72 a herd of nine hundred steers from New Mexico. With Baggs were four faceless trailhands long since buried by history in forgotten graves, his roving wife Maggie Baggs—the second white woman to enter the Hole; and by common consent of the legend, the good-natured, badpenny brown fox, Ned Huddleston.

# 33.

Ned never denied, neither did he ever define, his part in the bringing of the Baggs herd into the Hole. He would take credit if there were any profit in that. He would decline the honor should it cost him any convenience of safety or person. But the young Negro adventurer's sense of history, like his idea of lawful behavior, was hardly well drawn. He could smell an ambush a thousand yards upwind, or see trouble ten days off, if trouble were spelled "the law," or "bad Injuns," or "riled cowboys," or "hanging posse," yet to comprehend the peaceful potential of Brown's Hole was as clearly beyond him as the nearest star. His passion was to be free. Especially with other men's cattle. What worth to him the discovery of a winter haven for Baggs' cows?

But there was portent in that sanctuary.

The accounting for this was that, while awaiting its fame as a wintering ground for range cattle, the Hole had grown another crop of repute; it had become a retreat for Civil War slackers, a headquarters for hat-wavers, drifters, highline riders and hardcase fugitives from all honest trades. It was said, and devoutly believed, in Wyoming that it was "as much as a man's life is worth to go in there." It was into this atmosphere and arena of time-fused trouble that George Baggs brought his New Mexico herd in the early winter of 1871.

His New Mexico herd and his roaming mate Maggie.

Whether or not Ned Huddleston was guilty of the charge of bringing them there, Brown's Hole would never be the same after Maggie Baggs.

As for history and those hard bones:

Said the Old Brown Fox, from the mellowed remove of time enough and distance, "Maybe it weren't no Garden of Adam and Eden, but I reckon it were me what brung in the Sarpint, all the same."

# 34.

The winter of 1871-72 was a terror. Outside the Hole cattle froze on the open range by the thousands. But in the mesa-ed breaks and arroyo-ed draws and timbered bottoms of Brown's Hole a miracle took place. Baggs had nine hundred steers in the Hole when the snow blocked the trails in and out; when the spring melt came and the trails were open once more, Baggs trailed out his cattle to Evanston, Wyoming, and sold there to Crawford and Thompson—nine hundred steers. He had not lost a head in the hardest winter remembered. The future of the Hole, which Ned Huddleston could not see, was assured. But the present, which Ned could see very well indeed, was anything but safe.

During the winter he camped with the Baggs outfit. Due to the unwritten code of cow thieves the herd was not bothered. It had been brought in by a thief, and the residents understood plainly that one did not chew at the bosom of a fellow rustler with any profit.

There endured an uneasy but practical peace between Ned and Mexican Joe Herrera, who had vowed before too many witnesses that the Negro would return to the Hole only at the expense of his black hide. Terresa, who came to Ned and welcomed him with emotion, informed the latter of Joe's forbearance, but warned him also that it would be wise to consider moving on with Baggs' herd that spring. Ned thanked Terresa and welcomed him in turn, but something was gone. Each man showed a reluctance to look the other directly in the eye.

Yet when George Baggs pulled out his nine hundred steers for the Wyoming market, the Negro outlaw did not go with him. Neither did Baggs' rompsome mate Maggie.

The story was that Bagg's wife would wait in the Hole for him to return, but she was in fact waiting only for him to leave. For with the bursting of the willow bud and the burgeoning of new life in all things, Maggie Baggs had discovered Pablo Herrera, Mexican Joe's giant and uncritical brother, and it was love. Not twenty-four hours after her husband's departure for Wyoming, Maggie Baggs bid adieu to the Hole and fled southward, eloping with Pablo to Las Vegas, New Mexico. It is a social note, purely, to comment that Pablo never returned, while Maggie Baggs was back next winter with a second herd of New Mexican trail cattle and snug again with ex-mate George Baggs.

But the local damage was done. Mexican Joe, when he learned of the elopement, blamed the loss of the valuable worker brother Pablo on Ned Huddleston, vowing once more to skin-out the big Negro and feed his liver to the vultures. Ned was impressed enough to move out of the Hole to the camp of a rival rustler group headquartering at Charcoal Bottoms of the Green River, in nearby Wyoming. This was the Tip Gault gang, whose leader was the original "Badman from Bitter Creek," but whom Ned found to be the happiest of outlaw rogues and immeasurably preferable company to chili-tempered Joe Herrera and his *Latino* band of countrymen-cousins.

Joe's time, however, was tainted. Since Ned had last seen him the Mexican had imported a lawyer to help him administrate his growing affairs as the undisputed bandit king of Brown's Hole. This man was another physical giant, towering far over six feet and weighing two hundred and thirty pounds. He was a licensed attorney and had met Joe in South Pass where the latter had many times loaned him money to pursue his avocation, drinking himself unconscious. Hence, when Joe realized that legal brains would be a big need in the illicit sort of cattle ranching he planned, he sent for Asbury Conway The "Judge" showed up immediately, aching for the bottle. That had been in late summer of seventy-one. Now, a year later, Conway's keen intellect, with Joe's tremendous energy, had brought the Mexican *jefe* to his finest hour of outlawry.

It proved a short-count sixty minutes.

Up in Evanston, Wyoming, the new owners of the first Baggs herd were unable to market their steers for the right price and decided to hold them another year. To take the herd back into Brown's Hole was admittedly no sport for tenderfeet, so Crawford and Thompson hired one Jesse Hoy, a bullwhacker and freightline operator in the Rockies since 1864.

Hoy was a man with a secret, which possibly accounted for his daring. The son of a wealthy family in the East, he had gone to Paris as a young man. There a jealous Frenchman, finding Jesse unclad in company with the Frenchman's *fille de joie*, proceeded to castrate the American swain on the spot.

Whether he thought he had no more to lose, or not, Hoy went into the Hole as a man who feared nothing, asked no quarter, and quickly demonstrated that he intended to give no quarter.

Twenty-two men, not counting Indians, eleven white men, eleven Mexicans, spent that winter of 1872-73 in the Hole. There were two transient Texas trail herds in addition to Hoy's— twenty-three hundred head owned by the Adair brothers, and thirteen hundred head owned by a Dr. Keiser. These were the first of the numberless drive herds to follow the findings of George Baggs' "discovery nine hundred." Moreover, that same winter, the Spicer brothers, Wyoming cattlemen, moved in with three hundred head and the announced intention of ranching permanently in Brown's Hole. The place was "peopling up" and Mexican Joe sensed the vague unease which must come to the king when democracy threatens. His instincts proved right.

Jesse Hoy that winter took from the Herrera gang the very profitable monopoly it had enjoyed in the Ute moccasin and leather goods trade. Hoy did it by an extremely unfair tactic which any man of decent blood must resent—he treated the Indians fairly. By the time Joe understood the direction of this drain on his whiskey business with the red men, the never-sleeping Hoy had struck again. With the run off thaw and the opening of the Vermilion Creek wagon road in the spring of seventy-three, he brought into Brown's Hole the first mowing machine seen west of the front range of the Rockies. He put it to cutting the native hay which the Herraras had always scythed and bundled by hand for the lucrative market of the emigrant wagon teams along the California Cutoff. In six weeks Hoy put up more hay than the Mexican *guadañeros* could have cut in as many years. That did it.

Out came the whetstone and the knife.

"Terresa," said Juan José Herrera, "*Venga, por favor.* We are going to cut out the *hígado* of that *gringo menos los cajones,* and throw the rest of him into the *cascada del Lodore!*"

The "cascade of Lodore" was that fierce bore of white water

which rushed out of Brown's Hole through the awesome canyon of the Green. Into its dark hell had been thrown all manner of things unwanted as evidence, including three hundred head of cattle "rimrocked" off the highest lip of the canyon by the gang that past summer, when a very brave and very large posse of irate Wyoming cattlemen had pursued too far and too fast for comfort.

Young Terresa's sensitive features paled. *"Un momento, tio mio,* let me get my judge's wand."

By this he meant his Winchester, which he would keep leveled and cocked the entire time required by Uncle Joe to carve up Jesse Hoy. Should some reckless spectator try to halt the carnage, then Terresa would "judge" the infraction on the spot, and accurately.

But the preparations were wasted. Hoy, that so-far man of steel, lost his determination the instant big Joe Herrera entered his camp, hone and Spanish blade at the strop.

Hoy ran, as they remembered it, "like a rabbit."

But Valentine Hoy, Jesse's brother, was another kind of animal. He calmed his shaken kinsman, got on the same horse Jesse fled the Hole upon, turned the animal about, rode him back into the hideout, dismounted in front of the Dummy Bottom lean-tos and called out Mexican Joe Herrera.

Juan José charged forth like the black brave bulls of Castile to the trumpeters of the *corrida.* He was magnificent. Black eyes flashed. Coffee-brown body strained at every flexing muscle. Knife-steel glittered in the morning sun. *Olé!*

But Valentine Hoy, like Ned Huddleston before him, did not care to play at this Spanish game of hand swords. He hammered Herrera instantly with his fist and flush upon the point of his long Cordoban jaw, dropping him like a pole-axed wagon bull. However, unlike Ned before him, Valentine Hoy finished the job. He leaned down and neatly inflicted some knife surgery of his own upon the buttocks of the fallen *matador,* and so swiftly was the incision made that Terresa never moved, and neither did Mexican Joe, and for a good many weeks, and then only at great pain, and not in the saddle all summer.

The odor of the albatross set in at once.

By the summer of seventy-four, even Asbury Conway had deserted the Hole to return to civilization and the eventual honor of being made Chief Justice of the Wyoming Supreme Court, a not uncommon reward for the virtues considered.

When, later that autumn, Joe's nephew Terresa went to Charcoal Bottoms and joined the Tip Gault gang, seeking out his old horse-stealing mate Ned Huddleston, even Mexican Joe could recognize the stench of the decomposing bird of evil hung upon him by Valentine Hoy. He stayed on in the Hole that winter, still blaming Ned and Maggie Baggs for his fall, but no one listened any more. It was ancient history that he repeated. If immoral Maggie had begun his decline, it was law-abiding men like the Hoys and Spicers who had finished it. Other winds were stirring now.

Into the society of hard badmen in Brown's Hole had come the new element of even harder goodmen. None of the other outlaws understood the change any more than did Herrera; Ned Huddleston the least of all.

When Joe was vanquished and Terresa came over to the Tip Gault side, it meant only to Ned that he and his old *bandido* comrade of the grand Texas days were at last together again.

But if the meeting had reunited the two greatest horse thieves of them all, history was hoodwinked. Or perhaps the legend simply forgot to tell Wyoman Bill Hawley and his four tough Hat Ranch cowboys of the feared reputations of the rejoined Texas raiders. But that must wait along. Its stark tragedy would not descend until the coming midsummer. For Ned, a twenty-sixth birthday intervened, bringing a present of unimagined happiness.

It was the first real spring day of that fading winter of 1874-75. Inside his lean-to cabin at the Charcoal Bottoms camp, Ned heard a gutteral Indian voice asking his whereabouts. For a moment the voice belonged only to any one of a hundred local Ute customers to whom he had peddled trade whiskey, but when he had gone to his door to peer forth into the dazzle of the mountain sun, he saw that he was wrong.

In the first place that Indian was no "him," it was a "her," and the "she" was no Ute and not local, but a Shoshone from far off.

"*Wagh!*" Tickup greeted him, seeing his dark face in the doorway. "Me come back, stay by you!"

But Ned did not answer her. He was looking beyond the ugly squaw to the rider of the second winter-shaggy mustang. Then his heart was pounding and the sudden, silent tears were standing in his dark eyes.

Mincy. It was Mincy.

# *35.*

On what terms Ned sought contentment with the dumpy, Mongol-featured Shoshone woman, he never explained. Most likely it was through a simple workaday arrangement of the times, wherein the squaw exchanged her menial camp labors for the honors of the ex-slave's blanket.

Ned, now fully matured, was a striking specimen of manhood. A rich bronze in color, his features were chiseled in the aristocratic manner of the Hamitic Galla people of Kenya's Sabaki River country, a people with warrior parentage and proud, yet also, like Ned himself, restrained by dignity and grace, with a great and gallant gentleness toward the young and helpless.

It was not at all mysterious what Tickup saw in such a powerful and dangerous mate. Here was a man among men, certainly the ample match for another partner of her past whom the squaw imagined might follow her to Charcoal Bottoms.

Mincy of course was the catalyst. Now nine years of age, she had grown into an exquisite small flower of dusky petal not shadowed by any on the mountainside. Ned said of her that spring morning, "She was purty as a hid-up fawn, all tremblylash and shy to be 'mongst them bad lots at the Bottoms, but when she see'd Old Ned you could have lit a lamp wick off that smile; I never seen the sun rise up in nobody like it done in her."

As for the dainty halfbreed child, it was as if but the blinking of an eye had passed since she entrusted her rawhide medicine doll to the dark stranger. Neither had known a true friend in the four years since and both somehow felt that, in this fifth spring, something beyond their simple understanding had brought them back together.

But there was no outward expression of the flood of feeling; they greeted each other briefly. Ned only walked past the gesturing squaw and took the halter strap of Mincy's pony and led the long-haired beast back past Tickup's mount walking tall; he said aloud to both mother and halfbreed daughter the words which somehow conveyed it all, and quietly.

"Come on," he said. "You is home."

The announcement impressed not only Tickup and her shy daughter; word of it quickly swept up and down the Green. Everyone who was anyone in the fugitive world of the Brown's Hole outlaw society showed up to chivaree the popular Negro night rider. Neither the Shoshone squaw nor the frightened halfbreed waif understood the demonstration, but the former knew all too well the powers of the white man's cornmash *puha,* and she hid the girl under Ned's bed and sat guard over her with a cocked double-barreled shotgun in hand. It was a wonderful party while it lasted.

For a little time Ned was lost in a world new to him. He was a family man now. He had a woman and a young daughter to support, and in the carefree errancy of his outlaw's mind this problem delighted him. Moreover, it brought him new status in the community. How many families were there in and about Brown's Hole, Colorado territory? Precious few. If Ned Huddleston had joined this select number, he had surely taken one more step upward in that long flight—and fight—to establish himself on the other side of that river about which the Old Squire had told him that long-gone night along the Rappahannock.

Tickup proved a good housekeeper. "Homely," Ned said, grinning ruefully. "Homely as a mud fence. And dumb? I vow she ain't the normal wits of a quill-pig. Stubborn, you say? A mule got a head softer by somewhat, and don't kick nowhere near so hard. But she do muck out the place and keep a fire built and long as I throw her in the crick ever so often to drown the gray-back nits and sort of keep her fumigated, we get along tolerable."

His life with Mincy was something far afield. Ned must instinctively have guessed correctly about the little halfbreed girl's
white sire having been what he called quality. Mincy's delicate
oval face and fine features, her willowy figure and straight un-
bowed limbs were not the only indications of an inheritance
other than the Shoshonean blood of her mother; her very nature
seemed alien to that of Tickup's people.

At least Ned saw her in that light.

The ex-slave was no admirer of the red man. The Indian was
as much an alien to Ned as he was to any of Ned's white or
Mexican fellow-members of the Charcoal Bottoms encampment.
Ned eschewed them, except to sell them whiskey, and the advent
of Tickup, except for its pronouncement that she had come to
share the big Negro's buffalo robe, might well have had a less
happy reception. Indeed, but for the fact that Fogarty, the civil
head of the outlaw settlement (if Tip Gault were its military
commander), had himself taken to mate a Shoshone squaw, Ned
Huddleston would probably have turned away Tickup.

But the entire touchiness of becoming a squawman was over-
looked in his simple joy at being with Mincy. The child was fasci-
nated by the tall and powerful figure of the black man, and by
his strange gentleness with her in contrast to the hard behavior
he showed in common with the other hairbrand denizens of the
Hole. Finally, as she and Ned worked out, with the swiftly drifting weeks into the high country summer, a language of their own
by which to communicate other things than the pagan primary
ones of eat, sleep, warm, cold, careful, quick, beware and thank
you, the halfbreed child fell completely under the spell of Ned's
half-nostalgic tales of the white world far to the East, where little
girls like Mincy wore pretty dresses and fine ribbons and bathed
every day and slept by night in beds of purest cotton, and went to
schools where they learned to think and to speak and to make
marks on paper and to count up to more figures than the largest
buffalo herd. That was a magic land the white man lived in and
one day, Ned always wound up the stories, he would take Mincy
there and she would see a thousand things more wonderful than
Ned had told, and she would be as good as any white girl, and
have fine dresses and go to school and learn not to be an Indian.

"You is quality, honey," he would conclude. "Don't never forget that; and don't never forget that Old Ned going to one day prove it to everybody that you *is* quality, same as you was white."

To Mincy, certainly, being white meant nothing. To Ned Huddleston, as certainly, it meant everything.

"I makes you one promise, Mincy gal," he said intently, as they sat on the sunny mountainside one day resting from a long exploring walk. His words fell softly, as when a man speaks of a dream he knows he cannot share, but may still bring about for another. "You ain't bred to live like no kicked-dog Injun; if I cain't make it across that river myself, I mean to set *you* safe down on the far side, and that's my life on it."

If the oath were of granite, or of sand, its giver was suddenly presented with news requiring immediate action, not future vows.

When he and Mincy returned from the mountainside, Tickup told him, "Heap trouble, me come by you, leave Ute husband, bad Injun named Pony Beater. Now long here this day come old Yampatika friend of Tickup. Old friend him say, 'Take down tipi, put things on pack-pony. Ute husband hear where you go. Hear you live by Brown Fox. Heap insulted. Him Pony Beater come down mountain, fast, trot-trot. Him say him whip squaw, girl, plenty time. Him take pelt Brown Fox, too. Peel skin from top head of Fox to end of pizzle.' Tickup no like peeled Fox. *Wagh!* Me, you and girl, we go fast!"

It was the longest speech the squaw had ever made, and at every word Ned's heart dropped lower. Lord, God, now what? Wouldn't anybody ever leave old Ned alone? Must even the heathen Indians turn on him and declare war? Wasn't the time ever going to swing around to where the rest of the world would let up on Ned Huddleston?

Hell, he knew the answer. There were lots of white men and Mexicans and Indians in the Hole and all about up and down the Green, the Yampa and the Little Snake, but there was only one Ned, only one nigger. Even a brute redskin like Pony Beater, with a ten-times traded squaw uglier than a lump-jawed mule, could feel insulted over that.

All at once Ned laughed. Hell, he had Mincy.

There was a whole chain of peaks out yonder and it was summer and the living was fat and he and that homely squaw and that pretty little new daughter of his would just go out and live on those mountains like the Indians did.

Ned would take his traps and all his drifter's outfit. They wouldn't simply live out there, they would set up a good trapline —most of the spring fur was still passable—and make a little money out of their absence from the Hole. When old Pony Beater had come and gone from the Bottoms, they would slip back into the basin.

Meanwhile, Tickup and Mincy had little to fear with Old Ned watching out for them. Pony Beater was a whiskey-soaked Yampatika bum, a redskin skunk and a heathen; he sure wasn't any hardeyed white Southerner like Croad, and Ned had no need to fear his ability to handle the likes of the Ute.

Waved and shouted on their way by the good-natured badmen of the Bottoms, the Negro outlaw and his new Indian family set out for the higher slopes. If Pony Beater could find them, he was welcome to try, but Brown Fox didn't believe that any Ute could follow the trackline of the best forager the Confederate Army ever had. And if he did, by damn, he would find Old Ned about ten whacks better than ready for him. *"Wagh!"*

*"Wagh!"* yelled Tickup in response to his sudden courage-cry.

The Shoshone squaw kicked her scrubby Idaho mustang merci-lessly, clubbed the poor beast with a dry-root cudgel as thick as a man's wrist. She laughed at the creature's groans of complaint. Shifting her cud of shagcut and vile trade tobacco, she spat uner-ringly downwind upon a cackling mountan jay scolding their passage. The bird screeched indignantly, shook out its drowned feathers and profaned the pines with blue-jay opinions of ugly Indian squaws who chewed tobacco and laughed like a jackass at wet Colorado jaybirds.

Following the tall colored man and the squat Shoshone woman up the winding trail toward Cold Spring Mountain and the Wyoming Roughs, thin-faced Mincy held fast to her small buck-skin pouch of personal medicine and prayed earnestly to *Nau-Nang-Gai*, the Snow Bird, her patron among the Shoshone gods, to be good to their journey and to protect her new father, Brown Fox.

# 36.

Ned found a stream in the Wyoming Roughs which precisely suited his plan. To get to the place he had doubled and redoubled upon his own track, laying the path so that even an Indian might not guess that strangers had transgressed that lonesome outland. The camp itself was set on a cedar-clad spur which gave a good view of the only approach possible by horseback. There was plenty of wood for fire and for cover, and a rushing torrent of green mountain water ran nearby. The grass was high and sweet, the silences, supreme.

"Here she be," said Ned to his companions. "Turn loose the stock."

The stock consisted of his own buckskin saddler, a new horse stolen that past spring, his old and ageless china-eyed packmule Jeff Davis, with the coat, like Joseph's, of many colors, the two potbellied Indian mustangs of Tickup and Mincy, and the woeful package of bones surrounded by hide which the squaw called War Eagle, and which was in fact the same packmule she had had at High Creek Bench. It wasn't a grand herd in Ned's view but it was something; it was theirs.

The lodgeskins which Tickup had brought along, with the new poles cut by Ned, made a snug tipi. When furnished by Ned's good blankets, buffalo robes and the mats of grass which the Shoshone woman quickly wove, the whole fragranced by pineboughs freshly cut each day by Mincy, well, it was some doings, the best by far that Ned had ever known.

For a few days he watched the backtrail for signs of Pony Beater, but the Ute chief, like most of his red color, made many speeches and performed few deeds. Plainly, the Yampatika had felt the need to save face by beating his chest a bit in tribal hearing. As plainly, he had no real intention of bringing trouble to the big Negro whose reputation as a dangerous and famous outlaw had no doubt been relayed up into the Yampatika country.

Mincy tried to tell him differently. Pony Beater, she said, was a very bad Indian. He *did* beat women and children. He was not like all the other fathers she had known to live with her mother. Mincy had felt a small sadness for each of them. They had all met the same fate and for the same reason. When Tickup tired of a mate, she would scan the horizons for a new victim. When this unfortunate one appeared, the squaw would ply him with piteous tales of the manner in which the present husband beat her and her poor skinny daughter, this in spite of the fact that, until Pony Beater, not a one of the many fathers had mistreated Mincy and but a few of them put whip or hand to Tickup, then only when she merited the punishment and would have had the same from any Indian lord. But the trouble with Pony Beater was his liking for the white man's whiskey. When he was in its grasp, well, it was not a pleasant thing. The new father, Brown Fox, would understand.

"Sure, sure," said Ned. "Don't you fret, honeychild."

But he didn't understand at all; he was caught in the same trap Croad had caught him in, almost to the same dead-still detail of stalk and surprise and nasty shock of the voice of the enemy grating behind him.

"Brown Fox no move," instructed the Ute. "Me come to takum back Snake squaw, half-Injun kid, beat like hell!"

Ned crouched, every muscle in his body taut.

There was no time for talk. He was either going to turn and tear the heart out of that Indian, or he was going to stand there and do exactly what Pony Beater told him.

Into the last moment of his decision came the hoarse voice of Tickup. "Two-barrel gun make bad hole close up," she reminded Ned. "Ruin meat. Brown Fox better stand like stump."

Ned's will turned to water, ice-water. "He has our *shotgun?*" he questioned waveringly.

"Yes," said the squaw. "Me lay down gun, go chop wood. Him come sneak in camp, pick gun up, me no see. A bad thing."

"Lordy Jesus," moaned Ned. "Skunked again."

"What him say?" growled Pony Beater to Tickup.

"Who care?" said the squaw. "Me strike lodge, gettum pack-mule loaded. These best thing me you ever steal. *Wagh!*"

*"Wagh,"* agreed Pony Beater. "Loadum all."

"Me do," said Tickup, and went to work. Within the half hour Ned was alone in the deserted camp of his new family life, bound with his own lariat to a downed log too heavy for a team of mules to break free. Gone down the mountainside with all he owned in the world, including the buckskin stockhorse and the old piebald packmule, was the philosophic Shoshone rolling stone, Tickup. He could still hear her singing some outlandish Indian song to the happiness of the new day, or some such trash, as she followed Pony Beater back toward Colorado.

Well, at least they had left him with a choice; he could either be eaten by prowling bears, picked apart by buzzards, or just lie there and starve to death. It wasn't the same as knowing your route to the Happy Hunting Grounds for sure, as say, if a man were to be pitched into the Canyon of Lodore.

One thing, anyway, it hadn't been the same as with Croad. Not really.

More important than that, even, Mincy had not seen it; she had been picking berries down the mountain. Tickup had even seen fit to tell Ned, after roping him to the log at Pony Beater's order, that she understood the delicacy of this matter. "Me not say to girl how happen," she promised. "She think Brown Fox heap brave."

"Yeah," Ned had answered. "Heap thanks."

"Me heap thanks you," the squaw had replied with all seriousness. "Where else me find outfit like this for only work at wife one moon?"

Ned could still grin, thinking of that. A man had to admit Tickup saw things right through to the core. She wasn't confused by the seeds or the peelings. That *was* a hell of an outfit to pick up for swamping out a bachelor shack for four weeks.

Why hadn't he listened to Mincy, instead of making the child sit still for all his whoppers about making her into a white girl? She had tried to tell him the simple truth about her mother's constant mate-trading trick, with its invariable gain to the squaw of the deposed husband's personal property. She had even told him about the end of Croad, wherein Tickup, meeting a younger white man along the trail and one with a better outfit than the southerner's, had told the stranger the identical story of mistreatment which she had given Ned on High Creek Bench. The only difference had been that the new white man—he was really a mixed-blood Canadian—had shot Croad in the back of the head for brutalizing poor Tickup. The justice in that execution lay in the subsequent fact that the new hero in his time was gotten dead drunk by a wandering visitor to their snug lodge—a visitor wearing a very fine outfit and wanting any woman—and left outside the lodge all night in an Idaho January night to "sober up."

"Him so stiff next morning," the child had explained to Ned, "that new husband knock fingers off hand with ax, like twig from branch. New husband laugh. Squaw laugh. Very funny thing. Mincy no laugh. Old husband nice to Mincy. Never beat, and one time bring candy all way from Fort Bridger."

"Hoo, hoo!" Ned announced to the listening stillnesses of the mountainspur. "Maybe I come out more a winner than most. Leastways, I didn't get nothing knocked off with no ax!"

The indomitable sunshine of his spirit broke through once again. He began to cast about for a way to escape the heavy ropes which bound him to the log.

There was nothing, however, which could free him. The smoldering fire, could he have reached it, might have been used to burn the ropes through, roasting him in the process but at least freeing him. Yet he could no more budge that log than the mountain it lay embedded in; and shortly the sunshine cooled within him and the spirit shriveled. He was done for.

If he lasted a week without food and only the water of the mountain night's heavy dew he could lick from his lips, it still would mean nothing. He had laid his own cute fox's trail into that high camp in the Wyoming Roughs. Only another Indian, like Pony Beater, might unravel it in time. And from whence would such an Indian appear? Why, there didn't even live a red being who cared if Ned thirsted or starved. He knew there wasn't such a one, not anywhere: not in Wyoming, not in the Hole, not in the entire total redskin world.

But Ned was wrong, and owed his life to it.

There did live such an Indian who cared. Or half of such an Indian.

# 37.

It was not long past high noon of the second day when Ned heard the fine Irish tenor of Tip Gault, supported by the rich baritone of Terresa, singing in harmony a bawdy song of the gold camps as they splashed their horses across the tumble of Little Bitter Creek, far below.

He at once set up the outlaw signal cry of distress—a version of the Ute fox yap sign for trouble—but the troubadors did not reply, continuing their music with, if anything, elevated spirit.

"My God," said Ned to the log, "they going to pass me by!"

But of course the rascals were only galling him. Presently they came up the spur trail and drew in their mounts in equal gestures of amazement.

"Nedito!" cried Terresa. "Lying in the shade at this time of the day? It is no wonder that you fail in life!"

"Faith, lad," added the merry-hearted Gault, "sure now your mother taught you better. You'll never earn a honest split snoozing 'neath a down-log at one o'clock of the afternoon. Who's minding the trapline?"

Ned blinked bloodshot eyes and demanded to know if they imagined he customarily took his pleasures in that kind of a rope hammock. Moreover, he suggested they think twice about turning him loose, as he might just attack them if freed in his current temper.

To this, Tip allowed he had lost his nerve, and wheeled his horse to go. Terresa swore aloud that he was not going to be left alone with any wild-eyed madman, roped tight or otherwise, and spun his mount to follow Gault's.

Ned knew they were badgering him, yet at the same time a rush of apprehension flooded his better judgment, and he hollered "uncle" in abject surrender, pleading less entertainment and more lariat loosening. His fellow bandits at once unleashed him and informed him that in the pitchblende dark of the night before, tiny Mincy had shown up at Charcoal Bottoms on the pinto packmule. Seeking out Tip, who had been kind and attentive to the youngster during her stay with Ned, she had told the outlaw chief the entire plight of Brown Fox, and concluded with a plea, which Tip said would make a "stone weep," for an expedition to be sent at once to rescue her "poor dark father." The plea had been fortified by an accurate Indian instruction of precisely the way to find Little Bitter Creek Mountain and the cedar spur of Ned Huddleston's "happy camp."

Tip had tried to get Mincy to stay with the Shoshone wife of Fogarty. But the child had been so terrified of being found absent from the tipi of Tickup and Pony Beater, that she had galloped away on the Jeff Davis mule before they could restrain her. They surely hoped, said Tip fervently, that the precious mite had made it safe back under the rearskins of her mother's and the Ute chief's lodge, but all they could do of a practical nature was to follow up her directions for finding Ned; the kid was gone and nobody could help her.

Here, Ned disagreed vehemently. He was going after Mincy, he said, to free her from that lice-infested squaw and that plug-ugly "Injun" chief, or, by Jesus, would break the last bone in his backside trying.

"Hell," said Tip, sympathetically, "trying ain't going to knock no feathers out'n that red eagle's tail. A steer can try, lad, but it don't do him no notable benefit. What you got to have is a plan of pursuit, me boy, and stout comrades to side you through on it."

"What a pity," said Ned, scanning the raffish pair. "I can figure all manner of plan, I reckon, but how do a man locate those 'stout comrade' fellers? You know of any such what hunts close by this range?"

"Hmmm," said Tip, fingering his broad Celtic jaw. "Faith, now, and I don't," he admitted honestly. "But me and Terresa might try filling in for same, lacking better."

Ned nodded thankfully. "You just say trying ain't no good, but lemme tell you she's good enough for this nigger."

"I don't see any nigger," answered Tip Gault, looking around

[125]

the camp clearing. "But if the wise Brown Fox or the poor dark father wants two friends to ride along with him and get his outfit back, by God, I say he's found 'em."

"But of course," said Terresa, with a graceful Latin bow to the rope-cramped Negro. "What are stout comrades for but to rescue the weak-minded and succor the fair. To horse!"

They all laughed, and Terresa, being the lightest, took Ned up behind him and they went down the mountain. At the Creek Ned picked up the trackline of Tickup and Pony Beater and followed it afoot. His pace was a loping trot held with iron limb and deep lung. An hour before sunset he halted to examine a particular run of droppings in the trail. "My own hoss, and fresh," he said to his mounted companions. "We'll catch up to them while we still got good shooting light." Tip and Terresa nodded, no smiles now, and the pursuit resumed in silence.

It was surely no more than half an hour later when Ned halted again, dark hand upheld to lips, head bent, listening. "Hold them ponies' muzzles," Ned warned. "Take them back in the brush and tie them tight. We's here."

"*Ya lo creo,*" said Terresa, low voiced.

Tip Gault, examining the utter stillness about them, taken with the sudden nervousness of their horses, added his nod to Terresa's.

"Faith, now," he muttered, "I believe so too."

Then, turning with Terresa to hide and tie their mounts, he said, beyond Ned's hearing, "I don't like this, *amigo;* he's found something never figured in the plans of neither of us: it's way too damned quiet here!"

Terresa pointed upward to where a break in the pine timber showed open sky just ahead.

"It's always quiet where buzzards wheel," he said.

"Jesus Mary!" said Tip softly. "I didn't see 'em—"

"Nedito did," answered Terresa, tight-lipped. "He always does. They are the patron birds of his life."

"*Ya lo creo,*" said Tip Gault, and pulled the Winchester from its saddle-scabbard; he did not smile when he repeated the Spanish phrase.

# 38.

There seemed no need for haste in the journey. To begin with, they were not going any particular place. Then the matter of pursuit by the humbled Brown Fox was surely not of consequence. Both Tickup and Pony Beater now disdained Ned. The squaw had seen him twice overcome by men whom he might have fought, and did not. Once before she had seen him fail to come after Croad. Why would he then trail Pony Beater? The latter, a true pagan, almost a Neanderthal redman, feared little in life. The idea that the black rider whom he had subdued so easily might even yearn to pursue a chief of Pony Beater's reputation, well, it was simply not in the Indian's thoughts.

Presently, not many miles from Little Bitter Creek Mountain, the Ute decided to camp. If Tickup believed the distance unsafe, she made no complaint. Surveying the site which Pony Beater had indicated, she grunted her agreement. And why not? Brown Fox was tied to the old log. Probably the first to find him there would be the vultures. If some chance traveler should release the Negro cow stealer and pony thief, it still would make no difference. He was not a fighting man. Strong, yes. Kind, even, and good to children. A medicine chief with horses, he had some magic with all other animals as well. But a warrior? Never. Pony Beater would kill him next time they met, if the buzzards did not finish the job before him. And if the Ute were too drunk or lazy to undertake the business, then Tickup would see to it herself.

One thing to be certain of, she was not going to give up any of the splendid outfit of Brown Fox. His shiny new Winchester alone was worth everything in the lodge of Pony Beater. When, in the natural course of her line of work, Tickup should return to her Fort Hall, Idaho, homeland with all of Brown Fox's fine things to add to the estate which she was accumulating amid the safety of the Shoshone band of her birth, she would at last be the wealthiest Indian woman in that country. And not only that. In the camp of her Fort Hall people waited a virile young warrior who would be hers when she returned from this final summer's harvest. Indeed, if the handsome rascal were true to his word, the wanderings of Tickup would be over. Well, about time perhaps, for she was growing old for this sort of labor. She could not command the same attention as of the old days, and the quality of her victims had declined steadily since Croad. When the pickings of the hunt reduced themselves to Yampa drunks like Pony Beater and cowardly smoked thieves like Brown Fox, well, it was time to retire and go home.

As Tickup enjoyed this vision of a comfortable old age, she made snug the camp of her Ute mate of the moment. She even sang a little Shoshone song of her youth, something about the birds and the sunshine, sounding very much like the same tune she warbled croakingly when leaving Ned at the Little Bitter Creek Mountain betrayal.

Hearing the happiness of her mother, Mincy grew only the more uneasy. She helped Tickup, very careful to be quick and willing, but she had her own thoughts.

Something had been bad about leaving that camp of Brown Fox's. The child had not believed the tale told her by Tickup and Pony Beater when they found her at her berry picking and commanded that she come along without questions. She knew her mother better than to accept the claim that Pony Beater had purchased the outfit of Brown Fox, and she knew the Ute chief better, too, for he had never had one decent blanket to roll within another. So in all of the unhurried ride from the Spur Ridge campsite, she had been thinking of Brown Fox, her dear "dark father," who was the best and kindest she could remember in her nine winters. As the day ended, and with it the work of the new camp, Mincy lay in the tipi, listening to the boastings of Pony Beater and to the groans of pain from Tickup, very stiff and sore since the hard beating given her after she had finished arranging the camp and cooking a fine meal for Pony Beater.

"You were wrong to run away to Brown Fox and leave me with no whiskey to drink," the Ute had suggested, before seating himself to be served. "For this you will be whipped now; and also it is a good thing to have some exercise and to stir the blood of the stomach in advance of filling it."

The child he had not harmed. In this case, he told the squaw, the halfbreed cub could not be blamed, since it only went where its verminous Shoshone bitch-mother went. But let them both be warned that the least peeping of a sound from the skinny mixed-blood whelp, and he would beat the brat's pale body dark with bruises.

Tickup had said nothing, possibly because her own contusions hurt too much. Yet she looked at the Ute in a stabbing way when he turned his back to her for a moment, and she made a noise deep in her lungs which did not sound like any word, but the growling of an injured thing, of a wounded beast.

Now, the silent supper finished, and the Ute interlarding his boastings with belchings and more bestial reliefs, Mincy's fearful ears heard a command in guttural Yampatika which made her heart leap.

"Listen," said Pony Beater to Tickup, "you are not too sore to ride, and I have had an inspiration of the mind."

"May the gods protect us," muttered the squaw, but the Ute did not hear her and continued to grunt his orders.

"Take the best horse," he said, "that buckskin of Brown Fox's, and go to Mexican Joe's place and get me some whiskey. You can make it there and return before daylight."

"Money," said Tickup, "what about some money?"

"Take one of those fine new traps of Brown Fox's and make a trade. You should get three bottles, maybe four."

"Two," said the squaw. "Two at the most."

"Return with no less than three," answered Pony Beater, and reached over the fire and struck her beside the head and knocked her the length of her body, sprawling.

Tickup got to her feet, took the buckskin horse and departed without a word. In the tipi, Mincy's imagination raced.

If the night would cover the journey of her mother to Dummy Bottom, it would surely protect her own journey to Charcoal Bottoms, which was closer. When Pony Beater snored, Mincy would take the trusted old packmule, Jeff Davis, and ride to the camp of the kind Tip Gault, telling the white man where Brown Fox was.

The full-bellied chief snored soon enough. Mincy saddled Jeff Davis and made away safely. She arrived at the outlaw camp in good time, told Tip Gault what had happened, and was on the return trip with all things going well. Then she lost her way, and it was graying in the east before she found her trail once more.

When she came to the camp of the Ute, her alarm redoubled, for the buckskin horse of Brown Fox taken by her mother was not grazing with the other mounts beside the stream; either Tickup had not come back from Mexican Joe's camp before the sun, or else Pony Beater had done something very bad to her.

Mincy hid in the pines and waited, quieting Jeff Davis.

Noontime came and passed. It was about four o'clock when the horses raised their heads from the grass by the stream and whickered to warn of someone approaching.

Pony Beater now came out of the tipi, where he had been sleeping all day, and Mincy could see that his face was heavy with rage. But the one who approached was Tickup and she had not three but five bottles of whiskey. Pony Beater greeted her with a great belch and a glad cry and seized the first bottle and broke off the neck of it by smashing it against the nearest pine trunk and put up the ragged neck to his mouth and drank one half of the quart before lowering it to spit out the shards of glass caught on his bleeding lips and tongue.

"Goddam!" he cried in the white man's way, "Heap good!" Before sundown he had drained two of the bottles and nearly the third one, and he was so drunk that he could not utter an understandable word, nor his legs command his moccasins to go where he directed them.

In this condition he commenced once more to punish Tickup. The squaw tried to elude him, which blinded his last sense. Berserk with drink, he threw her upon the ground and would have killed her by thumping her entire body against the fire-baked rubble of the cook site, had not Mincy, knowing this was no ordinary beating of an Indian squaw, run from the timber with a pine-knot cudgel and attacked the Ute like some small, hopelessly brave terrier rushing in upon a grizzly at the kill.

Befuddled by the rain of futile blows, the Ute tottered to his feet and by a clumsy sweep managed to capture the child. Taking from her the cudgel, he knocked her to the ground with it and began to strike at her, helpless there, as he would at a snake.

Tickup, recovering, staggered up and dove at him, her thick body hitting him behind the knees and bringing him caving down to earth atop the bleeding child. In the fall his head struck with some force, and his rage disappeared as suddenly as it had erupted. He swayed to his feet, grinning and babbling foolishly, commenced to sing a Ute song of welcome to the summer and stumbled weavingly toward the lodge. By some miracle he made its entrance, lurched and swaggered and shouted a Yampatika war cry and disappeared, rump over camp kettle, into the interior.

Tickup followed him ploddingly, halting at the entry flap to peer inward. Satisfied that her lord had passed out, she stooped and went in. From the tipi's rawhide utensil rack upon which she hung her array of Indian housekeeping aids, she selected a wooden-handled butcher knife. Taking up the burlap bag in which she had brought the whiskey from Dummy Bottom, she emptied it and went to stand with it and the bared blade over the unconscious Ute. "Warrior," she said, "there is always a last bottle." Then she knelt, unhurried, to the work.

# 39.

Because of the buzzards and the stillness, Ned moved up most carefully. Terresa and Tip Gault flanked him, covering his advance. At the edge of the silent clearing, Ned halted and signaled them to join him. They came in and the three outlaws studied the seemingly lifeless camp of Pony Beater. After a long look, the other two turned to Ned, waiting.

"Hoo," nodded the latter softly.

"That all you got to say?" demanded Tip. "We ain't paying you to imitate no barn owls. 'Hoo' don't tell us the time of day, lad. Speak up."

"*Si,*" breathed Terresa. "*Que pasa alli?*"

"*Nada,*" said Ned. "That peers to be the trouble; ain't nothing going on over there."

"There are vultures flying, *amigo*."

"Hoo," said Ned, nodding again.

The stillness returned. Overhead the dark birds wheeled.

"Tipi's gone, horses gone, packmules gone," said Ned. "I don't know." He furrowed his brown forehead, rubbed his chin with the ball of his thumb. "Got to creep in there," he decided. "Gimme cover."

He went across the open grassland toward the ring of boulders which marked the most likely tipi-pitching site. His muscles twitched with each step. It didn't seem to be an ambush. They would hardly take that course to ward against pursuit. It was more likely they had spooked and pulled out after setting up the lodge. But then what about the buzzards? He glanced up at the circling shadows.

"Old black bird," he said, "you foller me from my borning place to my burying." He paused, shivering in the mountain gloaming. "Now who you got yonder there for Old Ned? Or is you a'waiting for me?"

He went on, coming to the boulders. After a moment he picked up a small pebble and flung it off to his right, in view of the tipi site. It rattled loudly. Only the stillness greeted its disturbance. He moved to his left, going around the boulders in the opposite direction. When he came to the last one, he hipped his Winchester and leaped into the open sweeping the site with the weapon. It was then that he saw it.

"Damn!" he hissed, the word issuing slowly, as he stood up straight. "You ain't never get use to it."

Pony Beater lay on the ground before him rolled in his shabby buffalo robe, head and body covered, feet protruding. The toes were turned inward on one foot, outward on the other, awkward, unreal, and they were a blue color that Ned recognized; the Ute chief was not sleeping in that moth-eaten buffalo hide.

Ned waved the Winchester overhead, notifying his companions the way was clear. They came over and around the boulders and stood with him looking down.

None of them touched the robe or the dead Indian. They knew this time and place. It was a partner of their daily life and living. Yet they always paid it its due; they never laughed at death. At the idea of death they would make all manner of rude jest. They would scoff at the threat of the Old One catching them. But in the presence of blue toes turned the wrong ways they did not laugh.

"What you make of it?" Tip Gault said to Ned.

"Somebody done him in that owed him plenty," answered the gaunt Negro rider. "Blood all over the place. Smell of it is like squaws gutting out a good kill of curly cows."

"*Verdad indubitable,*" murmured Terresa. "It is why the vultures were here so soon. They smelled him."

"They can have him," said Tip.

"But of course," shrugged Terresa, "that is their job. In Coahuila, we call them the undertakers. Did you ever watch them prepare a loved one for the ground? They commence with the eyes, plucking them like grapes from the sockets. Then they go in through the various openings, the mouth, the . . ."

"The saints preserve us!" interrupted Tip. "Is nothing sacred to you, you pale-faced coffeebean? Sweet Jesus, and spare us the details!" He turned to Ned. "How you want to play it from here?" he asked. "Stay on their tails?"

Ned shook his head.

"Got to think," he said. "There's no trailing them tonight. If the squaw's tooken our scent and flew the coop, she going to travel till daybreak. Be forty mile away, happen she choose."

"Maybe they're all dead," suggested Tip. "There's enough gore."

"Who'd want to take them off, if they was dead?" asked Ned. "No suh. Iffen they was done in, they'd be here same as him. They done spooked and run when they see'd the chief all stiff and blue, or else that flea-bit squaw done made up to another man and got him to take into Pony Beater for serious. No suh, Tip. Mincy and her Maw, they is all right. Got to be."

"Sure," said the Irishman. "And did you ever think I doubted it?" He exchanged a look with Terresa. "Faith, now, me boy, we'll just camp up the line a bit and start on after them first thing in the marning. Certain it is that there ain't none of us hankering to spend the night with his Nibs, yonder. Phew!"

"I wish," said Ned, kicking one of the empty whiskey bottles near the body, "that whosomever tooken-off this heathen Yampatika had been brung up good enough to leave us a drop of the pizen. Lordy, Lordy, I could use a peg."

Terresa, running his dark eye about the campsite while they

talked, suddenly moved past the covered body. Bending, he straightened with a full bottle in each hand.

"Murder and treachery and the vile deceit of man by woman I am able to comprehend. But how is this? The abandonment of good whiskey in the bottle unbroken? There is more here, *amigos,* than just a little staling blood."

"Small wonder the squaw spooked," muttered Tip Gault. "This place would chill a salamander. Let's get long gone from it while there's yet light."

"Amen," said Ned, and turned and walked swiftly away through the long shadows of the meadow pines. It was a juju place, and he did not care to be there when the sun was gone.

As he went, the others following him, he looked up above the pines into the twilight sky. It was still all rose and pink and feathered with slim cloud, very high. "Listen, Suh," he said, "please to keep the child close 'neath your wing tills Ned can catch up to her again. Happen you does that for me, I ain't never going leave her go no more. I'll raise her and fend for her like she were my own, and like I promise her. The poor little critter, you is got to help her, Suh. Now ain't that so?"

Tip Gault scowled hard at him. He could not decide if the big Negro were praying or wandering in his mind or might be fevered from his two days tied to the log. He did know that whichever it was, he didn't like the sound of it.

"Ned, cease off that sky-talking," he said. "It's enough to give a horn toad the heaves."

If Ned Huddleston heard him, he did not reply. He was thinking of Mincy. Nothing else in the world mattered beyond the small halfbreed waif.

# 40.

That night Ned did some thinking. Next morning he told his companions he had a plan: they should return to Charcoal Bottoms and fetch back a couple of packmules loaded with trade whiskey.

"You sees," he explained, "long as you all is determined to risk your necks for Old Ned, you mighten as well make a profit. We'uns will just mosey up the Fort Hall trail and into that Idaho Shoshone camp like we never heard of no Tickup squaw. We is selling whiskey and iffen we makes enough to buy back my traps and livestock off'n the squaw, well, that shine, don't it, boys?"

"It does," agreed Tip Gault. "But it don't get back the little halfbreed kid."

"It will never work, *hombre*," sighed Terresa. "Let us go back and gather up the gang and make a raid."

"On four hundred Injuns?" Ned was incredulous.

"Faith, lad," answered Tip, frowning. "We got to figure it some way."

"I already is figured it," insisted Ned. "Go fetch the whiskey and leave the brain part to me."

"The Old Brown Fox, eh?" Gault grinned with good feeling. "All right, we'll do it. Where will we meet?"

"That orange cliff butte above the Fort Hall cutoff." Ned waited for Tip's nod, then concluded. "See you there in three days, God willing and the crick don't get into the willers."

"She's done," said Tip Gault, and wheeled his horse.

"*Hasta lo vista*," waved Terresa, following him off.

Ned watched them go, feeling the lonesomeness close in about him.

The whiskey plan had been a trick. Ned had been up before sunrise, while his comrades were still asleep. He had run the trail

[135]

of Tickup far enough to find that her trackline lay straightaway for Idaho. He had also found something else. It was one of his own wolf traps. It was set in the middle of the trail, out in plain sight, and baited with a gristly chunk of something the Negro rider did not recognize in the early light. Going closer, he saw a discarded gunnysack left to dry on a nearby bush. The sack stunk, and Ned guessed the squaw had used it to transport the bait meat. He was right. The bait in the trap was the severed head of Pony Beater.

Ned understood now. Tickup was warning him, Ned, not to come after her. She had somehow gotten onto the fact that he was behind her with Tip and Terresa, and had put the head in the trail to show him what awaited him should he persist. It was a heathen thing to do. It made a man's skin crawl. But it spoke its message with an eloquence only an Indian could have achieved.

He had said nothing of the head to his companions, but had instead invented the whiskey plan on the spot to get them safely out of the game. It was all he could do for good friends.

The Idaho Shoshone were not overly friendly to the white man, despite all the missionary hogwash that claimed they were.

True, old Washakie, their head chief, had preached a lot of peace since his tribe had elevated him to take the place of his father, who had been chief when Lewis and Clark came through the country sixty, seventy summers ago. But his Snake tribesmen didn't always practice peace with the same hand they preached it. Going into one of their camps to spirit out a man's stolen horses and outfit, and to kidnap a little half-Shoshone girl, just wasn't decent work for white friends, or even for Mexican.

It was the chore of a fool, and Ned had been a fool.

"Happen a man got a weak brain," he said to the bull pines and cedars about him, "he got to have some purty big *puha* to go along with it. *Wagh!*"

Thinking of the Indian courage word and the way Tickup had used it on him in the past, he nodded to himself and set out doggedly along the trail westward into Idaho. He wasn't feeling exactly as haired-up as an ired grizzly bear, but somehow, between the *wagh* and the *puha*, he intended to get the job done.

"Could be, worst coming to worst," he grinned, "we'll just throw in a little dose of gitalong nigger juju."

[136]

# 41.

Ned became angrier and angrier as he went along. The weather
turned unseasonably warm. He growled and complained. The
trail stayed rocky. His boots shrank a size every mile. When he
met a nice emigrant family going westward and lost trying to
take a short-cut for Salt Lake, he took noon dinner with them
and pointed out the right trail. Then, while the good folks
napped a spell before spanning in, he stole the best horse they
had and decamped with it.

The loss would not cripple their trip and would surely put
wings to his.

"You is got to balance these things out," he said. "Take some
and leave some."

The borrowed mount took him as far as the orange cliff butte
and there played out. Ned abandoned the animal. It was better
to come into an Indian camp on no horse at all than on a poor
one. The Indians judged a man by the horse he rode. If he had
no mount whatever, he was just a poor fellow deserving of sympathy. If he bestrode a spavined plug, he was trash.

Thus he arrived at the Fort Hall encampment afoot. It was
mid-afternoon of the third day. Ignoring dogs, children, stray
packmules and screeching squaws, he bore himself with the total
disdain of the born fighting man. The Shoshone, or Snake Indians, a small, ugly-headed people, with bent limbs, long arms,
knobby joints and potbellies, were well taken with the tall brown
Adonis. None of them knew Ned. To them he was a curiosity, as
was any Negro. But they seemed to realize, too, that he was no
ordinary black man, no deserted buffalo soldier or simple-
minded slave. Accordingly, they granted him ready courtesy of
the camp, and assistance.

Why, certainly, they would conduct him to the lodge of the
woman Tickup. Only it was not the lodge, but the several lodges.

The woman was very wealthy, the visitor must understand, quite the richest Indian squaw in Idaho. Indeed, she had just returned bringing a final burden of fine goods traded from the white men in the Valley of Green River.

Oh, yes, the woman had a new husband. She had only now settled down with Moon Chaser, an own-son of Washakie. Moon Chaser was a warrior of reputation. He was not a pureblood Shoshone but sired out of a fierce tall Crow woman by Washakie. He was big and strong, with muscle nearly the equal to that of the visitor himself.

Coming to the place of Tickup's lodges, Ned observed that the squaw had three large tipis, together with a herd of some fifty fine ponies. These latter were being tended by a small child, and Ned's heart leaped up within him. He gave their secret call, *kraakkkeee,* the cry of the fish hawk, and Mincy ran to him, the tears of gladness rolling.

They were still hugging and laughing when Tickup came out of the master lodge. The squaw's ugly face turned to stone. She did not move but stood staring at Ned. He, not sensing the intensity of her regard, immediately moved to take advantage of the audience of well-wishers which had guided him through the big camp. He could not speak twenty words of Shoshone in a manner intelligible to Shoshones, but he made up for the lack by his mastery of the sign language. The Idaho Indians appeared interested, as were a delegation of Sioux visiting the camp. He greeted them all as brothers, urged them to take heed of what he now said of Tickup for the benefit of her fellow tribesmen.

The squaw was not the virtuous woman of hard work and honest trade which she professed to be, Ned began. She was actually a harpy eagle of lowest, most wicked cannibalism. She was a creature who ought to be horsewhipped out of the camp and made to return to the rightful owners all of the plunder which she had accumulated by murder most foul, and by intrigue and deceit worthy of a white squaw.

Lastly, she should be forced to surrender to some more fit and decent parent the poor small halfbreed child, Mincy. The latter, being of white blood upon her sire's side, would benefit most by being returned to the people of the father. This was the service that he, black Ned Huddleston, had come prepared to undertake.

When he had finished, he believed the ample silence to be in tribute to his address. His native enthusiasm for the role of the actor ran past his fence of outlaw cunning and reserve. Straining on tiptoes, he flapped his arms and crowed six times like a Barred Rock rooster. Then he made a twisting ballet leap high into the air and ended with a magnificently explosive WAGH!

"*Wagh*," agreed a voice behind him.

Ned turned around very carefully for a crowing cock of any breed.

"Moon Chaser?" he inquired politely.

"*Wagh*," repeated the brawny Indian. "Me new husband of rich squaw. New father of skinny girl. You want fight, we go in circle, take only knife. Me ready."

"Wait!" cried Ned, holding up a pink palm. "Friend New Husband, we can think of something isn't so final as knives. You likum whiskey?"

"*Wagh!*" answered Moon Chaser. "We drinkum whiskey first, then fight. You smart, heap smart."

"Oh sure," moaned Ned. "Brown Fox heap smart."

Now the Indians began crowding in on Ned and asking about the whiskey. He did his best to convince them he had comrades, stout and true as the course of the river, coming with two very powerful packmules loaded with the best of the white man's crazy water.

But Tickup made a counter speech, commencing by spitting on Brown Fox. She told lies about Ned that he could not imagine to spring from such a stupid and homely head. He was a spy for the Pony Soldiers. He belonged to a secret tribe of blackmen sworn to kill Shoshone Indians and in the employ of the Absarokas. He was there to spoil the peace talks which the Sioux had come to make with the Snakes. He was this, he was that, and the only sensible way to dispose of him was at the stake.

Other Indians came forward.

The Snakes talked. The Sioux talked. Old men and old women talked. Even young squaws were permitted to say a few words, and Ned began to worry for the first time.

Yet, just when things seemed to be getting out of hand, a wise elder spoke to calm the gathering tempers.

"Be generous, my brothers," cautioned the statesman. "A little courtesy, please. There is no fair question here of burning the black cousin as a visitor. The thing to do is to have him and Moon Chaser make the fight. Then let the winner take the squaw and the child. Let it be only the loser who is burned."

"Now thank you, uncle," Ned began. "You is making a heap more sense than all them other featherhats put together. I wants you to know that Old Brown Fox, he appreciate . . ."

He broke off, to stand with desperate glance darting around the circle of the dark-faced Shoshone jury.

"Like I was saying, brothers," he concluded, making all of them the courtesy bow, "So long to ever'body!"

He dashed for the thinnest part of the crowd, hoping to break through and run for his life. But he did not make it. War clubs thudded off his shoulders and head, and he was down. His next memory was that of being led into a large dirt ring with Moon Chaser, being handed a knife and instructed to make the best fight of it that he could, the outcome guaranteed in advance to be fatal to someone.

It was a fight which made material for the skin paintings of the tribe for a generation and beyond. Shoshone still live who heard it from parent or grandparent among the tales of childhood. Moon Chaser was strong and quick and not of a will to relinquish his new-found wealth; Ned was determined to survive for a better reason—for Mincy.

For what seemed like hours the red man and the black strove beneath the summer sunset. In the end Moon Chaser cut Ned with five passes of the blade, while the big Negro made not a single move with his steel. But then, unwarned, and as Moon Chaser tired, the brown-skinned fighter dropped his knife and drove his right hand into the Indian's jaw. His left hand followed into the pit of the warrior's solar plexus. Moon Chaser gasped and could not move, and a rain of blows to face and body drove him to the earth.

There was a great stillness then, for Ned could not honorably leave his fallen foe, as he would have left a fairly fought and vanquished white or Mexican opponent. In the Indian code, one fighter must die. Otherwise what decision had been made? If Brown Fox spared the Crow-Snake son of Washakie, the tribe would finish off Brown Fox. There was no appeal.

The panting Negro bent to retrieve his blade from the dust. Hefting it, he moved toward the helpless Moon Chaser. If he would have killed his enemy the legend cannot tell, for he was never brought to the moment. Even as he started toward Moon Chaser, Tickup came in behind him with her stone braining ax and smashed at his head. Twisting to the sound of her approach, Ned felt the terrible weapon graze the side of his head and knew, even as he fell, that his left ear had gone with the murderous swing of the weapon.

And that is all that he remembered until he regained consciousness with the caked blood on his head, his body bound hand and foot to the Indian burning pole, and the faggots piled close about him looming like the thorns of hell against the leaping glare of the dance fires which lit the night beyond.

# *42.*

Ned tested his bonds. The effort cost him a burst of raw pain. He groaned helplessly and looked about. The sole guardian was an ancient harridan who sat on her withered hams beating the heels of her palms together in rhythm to the dancers. She seemed unconscious of Ned.

"Hoo, mother!" he called to her. "How come me to be getting the barbecue? How come it ain't old Moon Chaser? I had him whupt."

The hag turned toward the sound of his voice, staring blankly. He could see the opaque moons of her eyes—she was stone blind.

Aid was near, however. The ubiquitous Tickup came lumbering up through the night, to answer Ned's query.

"You lose," she told the suffering Negro captive. "Because you no kill Moon Chaser."

"My God!" cried Ned. "You belted me fore I could count coup on him. You seen me start for him."

"Ha, ha!" The tabacco-ruined teeth were bared like those of an old mule to the lift of the leathery upper lip. "Me tellum

[141]

people you no swat fly. You catchum heart like mother coyote. No fight, just lickum cub and run. They see you make hug with Mincy. Know me tellum truth. People all say Tickup smart. Jump in quick. No let black quitter get away."

Ned's weary body sagged into his bonds as far as they would permit.

"Tickup," he murmured, "it ain't me nor old Moon Chaser what was the losers tonight; it's you what's the winner."

The squaw grinned again. It seemed to Ned that grin was like peering into a pocketbookful of cypress knees. Or like listening to the suck of the brown river about a circlet of sawyers bared against the current. But it was still a grin.

"You heap cunning, Brown Fox," she said. "Plenty smart sometime. You just catchum bad luck."

Ned set his jaw, watching her waddle away toward the dancers. He tried to make himself remember that he still had one solid chance remaining: this was the third day and Tip and Terresa, by outlaw agreement, ought to have made the landmark butte before sundown. If they had, and had then climbed its elevation to glass the country for his whereabouts, they might have seen the burning pole prepared. He knew Tip had field glasses and, by and large, when a gang of owlhooters made a "meet," they were careful to be there on schedule: the bandit business ran on schedules.

All right, say Tip and Terresa had arrived and did know of his predicament. Then what?

Well, for openers, there were those tough-looking Sioux guests of the "peace commission." Tip and Terresa would be more spooked by forty Sioux than by four hundred Snakes. With Snakes there was always the chance that Washakie might show up. Or that one of the local subchiefs might turn sensible in time to save a man's bacon from getting broiled, even a black man's bacon. But those Sioux were another breed of red cat. They had no Washakies, only Sitting Bulls. Odds were that if the Shoshone started to cool on burning Ned, the Sioux would heat them right up again. It was likely, in fact, that the entire idea of sacrificing a captive had been set off among the gentler Snakes by their ambition to show the savage Montana brother that he wasn't talking peace with any bunch of pullet-livered lovers of the white man, or of the black.

It added up, then, to realistic outlaw arithmetic: Ned's brave friends would have to let him burn.

It was a mighty poor way to go. The worst of it was there wouldn't be anybody left to worry over little Mincy. That hurt something fierce. All that moon-high talk of Ned's to the bruised, forlorn-eyed halfbreed waif in the happy camp at Spur Ridge was empty wind now. What miserable nigger lies those had been about how Ned would take her where the white man's main tribe had its tipis, and there raise her and send her to school in dresses made from cloth, not deer leather. But then maybe it wasn't all wind-rattle. Maybe for just those brief days he had made the little girl happy with his make-believe of the land of her white father. Maybe, for a smile or two, she had really thought Ned could change himself, too, that he could make himself into that white farmer he had promised her, and change into white man's clothes, instead of the horse boots, buckhide shirts, grease-fringed leggings and the wide hat of the owlhoot trail. Well, maybe. But if a man wanted at the last to be honest, he would have to say no. Ned had failed again.

The only thing in his life that he had known he must get done—seeing to it that Mincy was raised decent and made into a quality lady back in the settlements—he had not got done. His black man's luck was playing him the same old losing game right to the mealy end. He had come within vision of the dream, and that had been all.

God, though, there had to be something left for her.

"Lord, Suh," said Ned, turning drawn face to the night sky. "Iffen you is up there, which I ain't too sure you is from some of the fixes you done fetch me into, you got to help Mincy in my place.

"I knows you ain't going to run no good hosses windbroke a'coming to *my* rescue. But I gots to pray on you to catch up that poor little critter, and leave her to ride up behind you. Do it for a small ways, anyhow, Lord. Then she will maybe think Old Ned done told her *some* truth, at least. Use your *puha*, Lord. Don't stint on it for that child. You haven't another sparrow needs your eye on it any worst."

He started to say "amen" but his prayer was answered so swiftly he did not have the chance.

Over among the dancers a commotion arose. Someone was

coming into camp. In another moment the crowd parted upon shouted orders from the elders, and the grandest figure Ned Huddleston had ever seen rode into the Shoshone firelight. It was Tip Gault. Tip, and two big packmules loaded fit to break their backs with moss-padded gunnysacks full of bottled trade whiskey. *Amen* nothing, Lord, *Hallelujah!*

Black bacon would not burn tonight.

Yet Tip too seemed to be in trouble. The damned heathen were pushing and pawing like red apes to be at the whiskey. This was no trade talk going on; they were just taking that bottle-goods away from the brave Irishman. In seconds, glass was flying all over the place. Bottlenecks were smashed open with rocks, corks pried out with knifeblades, gun barrels, or bleeding fingers. It looked dismal for about ten minutes. Yet whiskey had charms to soothe, as well as to excite the savage heart. Shortly the tribe appeared to be mellowing to the cornmash. The people, grinning now as they wiped their chins, were pressing about old Tip to hear his sales pitch.

"Friends," the cheery Irishman declared in Shoshone far superior to Ned's, "you are welcome to the whiskey. It is brought to you as a small collection gift; what I would like to collect for it is the very worthless black man you have lashed-up to the burning pole. He is a bad fellow, a thief and traitor in my own band, and I would claim the courtesy right of punishing him in our own secret ways, which are too terrible to even speak out loud. I will take him and begone at your charity. *Wagh!*"

The Shoshone did not appear impressed, but rather inclined to take it under advisement while they finished the free drink. Tip, the moment he understood this, circulated through the thirsty mob with proper social grace but dead aim. When he had reached Ned's vicinity, and when no host Snake was listening nearby, he made another speech, and guarded.

"Lad," he whispered hoarsely, "you can see it ain't going to work. They are lapping up the bribe and never heard a word I said. But take heart, me boy. Old Mother Gault never raised no stupid children."

"Huh?" said Ned, sick to his stomach now, as well as cringing from the pain in his head. "She don't?"

"Not quite, Nedito! I was way ahead of them double-dealing redskin scuts. The whiskey was only to pull in the horse guards. Be ready to go when I slice you free." Tip whipped out his knife, looked around. "I got a couple of kickers stashed out yonder by the horse herds," he said. "In our game, lad, it always pays to keep an ace buried: I kept two on account of I double-value the pot this hand, meaning you."

It was a typical Gault generosity. Ned gulped hard.

"You always win, old Tip," he said. "What's the color of them hole cards you going to play?"

"Coffeebeans back to back," answered the Irishman. "I got Terresa and Cousin Casimero all set to run off a picked bunch of the Injuns' best horsestuff the minute I raises the war whoop." His knife flashed in the reflected firelight, and Ned's bonds fell away. "Don't move," ordered Tip Gault. "Run when I tell you."

He slid away from the captive and went into a circling war stomp about the burning pole. His imitation of a Shoshonean blood chant was no truer than the awkward white man's flop of his dance step, but the Indians understood both well enough to applaud the clumsy effort of the free-whiskey peddler.

Other listeners understood Tip's war whoop better.

Out by the abandoned Indian horse herd, Terresa and Cousin Casimero put spurs to their eager mounts, swept down upon the band of grazing ponies selected for the runoff that would rescue Nedito.

These horses were the very best in the entire herd of over one thousand head. They had been picked by the Charcoal Bottoms experts as the single band most likely to find ready sale along the emigrant wagon roads, as well as to provide the necessary diversion for Tip to get Nedito out of the Indian camp. That these particular ponies were being held on separate herd from the main Shoshone band, failed to serve any warning to the Mexican professionals. As far as Terresa and Cousin Casimero were concerned, it seemed merely that the ignorant *Indios* had only simplified their task for them. Moreover, the runoff worked in just that beautiful manner. The preselected animals ran in a tight bunch, with no breaking away, and the Coahuilan cousins had only to stay in their saddles to complete the easiest theft of high-quality horse stock in their careers.

In the Shoshone camp it went equally well for Ned and Tip Gault.

There was a moment's awkwardness when the big Negro voted

to find little Mincy and carry her along with them. But they scarcely broke fleeing stride when Ned realized that certain death would reward this insanity. He could never jeopordize brave Tip's life in this way. By the outlaw Book of Hoyle, Tip Gault had just put up his life for Ned's. That bet was never sand-bagged, nor undercut.

"Old Tip," he gasped, "forgive me. I only meant . . ."

"Shut up, you black imp!" roared Tip. "And *run!*"

"Yes suh," said Ned, and let out, full gallop.

In the darkness and confusion of the surprised camp, stam-peded horses were running everywhere. It was no trick for riders of their skill to catch and mount suitable animals and be gone from the tangle of half-drunken Indians and milling mustangs. Neither was it difficult, since they knew beforehand the precise route Terresa and Casimero would drive the stolen horses, to intercept their comrades.

The meet was made at the landmark butte. There the Fort Hall trail was abandoned. Through the starlight they pushed the lifted herd across open rocky country. This was that type of terrain called trackless by the uninformed, and known as the high lonesomes to the owlhoot bands. It was land wherein not only was a trackline difficult to follow, but the closing-in of any pursuit could be seen for up to twenty miles along the backtrail.

The only problem was to stay awake and not to go dozing and fall out of the saddle; it was all so boring and simple once away from the Fort Hall road.

But there *was* one other problem; just a passing small one. They discovered this when, with sunrise, they had a look at their backtrail through Tip Gault's field glasses.

Way back yonder, there were some Indians hanging on their trackline. And the problem was that they were not just *some* Indians, or *any* Indians, or even that they were the Fort Hall Shoshone.

Indeed, the problem was that they were *not* the Fort Hall Shoshone. Those were Montana Indians back there. Cutthroat Hunkpapa Sioux. The darkness had betrayed Terresa and Cousin Casimero. They had stolen the wrong horse herd!

# 43.

It was now mid-morning. Decisions must be made, and swiftly. The error committed by Tip Gault's two "coffeebeans" was the sort which could separate a man from his hair. Recriminations, however, were never in order among outlaws. Action was the answer.

"We'll turn loose of the herd," ruled Tip. "Let the devils come up to us close enough to see us do it, then away we go, free as birds in the air."

"I don't fly too good," said Casimero, Terresa's young cousin. He was a New Mexico Mexican and spoke the argot of the American range, as well as Spanish. "Besides, we're almost to the Wyoming line. Let's keep the horses. We can make it."

Gault, the merriest of men when circumstances permitted, was never the jokester when business entered in.

"You take your cut of the herd, *compadre*," he said, "and the luck of the trail be yours. I'm leaving my share of the Sioux seedstock right here in Idaho wheres you two geniuses dug it up for us. Them Sioux are Hunkpapas, Sitting Bull's boys. They been raising hell all spring and summer. Kilt thirty, forty folks over South Platte way, the Utes say."

Casimero nodded. "No use upping the ante," he said. "Thirty, forty dead folks sounds like enough. I'll pass."

That was it. Ned and Terresa picked out the two best Sioux ponies and swapped saddles. It hurt to let such horseflesh go, but losing hair hurt more.

They took no noon halt. Ned had borrowed Tip's glasses and climbed a nearby sentry pine to "see along" the backtrail.

"Hoo, hoo!" he called down. "They ain't stopping."

Terresa, who had already started gathering sticks for the coffee fire, dropped the kindling. "They *what?*" he said, unbelievingly.

"They ain't holding up to turn back with the herd," gritted

Ned, shinning down the tree. "They is done the same thing we done—swapped to fresh hosses and keep coming."

Now they were in trouble. The Sioux wanted horses *and* hair. The option for the outlaws was solitary: find a piece of high ground and fort-up.

"We can just about make it to Elk Spring," decided Tip Gault. "Any raise on that bet?"

"Nary," voted Ned. "Them springs is knowed; happen we got any chance, it's to get help from somebody passing through. Elk Spring's the place. Let's ride."

Since, in matters of the trail, the tall Negro's word was gang law, all mounted again and set out. If Ned led them right, missing no turns and going always the shortest way passable to a horse, they just might live to see the sun go down. The odds were understood and accepted. To men like these the run for the river, or the high rise, was not unique. If something less than a routine in their profession, it was still a constant of the outlaw operation. Like the unusually hard winter or wet spring, you didn't count on it, but you weren't exactly stunned when it showed up. So the short hours of the afternoon were ridden under without panic or pushing.

In the minds of each of the men, however, the same thought turned. It was making them tighten too much and Ned sensed it; he believed it might snap a nerve or two at the wrong instant if not relieved.

With that rare talent he had, Ned now expertly punctured the building balloon of tension. "I wonder," he said, "how one of them Hunkpapa haircuts compare to a hemp shave?"

Tip laughed, not too loudly, and answered that he saw no great choice involved, except that the Sioux ax might work more quickly than the posse's noose, to which Terresa demurred, holding that the hempen knot might be slipped—had not Nedito done it for him in Texas too many summers ago?—and that he, speaking as a Mexican and a horse thief, would vastly prefer to be tried by a jury of his *gringo* peers.

"*Yo concordo!*" grinned Casimero, who would fight a bear or a bull *mano a mano*. "Them damned Sioux don't think straight. Their brains turn crookeder than a hairpin trail. With them, it ain't a question of whether a man is guilty or innocent, but if they can catch up to him. That's your whole judge and jury with them Montana Injuns. Either you got the best horse or they have. *Es todo.*"

"*Ya lo creo,*" said Terresa. "*Mas pronto, mesteño!*"

He put his cartwheel Coahuila spurs to the flanks of his Sioux mustang. The little animal squealed and jumped, the mounts of the others responding to keep pace. Ned, easing to the lead again, was satisfied. These were tough brothers who had come to Idaho to bring him out.

"Hoo, hoss," he said happily to the painted pony beneath him. "They really is my friends."

# 44.

The Sioux pressed hard, determined to come up with the thieves before the latter might find safety in some white settlement.

Still, the Indians were five minutes behind when sunset brought the fugitives to Elk Spring. But, if the warriors had not beaten Brown Fox and his friends to the high ground, someone else had. Elk Spring was occupied when the Charcoal Bottoms outlaws whipped their flagging mounts up the last grade to its rocks and the water.

"Poor devil," said Tip Gault, when they saw the lone camper was a white man. "I reckon he ain't the faintest notion what company is coming to share his supper fire."

The "poor devil" proved indeed surprised by their news that some thirty or forty Sioux braves could be expected for supper; but, to the equal surprise of his worried guests, the lone wanderer seemed more interested in Ned Huddleston than in the angry Montana Indians.

He was a smallish man, in no way mean nor tough looking. Fair complexioned, blue eyed, he appeared to be of middle age. His straw-colored hair, bleached by rain and sun, hung to his collar, but he was fresh shaven and well washed. His clothing, if bizarre, was clean and patched right to the last rip. It was the patches, every cut and color of the dye vat, on his faded hickory jeans and denim jacket, which first took the eye. Only on the next look did a man note the "Injun" look to the rest of the stranger, and his outfit.

In fact, his New Mexico-type squaw boots, Comanche quill-pig necklace, Cheyenne beaded belt and the Hudson's Bay Company bright scarlet trade blanket under his pony's saddle, along with the Arapaho split-ear rope hackamore which the animal wore in place of a bitted white man's bridle, all conspired to alert the already frayed Indian nerves of the "guests."

But if this were a squawman, or renegade "Injun lover," he was an original model, not familiar to Brown's Hole and the drainage of the Yampa and the Little Snake.

"Casebeer," said the ruddy-faced camper, waving them to move in and share his provender. "You've time for a bite, before the uninvited arrive." All the while he had been studying Ned, and now he moved toward the tall Negro rider. "You're Ned Huddleston, aren't you?" he asked, in a dead-center, quiet way which nearly shot Ned out of the saddle. "You don't remember me, but I was in the posse which ran you from Fort Worth to Brazos Crossing. That was in the summer of sixty-five."

"I knows when it was," said Ned, feeling his stomach grow small. "You a lawman, mistuh?"

"If I were," grinned the mild-looking drifter, "I surely would never admit it to such an obvious band of cutthroats as you fellows. I may be carefree, friends, but not in any proper sense demented."

A little silence fell, and into it peppered the sounds of the Sioux ponies crossing the stream of the spring far below. Tip Gault took charge.

"Well, lad," he smiled back, appreciating the other's cheek, "whatever you be, or us, we are surely pals now. Leastways, till the Sioux do us part—from our hair."

"Aye," nodded Casebeer. "And that will be right about now."

"You riding out?" said Ned, amazed. "You never make it, man. They is near on us."

"I'll make it, Ned Huddleston," said the other. "For if I do not, then none of you will see tomorrow's sundown."

"Here," said Tip Gault, frowning. "Are you saying that there's a way to fetch help?"

"There is," answered Casebeer, going for his saddled horse. "Yesterday I passed a herd of Texas cattle on the drive for South Pass. Those Texans are tough and they do not care for Indians. Providing you gentlemen will give me one hell of a covering fire, right about now"—he was in the saddle, swinging the pony—"I will make bold to slip down the other decline, while you keep the Sioux busy. I have an idea I can convince those Texans to let me guide them back here for a feathered turkey shoot. Good luck!"

With that he was gone and Tip Gault was yelling after him, "Up the rebels, by Gawd!" and wheeling to run for the rimrock which cupped Elk Spring, levering his Winchester on the lope.

Ned, Terresa and Casimero got into place with their own carbines, and when the Sioux horsemen shortly probed up the front slope, they were met with barrage enough to discourage any thought of "easy meat" that sunset. Also, the gunfire, plus the Indians' subsequent retreat to cover, lasted long enough to get Casebeer out of sight down the rear slope.

The unruffled, straw-haired stranger might never be seen again by any of the desperate men remaining in the rocks behind him, but they had one consolation dear above all others to men in their situation. They had gotten a rider out through the surround. After that, with Indians, you just prayed.

# 45.

It is doubtful if any of the beleaguered men actually prayed. Ned Huddleston was given to talking out loud with the Lord, whom he sometimes addressed as "Sir," and other times commenced upon with, "Now, lookee here!" But the legend does not recall the offertories at Elk Spring. It only insists that at about eleven o'clock of the following morning, the Sioux having been on the attack since first sunrise and having nearly worked around the camp to deadly shooting spots above the spring, the Texas cowboys showed up on the gallop.

In their number, Ned, missed the stranger Casebeer. The action was too warm, however, for any reflection on this absence.

The battle was soon over, however, and indeed it was no battle, really. For the Sioux did not wait to make it one, once they had identified the relief force as Tall Hats. The Texans always brought a different feeling to an Indian fight than did their northern cowboy counterparts; they did not fight as fair and they would not quit when it was time to quit. Indeed, the Tall Hats were known, all too frequently, to chase the Indians in the same way that the Indians liked to chase the white man, and then to treat the Indians like other Indians would treat them. They would cut off the red man's hair and hang it on their gun belts to let it dry, and it was not a good or a fair sight to see a white man wearing Indian scalp locks like that, dangling from his cartridge belt for everyone to see.

Hence, the visiting Sioux departed without even their customary jeering and bravado when abandoning a field through discretion. They spun their spotted horses away and kicked them down the slope and off toward Idaho, cowboy lead singing their only sad song of farewell.

The trail crew apologized to Tip Gault and the gang for the failure to follow up the redskins, explaining that they had simply run their horses out in getting to the fight before the fun was over.

Tip, as would be his way, accepted the apology with large courtesy. "Faith, now, boys," he said, "I like the way you handle yourselves. If, when you get them scrawny beeves sold, any one of you would like to winter on a range where you can make more wages in a fortnight than trailing cows in a year, come see old Tipster at the Charcoal Bottoms of the Green. I am the original 'Badman from Bitter Creek,' lads, and pays off on promises as certain as Wells Fargo or the Overland Mail."

The cowboys, little doubt understanding that the "original Badman from Bitter Creek" was not engaged in the legitimate droving of fee-owned livestock, declined to a man Tip's invitation to winter in sin at Brown's Hole. They were privileged, they said, to be of service in such a matter as routing redskins, but for wintering through in that arctic clime they had little southern stomach.

At this point, Ned finally asked about the destination or whereabouts of their savior Casebeer.

"He didn't say," answered the head drover. He reached inside his calfskin vest, bringing forth a crumpled piece of paper. "Howsomever," he added, "he did give me this here letter for the colored man, and I reckon that will be you."

"Yes, suh," said Ned, reaching for the paper. Unconsciously he knuckled his brow with the nod, for these were southern men, fresh from the South, and ten years and ten times ten hundred miles of trail had not changed the way that they affected Ned. "Thank you, suh," he concluded. "I is beholden for the courtesy."

"Nothing to that," shrugged the other.

"No suh," said Ned. "I knows there ain't."

"Remember," waved Tip Gault, "my offer's good till first snow flies. Be careful of them milk-legged women in South Pass!"

"Yahh-hhHHOOOO!" yelled the cowboys in chorus, and raced off down the rear slope as they had come, young men, wild men, rowdy and uncurried and profane, and as gallant and courageous as they were crude.

"Stout lads," said Tip, watching them go.

Ned nodded, something stirred in him by this reminder of his past. Those Texans had brought a breeze from home to Ned Huddleston, and he straightened proudly.

"Yes, suh," he said to Tip Gault softly. "That's southern quality, *my* folks . . ."

# 46.

Pushing on, they made Charcoal Bottoms the following night. When they had eaten, Ned brought out the letter from Casebeer. He turned up the wick of the coal-oil lamp which guttered on the stump outside Tip Gault's door, and gave the piece of paper to the Irishman.

"Here," he said. "Tell me what it say."

Tip cleared his throat, held the letter off from the light, squinting at it with a definite air. Then, remembering, he snapped his fingers.

"Pshaw," he regretted. "Plumb forgot I ain't had me spectacles fixed. Here, Terresa, you do the honors."

"Spectacles?" inquired the Mexican, taking the letter from him. "You who see ant droppings on every tablecloth?"

"Sure enough," agreed Ned. "I never knowed you to use eyeglasses, Tip."

"You never knowed me to read no letters without them, neither!" snorted Gault. "Now get on with it, Terresa."

The latter, with some reputation as a scholar to maintain, struggled momentarily. At the need, Cousin Casimero appeared. *"Ah!"* cried Terresa. *"Primo hermano mio! Por favor,* read this letter to Nedito. That sun today, or something. My eyes swim. I protest. It is perhaps this damned perfidious lamp smoke. *Ai, Coahuila!"*

Casimero, an honest cow thief, took the ragged sheet and turned it thitherways and yon.

"I can tell you she's handwrit," he allowed. "Ain't nobody lying to you about that, Ned. Here." He returned the manuscript to the big Negro. "What does she say?"

Ned accepted the letter, shaking his head.

"Something, I vow. Wish I knowed what."

Two more white knights of the Bitter Creek roundtable

[154]

loomed through the summer darkness. These were Johnny Simo, a newcomer, and Joe Pease, a cowboy outlaw of the region. Neither was more sophisticated than a Senora sheepherder, nor educated beyond the level of the big print on a plug of *Brown's Mule*. But Joe Pease had the soul of a card shark, the brass of a sawdust-floor spitoon.

"Here," he swaggered, when young Simo backed away from the chance to read aloud for the dusty group. "Give me the little sonofagun."

Ned handed him the letter and the gunman hitched his cross-belted Colts to a more comfortable hang, tilted his hat brim back and cleared his throat confidently.

As if merely to be certain he was violating no man's innocently given trust, he inquired, "Who's it for?"

"Me," said Ned.

The volunteer's eyebrows made twin pyramids. "Oh," he said. "Well, all right, here goes anyway."

Once more clearing throat, he shot his jaw, readjusted his head to proper scanning tilt.

*"Darlingest Ned, iffen you only knowed how much I have missed you since that there thrilling night in Rock Springs, and them two forgetable-less weekends in Greenriver, you would surely rush to yore fastest hoss and spur . . ."*

"Oh, for the love of Jesus!" cried Tip Gault, snatching the note away from him. "It ain't that kind of a letter, you feeble-brained spalpeen!"

"The hell it ain't!" declared Joe righteously. "By damn, leave me finish it. I want to know what happent!"

"Hoo," said Ned sadly. "Me too."

They all sat or stood or squatted there, warming their hands foolishly by the light of the lantern on a sultry August night of mountain balm. They said nothing, communing, as wise men of ignorance will, with nature, and little else.

"Well, faith!" said Tip Gault, at last and exasperatedly. "We ain't supposed to be no blasted schoolteachers!"

Ned nodded, dark face grateful.

"That the gospel truth, old Tip," he said. "Let's go to bed."

# 47.

Next morning the gang was late arising, the four who had been Indian-chased needing some extra hours to recoup their ordinary animal energies. It was nearing midday by the time Ned had washed in the creek, scrubbed his teeth with pumice and grain salt, tallowed and combed back his heavy hair. High noon had arrived before he had broomed out his lean-to cabin, fried some breakfast backmeat and gotten settled on his favorite stump in the sun outside the cabin's door.

It seemed to him he had no sooner closed his eyes to lean back against the warming logs, when the barking of Fogarty's old sheepdog announced a visitor to Charcoal Bottoms. The nature of the dog's greeting being mild, Ned understood the intruder to be one of the brethren of the owlhoot. Hence, the lazing Negro opened but one of the heavy-lidded eyes, the nearest one to the disturbance. When he saw that it was Jack Leath, however, he raised the other lid and cocked his head to whatever business had brought Jack down the Green so bright and early in the day.

Jack Leath was the operator of the Laclede stage station on the Overland Trail. This emigrant route, known locally as the California or Bitter Creek Cutoff, was of primary commercial importance to the Tip Gault gang. Its counterpart farther north, the Oregon Trail, formed the other mainstay of livelihood for the industrious road agents. The neat and nice combination of the twain was that whatever was stolen on the one trail could be conveniently taken for resale to the needy travelers of the sister route. To economize on movement back and forth, a little something would always be lifted from the purchasers' fellow-pioneers, so that the return journey of the bandits to the other trail would not be made "light."

As there was no law in the wilderness areas of either route, and precious little civilization of any sort, the outlaw trade was both brisk and comparatively risk-free.

Good judgment, of course, was required. When nipping at the supply of wagon teams, for example, in any given caravan of emigrants, the gang was precisely careful to take only so many animals as to leave just the minimum number needed to keep the wagons of the group rolling. In this way the shorn pilgrims could not afford to stay and hunt for their purloined teams—or were not forced to stay—and they would invariably vote to hook-up what stock the gang had left them and get out of the infested region as quickly as they might. Amateurs who ignored this trade law of Tip Gault's by running off the entire herd of any emigrant outfit, soon found that the mild homeseekers could turn into quite a hornets' nest of pursuit. However, amateurism in the outlaw business was self-liquidating. The old pros, like Tip and his Merry Men, stayed solvent, and far from discouraging such untrained ambition, they encouraged it heartily. There was nothing like a few bumblers ambushed or caught and strung up to soothe the irate pioneers and keep the traffic fat and flowing.

Being a professional among professionals, Ned thus watched the advent of Jack Leath with more than normal interest. The latter, aside from using his stageline trading post as a false front for the liveliest whiskey pipeline into the Indian country, employed it as a screening point for potential easy strikes. He had the instincts of a timber wolf for picking the prey which could offer the most reward for the least gamble, and when he rode the owlhoot trail into the forbidden roughlands of the Green, he did not come bearing empty or unprofitable tales.

Profit was a word which concerned Ned Huddleston more than somewhat that August morning. When Tickup and Mincy had moved in with him at Charcoal Bottoms, the tall Negro had squandered his "whole belt" on making them, and himself, through the child, the "most happiest household ever knowed to Brown's Hole, or anywheres."

Money belts were the banks of the bandit business. An outlaw's weight might vary up to thirty pounds in a given season along the twin trails, depending upon how lean or prime the work proved. Since honor among thieves was a sometime slogan to the badmen from Bitter Creek, a member of the firm did not leave his winnings in the sugar bowl at home, or buried under the floorboards of his cabin. Rather, he unfailingly took his pay in gold dust, or fenced it for the same, then carried the dust wherever his body went in the compartmented pouches of his money belt. It was an accessory worn next to his navel, not even removed for the ordinary ablutions. Indeed, he was wedded to it and nothing short of death would separate a man from his belt, except perhaps surgery or, as in Ned Huddleston's present case, starvation.

The big Negro, observing the urgent council now going forward in front of Tip Gault's wickiup, pulled up his hickory shirt and shook his head at the unfed sag of his personal buckskin bank vault.

"Well, Slim," he said to the money belt, "you and me is just about went under, ain't we? But, say, ain't we done lit up that little old Mincy's eyes while we had her here? Sure we did. Why, I wouldn't dream to take back a dime of it. No suh!"

The moment's memory faded from his dark face.

Well, maybe not a dime. But a man would surely like to have a crack at getting back what he had spent on the ugly squaw by way of outfitting himself like some Scotch duke or Irish earl, for that hunting and trapping trip into the Wyoming Roughs. Hoo, boys, it was raspy to lose personals like that, guns, traps, powder, lead, molds, horseflesh, packmules, all manner of tack and furnishings worth a year's work in gold, and maybe more. Now he had not only an empty belly, but an empty belt, to fill. He leaned yet farther toward the conversation in front of Tip's hovel. "Old Belt," he said, "I cain't make out one word they is saying. But I will lay you a sack of weevily beans against two slab of grease-mold bacon that it'll add up to better times for both on us. And sudden-like."

Ned's face lit up once more.

"You see?" he said, nodding to where Tip Gault was now beckoning him to come over. "Old Brown Fox no more'n get the word out of his brain, than, whoosh! yonder old Tip he start to flagging his wingbone thisaway." He got up and walked over to the outlaw leader. "Morning, Mr. Leath," he greeted the Laclede trader. "I hope you done prospected a deep streak."

"Deep," said Jack Leath, "and high grade."

"California horses," translated Tip Gault. "Big herd and creamy, even for California stuff."

The phrase "California horses" was, of itself, explanatory. When an outlaw felt called upon to gild it with a qualifier, Ned knew big doings were upwind.

In California, the old Mexican tradition of a horse culture, together with much of the fine old Spanish blood of the original Arab and Barb horses of the Conquistadores, prevailed. The stock, which came from the great grasslands of the San Joaquin and Sacramento valleys, trailed over the High Sierras, was of premium quality and in the highest demand. And the California herds were usually much larger than those moved over from Oregon, or up from Texas and New Mexico, making them easier prey by far, and their captors immeasurably richer. California herds were in fact the largest single staple in the outlaw diet of the Charcoal Bottoms camp.

So Ned tuned his one remaining good ear even more sharply to the comment of Tip Gault. The effort twinged the raw wound of the left ear, where Tickup had tried to end his life and left him only the fleshy lobe to help him remember her. But he winced through the pain long enough to nod in acknowledgment of the information, and to ask, "How long we got to get set for them, Mr. Leath?"

"No time," answered the Laclede lookout. "They're driving fast and smart, and we will have to move right lively to get our whack at them."

"We?" said Ned, puzzled.

"Jack's going with us this trip," said Tip. "Got to. Not enough time to work it without him. Also, let's say he's took a fair-sudden yen to look personal after his invested interests. That about cut it to fit, Jack?"

"It does," said the sober stage-station keeper. "A man's got to get his feet wet sometime."

"He sure do," agreed Ned, "happen he ever wants to get dried out behind his ears. Leastways in this business. Who all's going along, old Tip?"

"I figure me, you, Jack here, Terresa, Cousin Casimero and Joe Pease, with maybe Johnny Simo."

"I wish we still had old Billy Buck Tittsworth to go along on

[159]

this one," Ned frowned. "Nobody got a keener scent for the wrong smell on the wind than old Billy Buck."

"Well, Tittsworth is long gone, and you knows it well as the rest of us," answered Tip. "When a man vows all on a sudden to turn honest, you got to think he's been took for final keeps, fars being any good to our kind."

"That's so, Ned," said Jack Leath. "A man like that Billy Buck friend of yours is never the same once he turns pure. It doesn't matter that you knew him as a boy back in Arkansas, or that he was your own age and decent to you, like you're always telling. Once a man decides to go straight, he can't be trusted. The trouble with being decent is that nobody rightly knows how to do it. Whereas, if you want to be smart and shifty and make a living, why it just comes natural."

"I don't know," said Ned. "I been thinking about going straight my ownself."

"You ain't!" Tip cried, horrified.

"I is so," answered the tall Negro softly.

"It's that breed kid," accused Tip. "You're still pining and mooning over making her into a white lady, and all that clabber. Forget it, Ned. Mincy's a sweet little thing, and God knows old Tip's the first to say so. But, lad, you got to be realistical. That child's near onto as dark as you be. You ain't going to be able to make her into no white girl, no more than you been able to bleach your own hide. I ain't aiming to rustle your brain of no decent thoughts. Just trying to hammer some facts of life into that mulehead of yourn."

"What you mean?" demanded Ned stubbornly.

"Faith, now, and it's as plain as your picture on them Texas reward posters, me boy. You're squeezing me to be unkindly, but the simple truth is that, even should you figure some outlandish scheme to spirit the tot back to the settlements and raise her up to be a lady—not white, mind you, which you'll never bring off—but just only to be a halfbreed lady, you still ain't got a greenhorn's chance in a crooked crap game to get her out of that Fort Hall Shoshone camp. Now you tell old Tip where's he made one slanchwise step in laying out that trail for you, and he'll buy the drinks from now till next Christmas. You go near that Idaho camp again and them Injuns will stretch your black hide over one of their dance drums quicker than you can say 'Old Brown

Fox.' Then what's your little Mincy to do for her set of wings to fly away on? *That's* what I mean, Ned, lad."

Gault was right, and all the way right. Ned knew it and yet it was just like everything else in his life before Mincy, if he admitted it.

But he would not do that. Mincy *had* made something different happen to Old Ned. His life had *not* been the same since that little halfbreed girl touched her fingers to the whip welts Squawman Croad had cut into him.

Unconsciously, his hand went to the one pouch of his money belt which was still inhabited, the one where he carried Mincy's tiny rawhide medicine doll and Colonel Huddleston's faded letter blessed by General Lee.

"Well," said Tip, worriedly, "come on, Ned. What's it to be? You going along, or ain't you?"

The big Negro straightened. Nothing was done in the white man's world, or the Indian's, without one thing. The red brother called it wampum, the white man spelled it money. It bought everything a man needed—maybe even a little halfbreed girl.

"Going," he said to Tip Gault. "Let's ramble."

# 48.

It was a hot August, one of the hottest in memory. It was weather that made the horses pant, and the stink of their lather pungent. Heat like that made men tense, tempers snappy, and Ned didn't care for it.

"Listen," he suggested at the noon halt, "iffen you two don't want to do what old Tip told you, include me out."

Cousin Casimero grinned. Young Johnny Simo scowled.

"What's wrong with a little extra pay for hardly any extra work?" said Casimero. "You heard the feller. Don't it sound like easy pickings to you, too?"

Ned glanced over the coffee fire. The drifter they had met was busy with his horse, fussing with the adjustments on a stirrup strap. Ned studied the stranger, shaking his head.

It was too pat, he told his companions. Here they were, the three of them, professional horse thieves on their way to Fort Steele to lay in the supplies they would need to trail the California herd eastward into more hilly country, where the strike would be safer. They spot the herd sure enough, back yonder in the vicinity of Fort Bridger, and ride on. Then, the same day, at their noon-halt camp, in comes this rider none of them knows, mumbling and snapping at himself. Claims, without being asked, that if he ever gets the chance to get even with the son of the she-dog who is driving those California horses, he will surely give him his level worst. Appears the head drover has fired him and not paid him his wages. Fellow then allows that if he wasn't alone—if he only had two, three smart helpers to go back with him—he would take his wages out of that herd by stealing horses. He would get his back pay and whoever sided him would make right smart wages, too.

"Now, hold the drift on that," said Ned, concluding. "Don't it strike you as almighty convenient that we just happen to be hoss thiefs and he just happen to be a'looking for some hoss thiefs to join up with him?"

"Aw, hell," grinned Casimero. "That's only what they call a coincidink. You know, something that pairs up accidental-like. It ain't got no true meaning."

"No," said Ned. "Not no more than drawing three cards to an inside straight."

"Aw, hell."

"What you mean?" demanded Johnny Simo, a youth who frowned a great deal but not with thought.

"I means," said Ned, "that Tip told us to go to Fort Steele and lay in them supplies, scouting on the way. If we seen the herd, we was only to scan it, mark the direction it was going in, the number of hands along, and like that. We wasn't supposed to pick up with and then foller along with no Judas goat, like this here Shorty feller. He give me the fantods."

"Well?" said Simo.

"Well," the tall Negro answered, "we is come the whole way round the herd. We is right back where we commenced. You two want to split-off with yonder stranger, forget you started out with Old Ned. *Adios*."

He got up and started for his horse.

Simo and Casimero stayed on their haunches at the fire. They watched Ned mount up and ride off. Johnny Simo tugged at his ear, spat into the coals. "It's funny how a man gets edgy when he gets old," he said. "They're always shadder-jumping."

"I don't know," said Casimero, brown face sobering. "Ned ain't all that old. I never knowed him to spook, neither. Less'n it was to some hants or voodoos or something. You know them colored fellers is pretty superstitched about them sorts of things."

"All right," shrugged young Simo. "So maybe he seen a ghost."

"Not likely at broad noon."

Johnny Simo came up off his heels. "Suit yourself," he said. "I'm going with the little feller, yonder."

Casimero, who would fight the black bull without cape, *muleta*, the blessings of the Virgin, or even the benefits of mortal clergy, was on his feet at once.

"You saying I ain't the sand for it?" he demanded.

"Hell no," said Johnny Simo, quickly. "It's just that I ain't so hard-tied to Mother Tip's apronstrings that I can't take a little side stroll on my own."

Cousin Casimero hesitated.

The little stranger come over from fussing with his stirrup buckle. "What's the debate about?" he asked, sharp blue eyes flicking after the departing Ned. "You two fell out with the colored man?"

"Naw," said Casimero. "We was just tossing a coin to see who'd get to go with you, and who had to ride on to the home-place and tell them not to set no place for us tonight. Colored feller lost."

The quick-eyed stranger nodded. "Some people have all the luck." He wasn't looking at them when he said it but at Ned's dwindling back. "Well, come on; if we're going to get set for our swipe at those horses, we got to push on. I'd say hit them about dusk. You agree?"

"Don't ask us!" said Casimero, sniggering. "We ain't no horse thiefs!"

"Not ever," nodded the sober Johnny Simo. "Let's ride, Shorty."

Shorty blinked his blue eyes. "Too bad the other fellow couldn't make it. He would have liked the pay."

"Hell!" said young Simo. "What you think we're doing it for? Fun?"

"Yeah," grinned Cousin Casimero. "Don't worry about Old Ned. Just lead the way for us. We're more your speed, Shorty."

The small man looked at them and swung his mount. "Reckon you are, at that," he said. "Come on."

# *49.*

Fort Steele was a frontier settlement twenty miles east of Rawlins, Wyoming, on the Union Pacific mainline. It consisted of a trading post, depot, telegrapher's shack, saloon, hotel, livery barn. The saloon was bigger than the hotel and the barn was cleaner than the trading post and the telegrapher's shack was busier than the depot. "It were some place," said Ned Huddleston.

Ned liked the telegrapher. Unknown to any but himself, the Negro outlaw had picked up intimate knowledge of Morse code during his Civil War service. It was his keenest entertainment, while luxuriating in the wiles of civilization, to hunker in the shack with the old railroad man who manned the key, swapping local lies while the messages chattered in and were answered. The shack was his first target, once the buying and packing of the gang's supplies had been attended to. Carmichael, the telegrapher, was in a decent mood, hungry, too, for the exchange he could expect from "that crazy Huddleston."

The two had been in several of the same actions during the war, on opposing sides. The telegrapher, being Union and Yankee, seemed to relax their friendship for Ned's part, and to intensify it for the telegrapher's. Carmichael was interested in the Confederacy and could never hear enough of Ned's wild versions of his personal contacts with the Southern High Command, which contained just that grain of realism necessary to the art of all master liars.

On this day, the heat still obtaining, Ned sought the shady side of the shack for his packmule and his saddlemount, then offered the proprietor of the shack shares on a gunnysack of warm beer purchased at the back door of the Golden Spike Saloon.

Carmichael contributed a wedge of cheese, which Ned estimated must have come out the Trail with the first wagonload of Forty-Niners, and a copy of the Denver *Post,* which was evidently printed sometime before Zebulon Pike found his mountain. Ned declined the cheddar but pried off the cap of a bottle of brew and sat down in the dirt and leaned back against the shack to catch up on the Denver doings, as per the *Post.*

The fact that he couldn't read a word disturbed him not in the least. It gave a man local importance to be seen looking at a newspaper right side up, and Ned knew which way that was because a priest down in Durango had once shown him which way the printing ran, in any language except Chinee. So he lounged and gulped his hot beer and absorbed the paper in heady silence, the while listening to the music of the telegrapher's key clattering happily in the shack.

Of a sudden, however, a gray look drained the healthy bronze of his weathered features.

"Excuse me," said Carmichael, taking his beer and sprinting into the shack to scribble down furiously what was coming in over the line from Fort Bridger.

"Sure, sure," said Ned, and eased to his feet, loosening his knife in its hidden scabbard beneath his horsehide vest, and looking up the street toward the saloon and the hotel with vast unease. He hesitated only long enough to be certain of the message . . . *two men killed by guards of the Anderson horse herd, trailing from California to Kansas City . . . the men known hard cases of the area, one Casimero and a comrade named Johnny Simo, the culprits shot down while attempting to run off the California stock . . . no further details known at moment . . . hold for confirmation.*

"Hold for nothing," muttered Ned. He leaped up onto his saddle horse and kicked him into a high lope, the packmule lumbering at a gallop which threatened to distribute the Tip

Gault gang's supplies all the way from Fort Steele to the Laclede stage station.

Once away from the settlement, however, Ned pulled his animals down to a sensible gait and abandoned any thought of desertion. Old Tip and the others must be warned. He knew the dangers. That telegrapher would have that news about Casimero and Simo spread all over southern Wyoming by nightfall. Everybody in Fort Steele and Bridger knew those boys were members of Tip's Bitter Creek bunch. The whole country would be watching out for the light-hearted Irishman and his badmen from Charcoal Bottoms.

Well, only Ned knew where they were. Ned and Jack Leath. And old Leath, he could just take care of himself. Ned's whole loyalty lay with Tip Gault.

The road camp of the outlaws was just south of the old Sulphur Springs Indian rendezvous, in the high lonesomes of Muddy and Wild Cow creeks. Ned found it and delivered his dark news. "Boys," he greeted his comrades, "this here hoss ain't been rode to blowing blood spray for nothing. We got trouble in bundles." He dismounted, went to the fire, poured himself a cup of coffee, downed it at a gulp. "Casimero's dead, and that Simo boy with him," he finished, dropping the cup into the dust. "It were my fault, Tip; I left them get away from me."

Tip Gault took the blow as he did everything. "It weren't no doings of yours, lad," he said, when he had heard the full story. "The fault is me own."

Ned did not argue. Neither did he understand in what way Tip could be blamed for the deaths. But in a moment, after Terresa had recovered enough to fly into a wild Mexican rage over the killing of a kinsman in what, after all, amounted to the line of duty, Tip explained.

It seemed that some years back, he himself had been in California and had worked for the father of the present Anderson who drove the herd they were planning to attack. The old man was a devil. Had Tip realized it was the old man's son who drove the California horses reported by Jack Leath, there never would have been any tragedy. Old Anderson, the outlaw leader went on, had used a plan of trail herding his horses which was practically guaranteed to sweep the country clean of potential thieves in advance of the herd. He would give a picked man extra pay to

ride ahead a day or so, putting on an act of having been cut off
the payroll with no reason, and aching with revenge to get back
at the owner. The man would claim he could not hit the herd
alone, but if only two or three stout fellows of local origin would
throw in with him, oh, what a haul could be made.

Pausing at this point, Tip looked at Ned and said. "Well, now,
and there's your Judas goat, me boy, sure enough. Yet it weren't
you what led them poor lambs of ours to the slaughter. It was old
Tip himself. Had I took the ordinary trouble to have Leath get
us the name of the owner of this herd, well, you can see the rest;
it would be that Shorty man, and not our two lads, eyeballing
the sun without seeing it."

This confession, far from calming Terresa, infuriated him further. If what Tip said were true, then his cousin and young Simo
had been murdered in cold blood, lured straight into an ambush
set up to slay them. Nothing could stop Terresa from going after
Anderson's herd and killing Anderson. This was no longer a
matter of horse theft, but of the family honor.

Ned could see that here was a serious error on Tip's part. It
had not only gotten Casimero and Simo killed, but it had done
something else—it had put the lives of the rest of them in danger.

Ned said nothing of this, however. He owed old Tip one. This
would be it. He would just keep his mouth shut tight. But he
wouldn't tie down his brain. For him, the trip was all of a sudden turning mushy. From now on Old Ned would be found
riding in last place, his eyes as wide open as his lips were sealed.
There would be no baited traps for him. Black sheep didn't
follow Judas goats the way white sheep did. Black sheep were
bunch quitters. It was time for Old Ned Huddleston to think
about quitting this bunch, about looking for another land and
another life.

"Happen you hang with me, old Lord," he muttered fervently,
"I'll take a new trail, soon's I get my cut on this job." The sun
was sinking now, the roughlands turning dark with shadows. At
the coffee fire, Tip still argued with Terresa over the Mexican's
hot-blooded oath to avenge his betrayed cousin. Joe Pease, the
friendly Wyoming cowboy turned bandit, was stoutly siding with
Tip. Watching them, Ned shivered, even though the August
dusk lay milk warm over the Sulphur Spring uplands. "I keeps
getting hunched, Lord," he said to the darkening sundown

clouds above. "Seems you is trying to tell Old Ned something which he ain't hearing. Well, Suh, it ain't so. I hears you, you understand? And I means to listen this time. Just you hold them buzzards back one more ride, Lord, one more ride. You'll see, you'll see . . ."

He broke off, startled. Tip Gault's hand was on his shoulder; he had not heard the Irishman come up.

"Sky-talking again, Ned, lad?" he said. "What was that about holding the buzzards back, me boy? Faith, now, and what kind of fiddle-faddle is that? Don't tell me you've lost your rabbit's foot, or got a sudden dose of silt in your craw."

"Who would lie to you, old Tip? I is scairt."

"Pah, nonsense. Get over here to the fire and help me with this crazy Mexican. Him and you have rode the river as far as she winds. Maybe you can hard-talk some sense into his coffeebean brains."

Ned nodded and followed Tip back to where Terresa was already tightening the cinch straps on his double-rigged Texas saddle. But the intercession of the big Negro rider was not required. Another rider, not Negro and not big, hammered up through the summer twilight. He was out of breath and his story was brief—it even convinced Terresa.

A decoy had shown up at the Laclede stage station who precisely fitted Ned's description of Shorty. He had arrived only hours after the telegraphed news of Casimero and Simo had come into Fort Steele. The man had attempted to pump Jack Leath about local help in running off some of the Anderson horses. Jack had feigned ignorance even of the decoy's meaning, sent him on his way, he hoped, convinced of the station proprietor's honesty.

"That's about it," said Leath, accepting the cup of black coffee and whiskey offered him by Joe Pease. "Except that I've likely killed this good horse getting here with the glad news. Now what in the hell are we going to do? Looks to me like you'd ought to back off, Tip."

Ned, watching the brash Irishman, saw his blue eyes glint. There was a devil in old Tip, and a man who knew him could see the fire sparking in those eyes at the very hint that the Badman from Bitter Creek had overmatched himself with any foe.

"Jack, me boy!" cried Gault, "it's exactly the opposite. Faith, now, can't you see what they'll think, with poor Casimero and young Simo out of the way, and you telling them that all the other local lads be honest men? Sure, and they'll be certain they've swept the way clean of ambitious horse thieves. All we need do is trail them three or four days, letting them get convinced of the wonderfulness of their dirty trick. It will be like robbing blind orphunts. The saints pardon the sin; I'm feeling guilty already!"

Gault's enthusiasm carried the evening.

Terresa could see that his revenge would be multiplied by waiting. Ned had committed himself, and the Lord, to the proposal before Leath's arrival. Joe Pease had neither the intelligence nor the instincts to inquire for higher goals than a good run-off of high-grade horseflesh. The sole question mark, Tip being naturally in favor of his own rash schemes, was Jack Leath. And Gault took handy care of him when, next moment, the Laclede man cautiously suggested that he believed the venture would be best served by his expeditious return to his trading post.

"What!?" cried Tip. "And leave me short-handed?"

"Short-handed?" scowled Leath. "You've four men, counting yourself."

"Precisely," nodded Tip. "And did you ever know me to buy into a big pot one card shy of a full hand?"

"Meaning?" demanded Leath.

"That you're me fifth card, lad. You fill me hand."

Ned thought briefly that if the Laclede station master held to his bid to back out, Ned would fold and go with him. Likely it would be that last hunch that the Lord and Ned had agreed on would be listened to.

But Tip Gault knew the game better than that.

"Boys," he raced on, "we ain't going to just carve a decent slice off'n this Anderson herd, we're going to cut the guts out'n it. From right here, the plan changes. I say we owes it to old Casimero and the Simo kid. Now who wants to play a little 'winner takes all,' and who wants to cut and run for home?"

"Hell," said Jack Leath. "If you're meaning to hit for the whole works, all right, you've filled your hand; I'll ride with you as originally figured. Go ahead, deal 'em."

[169]

Tip Gault took up a charred stick from the fire and began to draw with it in the dust of the fireside his plan for trailing and ambushing the Anderson herd. The men leaned forward, watching intently. Only Ned did not. The big Negro sat removed, looking off into the darkness.

"Buzzards, buzzards, gathering again," he muttered.

But the night was windy. The campfire's smoke filled the air, the ash curl blowing with it. No one heard him. No one noted. Tip Gault rattled on.

# 50.

They trailed the Anderson herd four days eastward. Several times the decision to strike was nearly taken. Each time Tip backed away, saying the country was too open. Better terrain, more hilly and cut up, lay ahead. They would wait until they crossed the North Platte, then move in.

The outlaw band then rode ahead and established camp in the vicinity of Pass Creek, overlooking the meadowland where Anderson would most likely halt.

Ned was not happy with the campsite. He said they had ridden past several bunches of local horses in the grassy draws and meadows of the creek. He remembered that somewhere nearby—or not far off—was the range of the Hat ranch cattle. If so, they had best be careful. Just their luck to make a good hit and then run into Hat ranch cowboys. It was Ned's hunch that somebody had better go and see if that horsestuff they had passed by was carrying the Hat brand, a stamp-branded small Stetson on the left flat of the jaw. If they were, then the strike had best be delayed until the Anderson herd got off Hat ranch land.

It was one thing to cut up a transient herd, and another to disturb local Wyoming stock. Drovers from far off, like young Anderson, were mostly anxious to keep moving. Even when you hit them, they always voted to push on. Stopping to run the thieves invariably meant losing more horses to other thieves, or simply through wandering or straying on graze. But if you got the Wyoming ranchers on your trail, they had nothing better to do than stay there, and they would run you to Laramie, or Omaha, Nebraska, if need be, to teach you the difference between California and Wyoming horses, cattle, or whatever. Even the sheepherders were mean in Wyoming.

Tip laughed at the tall Negro's anxieties.

"You're seeing spooks, lad," he assured him. "Sure now and old Tip knows better than to lift local stuff. Besides, them horses you seen was on the trail yesterday. I ain't seen any today. Have you?"

"No, suh," admitted Ned. "But yesterday is quite recent enough to satisfy Old Ned."

"Pshaw!" waved Tip. "Go and get your horse and come along with me. I want to scout around for a way to drive them hosses out of here when we lift them. Whiles we're away, the boys will build a brush corral big enough to hold what we get, until we can put them all together and move them out. That'll be sunup tomorrow."

"If you say, old Tip," murmured Ned.

Terresa, who was always Tip's second-in-command in matter's of horse thievery, asked to borrow Tip's field glasses before they left. He said that he expected to have the corral up long before sundown. When they finished it, he wanted to take the boys, Jack Leath and Joe Pease, and have a look at the country eastward, assuming Tip was going to cut back to the west, looking for the escape route to move the stolen herd out of the country. By the time the corral was in place, Anderson should have the herd on graze at the big meadow. Terresa could glass the horses while the sun was still shining, thus spotting the main bunch and figuring its location for running off, come twilight.

This was agreed.

Tip and Ned would return in plenty of time, but there was no reason for Terresa and the others to sit around waiting. Tip gave the glasses to the Mexican, and he and Ned rode out. Tip's last words to Terresa were a warning not to make any move, *no matter what*, until Tip was back to take charge of the run-off.

"It ain't," he assured the proud Coahuilan, "because you don't

[171]

know how to stampede a good herd and make away with it. It's just a matter of being absolutely sure that some of us ain't running one way, while others of us is heading the other. We have got to stay together."

Terresa understood this. *"Comprendo,"* he nodded. "Do not worry, *hombre.* Nedito is my good-luck charm, and I would not dream to gamble without him by my side. *Hasta luego."*

*"Hasta luego,"* answered Tip Gault.

Ned said nothing. The time had gone when things were as between true *gamelos,* true twins, with Terresa and himself. If he were, indeed, a good-luck omen to the Mexican, that was fine. But Ned didn't feel the favor was returned. Terresa was snake-bit. Where he was, there trouble was for Ned Huddleston. They didn't see things the same way. They never really had.

"Hoo, hoss," said Ned softly to his mount. "Be ready to run when I gives you the word."

"What did you say?" asked Tip Gault, back over his shoulder.

"Talking to the hoss," said Ned.

"What'd he have to say?"

"Wanted to know iffen you knowed your work."

"What'd you tell him?"

"Told him nothing. What the hell a hoss know bouten such things?"

"As what?"

"Stealing hosses."

"Oh." Tip shook his head. "You know something, lad? You *are* crazy."

"Gots to be," answered Ned. "I is here, ain't I?"

Tip did not reply. They rode on, but did not find the drive way out of the hills that the outlaw leader sought.

The afternoon was well wasted by the time they turned back. Coming about sundown to the pasture at Big Meadow, they ascended a ridge and saw that the Anderson horses had indeed made the night halt on schedule. Tip was much pleased by this proof of his astuteness and, in truth, Ned himself was somewhat relieved by the accuracy with which his chief had predicted the pasture spot for the herd two days in advance. It was this sort of planning skill which had led to Tip Gault's reputation. Maybe old Tip was getting back on the trail. Maybe those buzzards

Ned had muttered about back at Sulphur Spring had just been shadow birds.

They started to circle the herd to reach their camp and brush corral east of the Anderson halt. As they did, a commotion arose out of sight in the meadow. Anderson men were shouting top-lung, and horses—one hell of a lot of them—were running.

"Stampede!" cried Tip. "Come on!"

They put spurs to their mounts and were in time to intercept, at the lower edge of the meadow, a choice band of the stampeded Anderson stock. Horses were running every direction, having been wildly spooked by something in the Wyoming dusk. Tip was equal to the opportunity.

"Don't know what in God's world started them to run," he called to Ned. "But if we don't haze this here band of beauties right on along with us, we'd ought to turn in our horse thief badges. Flank 'em to the right, lad; I'll go left." Ned obeyed and there was no trouble in picking up the forty head. At least, no trouble visible in the summer gloaming of the Pass Creek hills.

But Ned's buzzards had not been shadow birds.

Of the forty choice head which he and Tip Gault hazed toward their hidden camp beyond Big Meadow, only thirty-three were Anderson stock. Seven head were local horses, taken along by the big herd when it broke and ran. And the small brand burned on the left flat of the jaw cheek of the seven head was one well known to the region—a crude tall-crowned Stetson.

# 51.

Ned and Tip Gault came to the outlaw camp. It was deserted. What had happened? The most likely answer was that Terresa and the others had started the stampede. But it was dark now and they ought to have returned. Well, it would be all right. There had not been any gunfire. Perhaps Terresa, Leath and Joe

Pease had also gotten some good horses together and were bringing them in. They might have a bigger bunch than Ned and Tip, encountering more delay in driving due to the greater number of animals.

"We'll put ours in the corral," decided Gault. "I suspect the boys have got off with the main mess of them."

But before they got their horses put away, Terresa showed up alone. He was extremely apprehensive, nearly incoherent. Tip got him quieted down, then the story came tumbling out.

Jack Leath and Joe Pease were back in the hills only half a mile from the stampede start. Joe was hurt badly. They had waited for Tip and Ned, but it grew late and a gift came to them with the twilight. A horse from the saddle string in the camp broke loose and ran into the hills dragging picketpin and rope. They had caught the animal, which was wild-spooked. Pease, the cowboy, had suggested this was too good a chance to jump the herd for them to pass up. All they need do was tie a big sage bush to the camp horse's tail, give him a swat on the rump, send him galloping back into the herd. If those Anderson horses wouldn't go every which way, Joe would buy the beer until next August. But in getting the bush fastened to the frightened horse, Pease had been kicked squarely in the head and chest. Leath and Terresa had hidden him off the trail and gone ahead to run the camp horse back into the herd. This worked beautifully, starting the wild run of stock into which Ned and Tip had stumbled on their return. But Terresa and Leath had not been able to get a driving bunch together in the darkness, and had returned to help Joe.

By this time the brave cowboy was in enormous pain, with jaw broken in two places, chest caved in and shoulder shattered by compound fracture. They had tried moving him but he had vomited with pain and some blood had come up. He could not keep quiet when touched, but cried out pitifully, and so, afraid of attracting the Anderson people, they had put Joe in a ravine. Leath stayed with him, and Terresa had ridden for help.

"In God's name, *hombres,*" pleaded the pale-faced Mexican, "what is it that we can do for him? He weeps from it. The life runs out of him. Yet we cannot leave him."

"Never," said Tip instantly. "Ned must go and stay with him." He wheeled to the silent Negro. "Lad, you have had some experience, you said, of nursing in the Confederate hospital at Tishomingo, after Shiloh."

"No," said Ned. "It was up in Maryland after Second Manassas."

"The same thing," nodded Gault. "You're our doctor; stay by the poor lad till either daybreak or he goes under. You agreed?"

"Maybe it don't matter iffen I am," replied the colored rider. "Maybe there's something else you'd ought to know 'fores we go to nursing old Pease. With Terresa, just now, something elst rode into this camp. We got to get out'n here, Tip."

"What the hell you talking about, lad?"

"Juju, man. My nigger juju is on me. It has squoze down fullway. This here camp is hoodooed. We got to go on tonight."

"We can't do it," protested Tip. "Not and leave Joe."

"Joe's a dead man," Ned muttered. "The juju say it."

"Don't matter. We ain't leaving a pal. Not alive."

"We can't leave without the rest of the horses, either," Terresa broke in. "There are two or three times as many as you brought in, still down there. Anderson has pulled on out with the main herd, precisely as Tip said he would. The only risk required of us is to remain here another day to gather those hundred head that are waiting back there."

"Another day!?" cried Ned. "You're daft, Terresa."

"No he ain't," Tip said. "He's right. We can't leave a hundred head just because your nigger juju is clamping down on your nerves. We'll stay over tomorrow."

"Not with me," Ned said softly. "I'll stay the night with old Pease, because maybe I can help him through the lonesomes and the pain. I got a little idee what both is like. Where at's that whiskey bottle, old Tip?"

Tip found the bottle and gave it to Ned. The big Negro left on foot. It was only a middling walk to the ravine where Joe lay, and Ned believed that the dark was better climate for man than for mount. Moreover, he wanted to rest his new horse, a lop-eared black gelding, against the daybreak departure which he had promised himself he would make.

Finding Joe Pease in the cold gully of stone where Leath crouched with him, Ned gave the orders to Leath, who gladly started for the base camp. Ned was able, with kindness, two warm blankets, some crude splinting of the splintered shoulder blade and copious use of the bottle of rotgut, to bring some rest to cowboy Joe Pease.

The latter was conscious at all times, but could not speak due to the grotesque sagging of his broken jaws. When morning and the sun came and Ned told him he was leaving, the cowboy only reached his hand up to shake Ned's, bobbing his head as if to say that he understood.

"Hell," said Ned, sitting back beside him and cradling the white man's tortured head in his lap. "You ain't think I acherally meaned it?" He squeezed some water from the canteen and washed the other's lips and face with it, clearing the caked blood. "You ever see me go home 'fore the bottle's finish?" he asked. "You got to have more faith in your feller hoss thiefs, old Joe."

If it were a grin which Joe Peas tried, it was a ghastly one.

"Don't fret," Ned murmured. "It only make you bleed more. How am I going to culture you back to health, happen you don't lay still and taken your whiskey like I say?"

He raised the bottle and Joe drank as well as he could. But the whiskey ran with the blood from the corners of the colorless mouth. The cowboy lay back.

When Ned asked him at noon if he wanted to be raised up, or if he could eat or would like another drink of whiskey, Joe held up a pale hand and shook his head very slowly. It was plain that he meant Joe Pease needed no more food or drink or raising up in that world, and he was right. When the late afternoon inked the hills with the long shadows which ran ahead of the sunset, a singularly dark-colored lobo wolf came out of the hillside chaparral to sit on the slope opposite, staring at them.

The animal seemed to know they would not shoot at him. As well, he appeared to know what they were waiting for. Seeing the wolf, Ned shivered. He glanced down and saw that the dying cowboy had also seen the lobo, and had come partly up on one elbow, trying to speak, to convey some overriding apprehension to Ned.

The big Negro understood what it was.

"Rest easy, old Joe," he said. He put his arm about the other's shoulders, supporting him. "I ain't going to leave him get you. You'll be put under, Christian."

The comprehension that he had been promised decent burial

[176]

brought last relief to the frightened eyes of the cowboy. Like the wandering drifter of the ballad, he was not afraid to die, only to not be given his full six feet deep 'neath the ground and proper wrapping in a blanket.

Perhaps that is why he held Ned's hand and was gone with a long quiet sigh of gratitude in place of the pain which had made his companion's heart weep before the wolf came to sit on the hillside beyond.

"God rest him," said Ned to the sunset shadows. And, shivering again, got up and went away from there very quickly over the ridge and down into the timbered flat of the outlaw camp.

# 52.

As Ned neared the outlaw camp he saw three horsemen riding into it. For a moment he knew great fear, then recognized Tip's flashy sorrel and realized they were his own comrades. At his approach, Tip gave him the whippoorwill whistle which was their signal for "all is well," and greeted him with, "Well, lad, I trust you've did better than us. We've rustled these damned hills the day long and picked up nary one head of stray stuff. Don't ask for no more whiskey; me and the boys done destroyed the other bottle. What else might you be needing?"

"A shovel" said Ned, and no one smiled.

"Ah, now," sighed Tip Gault. "And I'm sorry to hear it. You need any help over there?"

"None. I promised Joe I'd put him under decent. It eased him some."

"Praise God," said Tip. "Thank you, Ned lad."

"Hold on," said Ned, picking the shovel from amid the pile of saddles, panniers, blanket rolls and general duffle of the campsite. "I ain't done yet."

"*Por favor,*" interrupted Terresa. "Hurry with it, Nedito. We wish to go up on the ridge and take one last look around while there is light to see."

Ned nodded somberly, and began his statement by warning that any delay at the present point might make that look a last one for certain. He reminded his companions that they had already lingered an entire day beyond their ordinary schedule, which called always for a next dawn drive-out of any stock gathered on a strange range. To spend even the coming night at that camp was praying for trouble. If they had anyone on their track at all, they had given him one whole day to catch up to them, send back for reinforcements, or any damned other thing of damage to the Tip Gault gang. Ned had himself stayed the day because of poor old Joe. Joe having died and Tip having said that would be their signal to get out, what in the name of the many saints of Terresa, or the sweet Jesus of old Tip, were they doing still standing around arguing about it?

The big Negro was astounded next moment when Terresa replied that, not only had they spent one day, they were going to spend another. It was madness, the Mexican said, to make all the plans and take all the risks they had, and then to go home almost empty handed because "some of them" had suffered a relapse of the necessary *intestinos* to complete the job.

Ned understood that his one-time "twin" was referring to him. But he rode around the insult, understanding more than just the apparent meaning of the remark.

"Terresa," he said, "you knows better than that. So does I. Likewise, I knows something elst: you ain't wanting to gather no more hosses so much as you is pining to get a potshot at them Anderson drovers, specially that Shorty feller. You is talking hosses and thinking *venganza.*"

"A lie!" cried the hot-tempered Latin. "We have already taken our revenge."

"Hell," said Jack Leath. "Let's not start any family fights. It's been a bad run and I agree with Ned. We better get out of here and forget the whole damned thing."

Ned shouldered the shovel.

"Don't cook me no supper," he said. "When I get back, I is gone. This here keg of corn has turnt sour."

He went off into the sunset shadows, long-striding, not looking back. Tip grinned and said something about the nigger juju

working on him "overtime without no extry pay," but neither
Leath nor Terresa shared his lightness. Both instead went for the
saddled horses. For a moment, Tip Gault thought to let them
check out the ridge without him. But it was a little too quiet
when they had gone. The Irish had another name for it than
juju, yet it worked the same way. Leprechauns or voodoo dolls,
who cared? Both put the eye to blinking at shapes which weren't
there, the mind to jumping sideways at rocks that turned out to
be pebbles, or puffballs, or nothing.

Tip got up quickly, following his two comrades to the picket
line. When he had swung his mount away to catch up with
Terresa and Jack Leath, only Ned Huddleston's horse remained,
hipshot and tail-switching, in the camp of the Bitter Creek outlaws. And he wasn't there five minutes later.

Like a twilight shade, Ned drifted back to the camp and across
to the picket line strung between two jack pines at the edge of
the timber. Whether he had deliberately waited until the others
had gone up the ridge, or simply had a belated hunch to move
his mount, no man knows. But he took the bony black gelding off
into the timber and down over a rise of ground into a swale some
distance beyond the throw of the firelight, there tying him hard
and fast. He did not return to the camp but circled it wide,
shovel on shoulder, almost running now, feeling with each reaching stride the building forces of dark instincts within him.

In the camp, only the kindling of the newly laid fire cracked
and popped. Ten minutes passed, then fifteen.

Three hundred yards down the ravine which the camp headed,
the stolen horses in the makeshift outlaw corral raised their
heads. Their nostrils flared, ears pointing downslope. Several of
them made the mustang alerting chuckle softly in their throats.

Five riders came out of the jack pine from below. They pulled
up sharply at the sight of the corral. The man in the lead held up
a warning hand. All sat listening in the dead stillness of the
mountainside; then the leader turned his horse back down the
ravine, the others following him.

A short distance back into the timber, they dismounted. Pulling saddleguns, they tied and left their mounts. At the corral
again, they split up. Two went to the left, two to the right,
around the corral. The leader remained where he was, covering
the flanking detours of his men. The four stalkers, meeting on

the far side of the enclosure and finding no guard about, waved to the leader. He came straight into the corral, and they closed with him.

For a moment the five men studied the stock inside the crude cedar-pole, sagebrush and strung-lariat pen of the stolen herd. The thick-chested leader turned to the others.

"You count them the way I do?" he said.

One of the men, lean, lantern-jawed, mean-eyed, answered for the rest. "Yes sir, Mr. Hawley. There's our seven Hat-brand hosses. You was right. How'll we play it out?"

"Anyway it falls," said rancher Bill Hawley.

The five moved on, past corral and horses, crouched now, watching where they put their feet. There was still enough light for them to see and follow the line of shod-horse hoofprints which went on up the narrowing ravine from the corral. Seconds later, they were into the boulder pile which ended the ravine. Again, Hawley raised his hand.

He and the lantern-jawed foreman, Jess Liggins, went forward, the three others covering their advance. Beyond the boulders, Hawley and Liggins saw the small grassy glade of the Pass Creek camp. There was no mistaking the litter of saddles, packmule panniers, blankets, utensils. The owners that went with that duffle, and that fresh-laid supper fire crackling yonder, were the men they wanted.

"How's the wind?" said Hawley, low-voiced.

Jess Liggins wetted a gnarled finger, held it up to be licked by the evening breeze. "Downdraw," he said.

"Lucky," nodded Hawley. "But not for them."

They waved the others forward. The three cowboys came up, levering their Winchesters slowly, thumbs on cocking hammers to dull the sound of the metal's movement. They took positions in the boulders nearest the fire, spreading into a half-moon to avoid any crossfire among themselves, yet to guarantee a fire blanket of the campsite. No word passed after that.

Twenty minutes of nerve-crawl ensued. Then the clink of horseshoe iron tightened the bellies of the assassins.

Presently voices were heard, then the three outlaws loomed in the firelight, their horses seeming very tall in the early summer darkness. They did not return the animals to the picket line. Unsaddling, they slipped the bridles, hobbled all three mounts, turned them loose to graze. Gault went to the fire and put the coffee on. Leath and Terresa brought bacon, beef, some old sheep-herders' bread from the supply panniers. The Mexican and the trader flipped a coin to see which of them would help Tip cook. Terresa lost. Jack Leath went back to the pile of camp duffle, saying something about shaving before he ate. Terresa got up some fresh kindling, laid half a dozen good chunks to the blaze, Indian style, in a tipi-shaped cone. The new wood took light, burning brightly. Tip leveled the wood with a charred stick, settling the flame. He still had the stick in his hand, turning to speak to Terresa, when the guns began.

There were two distinct fusilades.

The first, from the three cowboys on the upper horn of the half-moon, struck Tip and Terresa. The Irishman spun completely around, was hit off balance, and fell sideways, twistingly, into the fire. The impact scattered the brands and overturned the coffee water, quenching the campfire as if covered with a thrown blan-ket. Terresa, still on one knee from stoking the blaze, dropped to the other knee, toppled over to his left in the same instant that Tip's falling body went into the fire, plunging the camp into darkness.

The second fusilade was delayed one-half heart tick, as Hawley and Jess Liggins tried to get a deadlier line of sight on Jack Leath, who was partially screened by the duffle pile. Their guns spoke, as the fire's sparks were sent whirling by Tip's fall.

The Laclede trader was deeply ripped in his shoulder, side, hip. So close were the explosions and so heavy the bullets, the shock drove him to the ground. He was up in the next moment, staggering for his horse, the assassins following the sounds of his crippled flight with a probe fire of murderous, timed shots.

Leath got to his mount, slashed its hobbles, swung to its back. But the horse ran erratically, drawing the attention of the five Winchesters down to the point of its blind crashings through the scrub. Its rider was struck twice more, quartering shots from the rear and side, lung and kidney. He reached for the horse's mane to hold on, but his hand closed on empty blackness. The horse was gone from beneath him, shot dead on the run.

Jack clawed onward, crawling like an animal. Acrid smoke and powder-flash stabbed after him. Each instant must bring the blunt-nosed slug which bore his name upon it. Yet Jack Leath heard a horse whicker now ahead somewhere, very near; it was only over that small rise, and he made it there to stumble by incredible outlaw luck upon the hidden mount of Ned Huddleston. Freeing the animal, he clawed his way into the saddle, started downslope and safely away from the continuing probe of the ambushing Winchesters.

But luck and time were done with the Laclede lookout.

The black gelding, confused, took the bit in its teeth and bore directly back upon the campsite. Jack groaned and sawed with last strength on the bridle to get the brute turned. His only response was the burst of cowboy rifle bullets which greeted him and the black horse at the edge of the campsite clearing. He died with the powder-glare of the gunfire blinding him and fell together with the dark gelding.

# 53.

Ned paused in the shallow trench. The shovel remained half-raised. The first round of distant shots he did not count. The second round, following almost immediately, he tolled off like the drumbeats of a death knell. The nature of the gunfire was precise; it did not, after the first burst, sound as though discharged at random, or frantically. Rather it was the volley firing of an execution. And then there was utter stillness from over the ridge after the last volley. The Negro outlaw knew that his comrades were gone. The juju warning had been right. The buzzards had not been shadow birds.

Ned picked up the lantern which lit his gravedigging, and blew it out. He lay the shovel down beside the unfinished hole.

Lord, God, which way now?

He was cut off on foot and without rifle or handgun. He had his knife, some cold food in a sack, a canteen, some whiskey left in the bottle with which he had been nursing Joe Pease. Should he drift right now with that much? Ought he to hole-in somewhere close, like the fox that he was, and hide until the danger had circled the area and gone away? Was there reason or sanity in going back to scout the death camp?

It was this thought which brought him to nod his head. Not real reason, maybe, or common sanity, but there was a factor to be learned about, a thing to settle in the mind. He had been made to think of it when, in preparing Joe Pease for burial, he had discovered the cowboy outlaw's full money belt to be missing. At the time he only resolved to ask Leath or Terresa which of them had relieved the wounded Pease of his wealth, so that gang shares might be declared all around. Now, suddenly, the remembered beacon of the cowboy's gold lit the trail over the ridge for the desperate Negro.

Somewhere over there in the dark of that murder camp were other money belts, and heavy ones. There was, in fact, if not disturbed by the killers, a considerable fortune over there on those dead bodies.

Question: why had Ned Huddleston come on this last raid, at all? Answer: to get the money to find Mincy and to buy her release, and relief, from the cruel Indian life she suffered with Tickup and the thieving redskins of both Shoshone and Ute tribes.

Well, the good book said that all that a man had he would give for his own life. But the other side of that old coin was that the same man would give that same life for something else, every time; he would give it for money, or for money belts. So the book was wrong. It ought to say that a man would give all that he had, including his life, for a little money.

Ned waited until the eerie-still part of the night; then he crossed the ridge and approached the silent camp. On the outskirts, hearing no sound, discerning no movement, and seeing clearly by the starlight the motionless bodies of Tip Gault and Terresa near the ashes of the fire, he moved on in.

Snaking inches at a time, he came to Terresa and took his belt. Tip was but two yards away, and his belt, too, was intact. But where was Jack Leath? It was plain that it was the Laclede trader who had taken Pease's belt. Had he, then, made it away free?

Ned's instincts of the hunt told him no. There was more death around here than he had come to yet. He circled outward to be sure that Leath did not lie nearby with the rest of the gold, before making for the thicket beyond the rise, where his black gelding stood tied and saddled, waiting for Ned.

He found Leath, and quickly, but he also found the black gelding, as dead as the stage station keeper. The solace for Ned was gold. Jack Leath did have the two money belts about his rigid middle. Unhooking them, Ned thought of the dead man's nature. Plainly, Leath had had no intention of reporting Pease's belt. It made the work of robbing his corpse easier, and Ned felt no pang for Jack Leath.

But the cold faces of Tip Gault and of the Coahuila poet, Terresa, would travel with the tall Negro many a remaining mile, would awaken him in a chill sweat for a hundred times in a hundred nightmares. It seemed to Ned, in the starlight, that both his friends had died with surprise. Terresa lay on his side, knees tucked, hands together like he was praying. Tip, old Tip, who had never said an unkind word to Ned or demeaned him in any way, was flat on his back in the ashes, his eyes wide open and pleading as though to ask someone to help him get up. Both men had their lips drawn back over the upper teeth. They were no different in death than a game animal shot down in flight or in covert. Neither of them had known what or who had killed him, or why. That is what their faces said to Ned Huddleston: *Why? Who? What for?* For stealing a few piddling California horses?

"Lord," said the frightened Negro, reaching the upslope of the timber in safety, "it ain't going to be thataway with me. I axt you for your help, and I told you how was it going to be, happen you stood with old Ned. I is through with outlawing, Lord. This here money ain't mine, it's Mincy's. I am going to use it to bring her out'f the wilderness, then I'm done, all done, Lord."

He went on over the ridge, back to the grave. There he worked until dawn, covering over Joe Pease. Some variants of the legend say that the big Negro did not bury the brave cowboy, but left him lying in the open gut of the ravine where Leath had dragged him. Ned knew far better than that. Any outrider of the high lonesomes would. Manhunters always watched the sky and went where the buzzards wheeled. If the legend wishes to challenge the ex-slave's motives for returning cowboy Joe Pease to the dust of his beginnings, let it. But let no western man believe that a fugitive with Ned Huddleston's history would leave buzzard bait exposed to broad daylight with a possible squad of Hat ranch executioners lingering in the vicinity.

*Ai, Coahuila!* as the dead Terresa would have objected.

When full daylight came, Ned lay nearby in the rocks waiting for riders, watching the ridgetops, taking the calculated gamble of the wild animal which for these stark hours he had become— to lie up near the dead prey, hoping to escape discovery, should the hunters trail that way, by being hidden virtually underfoot.

The cunning was not required. No riders came. With sundown and the certain feeling that the Hat ranch cowboys were gone, not dreaming of Ned Huddleston's escape, the desperate survivor crawled from the ravine.

He drank a little cold water and some whiskey, and set out through the gathering twilight of the Pass Creek hills, outward bound from the outlaw life.

It was him and the Lord and those four money belts gambling for freedom and a decent life for little Mincy.

# 54.

All that night Ned kept walking. He moved as a man will who senses his tomorrows telescoping, his time for restitution running short. Daybreak found him stumbling westward along the Overland Trail, twenty miles from Pass Creek. His feet were ruined, boots welded to blistered soles, the pain too great for the mind to command. In an aspen grove just beyond a ranch house he had detoured, he hid during the day to plan the coming night's travel.

Long before sunset, he knew what he must do; go back to the ranch house and steal a horse. Walking even that far would be all that he could force from his depleted strength. Even unfettered by the heavy money belts he could not have gone many miles without a mount, and the thought of abandoning, even of temporarily burying the outlaw fortune, was unacceptable.

"Gots to keep going for Mincy," he told the aspen trees about him, and their leaves, which never stopped moving, rustled to the nods of the slender limbs, and he seemed to hear them whisper back, "Sure,Ned, sure you is . . ."

Under cover of dusk he limped back to the ranch house and studied the layout. There were three horses in the workstock corral. They looked to be a wagon team and a saddler. That might be bad doings. Take a horse away from his friends like that, and the friends were all too apt to whicker or kick up a fuss at the parting.

The choice was barren. There were no other horses and Ned Huddleston either took this one or he quit. And that was no choice in reality. For by now the news of the Pass Creek ambushing of the Tip Gault gang would be spread broadside of the country. A Negro rider on foot would be target for more than polite questions. Particularly where Ned's repute as a gang member was known by so many of the locals, and no Negro body had been found among the dead of the Big Meadow massacre.

So it had to be that horse, and Ned, when full dark was down and he had allowed the ranch family two hours to get to sleep, went into the corral and with all the horse magic that was his, spirited the saddlemount out of it and away. Almost.

As he led the animal off into the brush, both of its corral mates whinnied querulously and very loud. A light sprang up in the cabin, a door was flung open, marking the outer darkness with its oblong of orange lampshine.

Ned scrambled to the mustang's back and, for a near-fatal moment, the stolen horse reared and fought the attempted mount-up. The rancher swung his Winchester toward the commotion and cut loose. Ned felt the bullets, one tearing through the flesh of his left arm, the other cutting deep into the meat of the thigh on the same side. But he was on the horse now, and able to kick it into a gallop for the roadway of the Overland Trail. Behind him the rancher levered more shots into the night. The dishonored ranchdog, awakened from its under-cabin bed in time only to run out and bark very industriously through the course of three complete circles of the ranch house, and the raging owner, who had in frustration let go his last two shots at the dog, made the night blue with vows of canine execution come daylight.

As for Ned, he was hurt worse than he knew. How long he drove the stolen saddler westward on the Overland, he did not remember. All he remembered was that he began to get very ill and to sway in the saddle. His hands felt ice-cold and could no longer keep hold of the mustang's wiry mane. He did not even remember falling from the back of the horse. When next he knew anything, it was the bright early pink of sunrise in his opening eyes and the discovery that he lay flat upon his back in the middle of the Overland Trail.

That, and one other thing.

He was still terribly sick and could not move even the twenty or thirty feet out of the trail into the roadside brush. Ned Huddleston was done; he either lay where he was and died with no man's hand to comfort him, or he lived where he was and faced certain capture.

Instinctively, he glanced into the cloudless sky above. Well, that was somewhat, anyway. The buzzards had not found him yet. But it was early, mighty early. Give them time; he was there and he would wait.

"Old dark bird," he said, letting his straining head fall back into the grass-grown wagon rut where he had lain the long night through, "you told me true. It was you I seen at Sulphur Spring. You try to tell me to turn back, but I figure me and the Lord got more *puha* than you, and I done sky-talk myse'f out'n listening to you, old turkey buzzard."

Eastward on the road, just out of sight over a rise, the tinkling of packmule bells broke off the wounded man's fevered mutterings. Packtrain coming west. Got to be six, seven head judging from the bells. Could be one driver, or two or three. Didn't matter. One would be enough for Ned.

No man who came over that rise in the Overland Trail would be a friend to a black horse thief dying in the middle of his four stolen money belts in the bloodied dust of the wagon road to freedom.

But the trackline of the legend was narrowing; the future was closing in on Ned Huddleston. The man who came over the eastward rise with the packmules that summer dawn was no stranger, no enemy.

"Lord, God," gasped the stricken outlaw, as the lone outrider of the packstring halted his mount above him. "Billy Buck. It's old Billy Buck . . ."

Just then the blackness rushed in upon him once more and he sank into it believing life had fled him the very moment when the Lord had sent a friend to find him.

As for Billy Buck Tittsworth, the ex-member of the Charcoal Bottoms settlement, he had not reformed so utterly as to fail his duty to an outlaw pal of the wilder days. A very small man physically, he somehow managed to hoist the big Negro to the back of one of the packmules and to lash him there securely. Then, with Ned still unconscious, he turned aside from the Overland Trail and from his packtrain's commercial adventure. Following the paths of coyotes and kit foxes which were familiar to him from the nights of his riding with the Tip Gault gang, the little man climbed high into the surrounding hills and there found a hiding place with wood, grass and water, and an unobstructed view of the approaches from all points.

There he commenced his vigil over the scarcely breathing form of the ex-slave with whom the warp of his own life had been strangely interwoven.

W.G. "Billy Buck" Tittsworth had been the son of an Arkansas cotton farmer. The neighboring place to the Tittsworth farm had been the flinty hill acres of Colonel, then Squire, Huddleston. As boys, Billy Buck and the young Ned Huddleston had hunted and fished and wandered the backlands of Siloam Ridge. The war, and the color-bar which was brought with their advancing age, separated the youths until their ways were by chance rejoined in the outlaw refuge of Brown's Hole. In this unbigoted society of thieves and murderers and plain misfits, Negro and white man had resumed the warm camaraderie of youth up to the recent decision of Tittsworth to get out of the Hole and go straight. Now chance, the greatest arbiter of men's lives, had brought the pair to yet a third meeting of their fates.

In that lonely hideout camp below Bridger's Pass on the eastern rise of the Continental Divide, Ned Huddleston would die— and Isom Dart ride forth.

# 55.

Ned slipped in and out of consciousness for two days. Then his whipcord constitution and animal vitality began to tell. On the third day he was lucid and on the fifth day able to stand unaided and to care for himself. At the end of the week he sat with his small Samaritan in the sunshine in front of the brush wickiup the latter had built to shelter him. In his mind was much of the gratitude, emotion, sentiment of the old days, and withal a great desire to talk.

"Billy Buck," he said, "ain't no way this nigger ever going to be able to pay you back."

He called himself nigger without thinking. Although not quality, Tittsworth was a southerner, and the use of the word fell naturally from Ned's tongue. His white companion thought nothing of it.

"Who said any word about paying back?" he asked the big Negro. "Hell, Ned, you don't leave somebody in the road to die. Not friends, you don't. Besides, all I done was brung you up here to croak. I never thought you'd be small enough about it to get well."

Ned nodded and went on to ask the white man if there was anything of advice he would give someone in Ned's place. Tittsworth thought about it and then shook his head. A man couldn't tell another man, he said, what would be right for him. In his own case, he was still not convinced that the pure life paid a profit.

Since leaving the Hole and the Bottoms, he had gone to Oregon and invested his outlaw stake in cattle, which in partnership with a Welshman he had driven back to Wyoming. They had put the stock on range between Rock Springs and Brown's Hole on the Salt Wells Creek drainage, and soon lost everything to hard weather and quarreling between themselves. Every dime

Billy Buck had left in the world was tied up in the packmules he now owned and in the trade goods on their backs. Pending how well he fared on delivery of the goods in Green River City, he was either dead-broke or just starting all over again with whatever small stake the packstring venture might bring.

"But if you're bound to try it honest," he concluded, "I wouldn't dispirit you, Ned. What did you have in mind?"

The gaunt colored rider sighed deeply, still very weak.

"Going home, Billy Buck," he said.

"Home!" cried the small white man. "You must be daft."

"Maybe," Ned murmured. "But let me tell you how it hangs in my mind, and why I has the idee."

He then told Tittsworth the wistful story of his love for the little halfbreed girl, Mincy, and of the vow he had made to prove something of his bad life by bringing it to a good end helping the waif. When he finished, Billy Buck sat scowling for several minutes, thinking very hard about what he had heard. In the end, he looked up at Ned and shook his head.

"You're daft, all right," he said. "But it may be that I know the feller what can help you lift that Injun kid. Ever hear of a bunch-quitter named Casebeer?"

"*Casebeer!*" The word illuminated Ned's memory like a lamp being turned full-wick. It lit up his face. Sent his hand to the first pouch on his money belt. Of a sudden his strange prescience, his slave's juju or horse thief's *puha,* was stirring him to great excitement.

Bringing forth the letter from the money belt's pouch, he gave it over to his companion. "What name you sees on the bottom of that?" he said.

He knew that Billy Buck had been to school. He had had to wait for him on too many long afternoons of their boyhood outside the Siloam Ridge schoolhouse to forget that. Billy Buck used to tell Ned what the printing on the boxes and bales and barrels in the general store said, and what the letters on the freight cars of the railroad train stood for. Billy Buck had even taught Ned how to recognize his own name in print.

Now the small man peered hard at the letter of Casebeer, then back to the waiting Ned.

"You want me to read it to you?" he asked.

"I reckon," nodded Ned. "Seeing's how God has brung me this far with it."

"All right," said Tittsworth. "Listen to this."

The letter, addressed to *"Ned Huddleston and Whom it May Concern,"* was a simple statement of the fact that the writer had been a member of a posse in Texas in 1865 which had sought to capture and hang the subject for a crime he had not committed, subsequent evidence establishing the guilt of the true criminal beyond reasonable doubt. As a result of his involvement with the near injustice, Casebeer had vowed to never again take the trail against a fellow-man in violence, but to spend his days in helping all who needed help and were themselves the victims of injustice or cruelty. In particular, the subject, Ned Huddleston, was owing of redress. Should he then have future real need for aid, he must send for Casebeer, knowing that the latter would not fail him. The brief note ended with an address in far Nevada, where the writer might be reached, and a signature in the same bold hand which read, clearly, *"Claude Casebeer."*

When Billy Buck Tittsworth refolded the letter and gave it back to Ned Huddleston, the Negro rider knew his life had changed in those few moments.

The white man sensed it, too.

"That Casebeer," he said, "is dafter than you. You two had ought to make some crazy pair."

"Yes, suh," Ned added softly. "God helping us, and the money belts holding out."

Three days later, fed to health from the very doorjam of death by a diet of venison, sourdough pancakes, black coffee and trade whiskey, Ned left the hill with Billy Buck Tittsworth. They went on over the divide and came to Green River City with the pack-string in the middle of a late August night. Halting the mules in front of Aaron Overholt's livery stable south of the railroad tracks, they said good-bye. Tittsworth would take no money and little thanks. "What the hell are friends for?" he asked. "And how much is a good one worth?"

Ned had no answer except profound, awkward gratitude.

The next dawn he was on the train for Nevada, and when he alighted at the dusty, coyote-lonely station named in Casebeer's letter, he did not give his name as Huddleston.

When he sought directions from the ancient occupant of the telegrapher's shack to find Claude Casebeer, the old man squinted at him suspiciously and demanded to know who might be asking.

"Isom Dart," said Ned.

And thus was put the lasting identity to the legend which had begun with his departure from Siloam Ridge, on the wagon seat beside his white master, another lifetime ago.

From whence he took the name, no man has said. It was simply that one man had died and been left behind in the hideout camp below Bridger's Pass, and another born with the delivery into the Nevada desert of the tall, quiet-voiced Negro on that windy sunbright morning in the summer of seventy-five.

"Isom Dart," he had said softly to the old depot-master's query, and the new life was begun.

# 56.

Casebeer clearly meant his vow to help his fellow creature. Isom found him fifteen miles from the whistle-stop, engaged in trying to teach irrigation to a bunch of jackrabbit Paiute Indians to whom a stone-age culture would have been considerable advancement. The effort, of course, had proven totally futile, and it was Isom Dart's luck that he arrived when the itinerant humanitarian realized it.

"Huddleston!" Casebeer cried, when the tall Negro limped up to his brush hovel and called to him. "God help me, it's good to see a friendly and intelligent face! Come in, come in!"

He waved the invitation, indicating the brush heap hut. Isom grinned, held up his hands protectively.

"I'd ruther you come out," he said. "That *hacienda* of yours ain't percisely no mansion. How you be, Mr. Casebeer?"

"Fine, just fine, Ned. How about you?"

"It ain't Ned no more, Mr. Casebeer, suh. I done changed it."

"You changed your name?"

"Yes, suh; new name for a new life. I done give up the outlawing business. Calls myself Isom Dart now."

Casebeer nodded. "It has a ring. Easy to remember and not unmusical. I'll miss old Ned Huddleston, though. I owed him a great deal."

It was Isom's turn to nod. "I done took over Huddleston's debts," he said. He dug out Casebeer's letter and handed it to the white man. "I need help to pay them debts off, suh. You still stand behind your offer as wrote in that there letter?"

"To help Ned Huddleston, you mean?"

"Well, to help Isom Dart to make good on Old Ned's last debt, you might say. It's thisaway, Mr. Casebeer."

He told Claude Casebeer the story of Mincy and of his vow to free her and rear her "white" in the settlements. "You see, suh," he concluded quietly. "Iffen you ain't raised white, you ain't got a rightful chance to be somebody. I spend my own life, so far, finding that out. My old master give me a good start, but he gots hisself kilt in the war, and I run off out here."

Again his hand went inside his shirt. A second letter, much more frayed and yellowed than the first, was brought forth.

"This here paper," he said, "was handwrit by my old master and says that I is turnt free by him." He made no motion to show the letter to Casebeer, but returned it to its hiding place inside his shirt. "Old master, he told me to go acrost the river and find the decent folks what would believe what he writ in the paper 'bout me." A fleeting look of sadness shadowed the dark eyes. "Onliest thing is," he continued, "I been a'crossing rivers ever sincst, and . . ."

"Ahhh," interrupted Casebeer softly. "Let me finish it for you; you've been crossing rivers ever since and you haven't come to the right one yet: and now you want to find that little halfbreed girl and put her over on the other side, in your place. Is that it, Isom Dart?"

"Yes, suh, that's it. Will you he'p me?"

"Wait a moment," said Casebeer.

He left Isom and went across the dusty furrows of his irrigated mission toward the lone Indian figure grubbing with a hoe. Even from the distance Isom could see that the Paiute field hand was using the implement wrong-side-to, trying to push instead of chop with it. He had piled up a considerable mound of dirt to block the very water he was trying to introduce into his furrow from Casebeer's master ditch running from the nearby source creek. The white man came up to him and patted him on the shoulder, as if to tell him he was doing a good job. Then he took the hoe from the Indian, very gently, and with a great swinging heave, flung it into the creek. He then shook hands with the interested redman, made the sign of peace to him, and waved farewell as the Paiute took off at a dog trot over the furrows toward the distant hills of his people. Watching the Indian Isom saw the the discharged worker pause on the first rise of ground beyond the creek. The fellow's laugh could be heard clearly in the still desert air. Then the Indian pointed at Casebeer and made the universal circular motion at the side of his own head to indicate his belief that the white man was less than whole of intellect. Laughing again at his own estimate, the Paiute turned and jogged out of sight.

"Seems," said Isom to Casebeer, who was just coming up, "like he don't cotton to having his lot increase."

"He's the last of an entire tribe I befriended and tried to teach," answered Casebeer. "And maybe he is more right about me than I about him and his people."

"Yes, suh," nodded Isom. "Maybe."

Casebeer did not reply, except to excuse himself and disappear around the brush wickiup. He returned in a moment leading a desert jackass of dubious breeding but patent endurance. He told the puzzled Negro to mount up and stand by, then went to the door of the hut and struck a match to the tinder-dry structure. It was burning fiercely even in the few seconds required for Casebeer to mount up behind Isom on the overburdened mule.

"Indian law," he said, turning the mule toward the railroad track and the distant beacon of the water tank at the whistle-stop station. "Leave the land as you found it."

"Good law," Isom gritted between set teeth, and was glad his feet hurt so badly from walking out to the abandoned mission; if they hadn't, he would have had to worry about the pain of the jackass's razorblade spine which threatened to saw him in two before ever they made the sagebrush depot.

[ 194 ]

"Don't try to talk," advised Casebeer, noting his companion's plight. "It's far more comfortable in the shade under the water tank, and we shall have plenty of time there to discuss terms. The next train eastbound doesn't come through until tomorrow night."

"Hoo!" winced Isom Dart. "I never reckoned walking could beat anything. But it gots this here mule whupt six ways from Sattiday."

"Seven ways from Sunday," corrected Claude Casebeer.

Isom Dart looked at him.

"Yes, suh," he nodded. "At least."

Beyond the sun-cracked station they sought the shelter of the water tank and there, amid desert heat, ragweed pollen and blowing sand, made the deal which would irrevocably alter the lives of both men, and that of the nine-year-old Mincy.

To begin with, Casebeer believed the abduction or purchase of the halfbreed child would be the least of the matter. When he saw the amount of money which Isom Dart had in the four fat money belts of his dead outlaw comrades—it was no ordinary "stake" but a genuine fortune by the standards of the time—the sometime Samaritan expanded the mutual horizons of himself and his Negro solicitor far beyond the rescue of Mincy from her bondage with the Fort Hall Shoshone, and her mother, Tickup.

Why not declare a real partnership? The money was all Isom's, Casebeer wanted no dollar of it for himself. But Dart was still a Negro and could not hope to make his vision of a white tomorrow for Mincy come true. However, suppose that they employed the money through Casebeer back there in the settlements? Suppose they let it be thought that the white man, not the Negro, held the purse strings? In the same way, and even more vitally, the little halfbreed girl could be called Mincy Casebeer—if that was the way the settlement would prefer it—and Isom and his white partner would be free to make of their venture together whatever they might by brains and sweat, not vitiated nor made sick to ruin by the color bar.

Isom Dart understood every word, spoken and unspoken, in his new friend's proposal. The heart of it was sound and the sound of it was sweet to a freed slave whose ancestral instincts told him that here, at last, in far Nevada, beneath a lonesome desert water-tank on the Union Pacific railroad tracks to California, the Lord had finally sent him a friend that he could trust.

What a strange and puzzling thing, he thought, that it should prove to be a white man.

Looking at Casebeer, his heart too full to speak, Isom put out his dark hand and the two men gripped hard.

After a suitable moment of awkward recovery from the emotion, the tall Negro grinned in that quick-bright way of his so well known to the legend, and spoke in the deep, soft voice equally remembered.

"Old Claude," he said, "where at all this going to be?"

"Oklahoma," answered the white man, unhesitatingly.

"Never been there," mused Isom. "Save on the run."

"We will lease cotton land in the Indian Territory," continued Casebeer carefully. "That way there will be no tracing of a title to either of us, no need to put your name to anything. I know the precise bottomland and the Indians who hold it. I know they will rent it to us."

"Go on, go on!" cried Isom Dart. "Luvva God, go on!"

"We will put Mincy in the best boarding school your money will buy," said Casebeer, seeing the hope shining from the dark eyes watching him. "There she'll be made the white lady you want, or come as close to it as human dreams will buy."

"I knows it, I knows it, old Claude; praise be!"

"Then," said Casebeer, "you and I will get onto that land, Isom, and we will make it flower like nothing any man in the Territory, red or white or black, ever saw in his life before. It will prosper because it must. And because both of us are tired of wandering. And because God brought us together, giving you the money and me the chance to use it for you, and giving both of us the little girl and our new lives to lead—together."

"Lord, God," whispered Isom Dart. "I cain't believe it. Just like the promise land. Me and you, old Claude, and little Mincy. Rich ain't even the word for what we'll be."

"Likely it isn't," answered Casebeer, and that was all he said.

Isom Dart didn't hear him. He was day-dreaming, eyes wide open and far-fixed upon a distant river.

"*Jesus,*" he said. "*I can see the other side.*"

# 57.

It was decided that Isom Dart should stay on the eastbound Union Pacific to its terminal in Omaha, Nebraska. There he would wait for Casebeer and Mincy. The chance that his connection with the Tip Gault operation might be of interest to some certain southern Wyoming cattlemen led Casebeer to rule against Isom's participation in the rescue of the halfbreed child. There was, as well, the reservoir of animus among the Idaho Shoshone to be considered. Casebeer had heard, along the wilderness telegraph of the red men, that the big Negro was given full credit among Tickup's people for the failure of the Sioux peace mission, together with the attendant renewed horse-raiding by the Sioux upon the famed Shoshone herds. Isom, for his part, was inclined not to argue the matter. Indeed, under the terms of his new life, it would scarcely be proper. Kidnapping was a crime, and it wasn't right either. So he remained upon the train when it stopped in Green River, Wyoming.

Claude Casebeer, with that part he needed of Isom Dart's money, swung down to the depot platform. His plan was to outfit in Green River, journey into Idaho, make his arrangement in the vicinity of Fort Hall for the spiriting-away of Mincy, return with the child to Green River, board the Union Pacific with all due urgency, chuff away eastward to join Isom in Omaha. The last the departing Negro saw of him, the mild-mannered Casebeer was starting south over the ruts of Main Street toward Aaron Overholt's livery barn.

"Good luck, old Claude," said Isom through the soot-grimed window of the chair car. "I sure hopes you and our money done win the pot. You don't show up in Omaha with Mincy, it'll be some sad and lonesome cotton patch we'll plow."

But Casebeer was as good as his word—and better. He showed up in Omaha not only with Mincy, but with Tickup. And even that wasn't the end of his surprises. In a special stall in the express car was old Jeff Davis, the piebald packmule. It was quite a reunion.

It was also quite a problem.

Shipping the ménage down the Missouri via paddle-wheel steamer to Kansas City, and then transporting it to the Indian Territory by wagon proved a journey not easily forgotten. The Shoshone squaw was a particular highlight of the difficulties. At one point Isom had to be restrained from tossing her over the stern-rail of the river packet.

But Casebeer was able to convince Isom that Tickup could be handled. "You can afford her," the rescuer of Mincy insisted. "She loves to ride the cars. Just plain crazy to get on them. Any time you tire of her, or she gets in the way, we just buy her a ticket back to Idaho. Make it a one-way stub and leave it to her how to figure to get back to Oklahoma without the Iron Horse."

Moreover, he explained, the Shoshone squaw had caught him making away with Mincy—after accepting Isom's good money in payment and honest purchase of the child—and had demanded she be taken along to see her old mate Brown Fox as the price of her co-operation.

"In a word, Isom," said Casebeer. "Blackmail. She took our money, then threatened to tell the chief I had stolen Mincy. You know first-hand a little something of the temper of those Fort Hall Shoshone, I believe."

So Isom put up with the squaw, who after all her years of hardworking abstinence had now acquired a monumental thirst and carried a bigger head-of-steam all the way to Kansas City than did the boilers of the *Prairie Belle*.

He did it for Mincy. Tickup was, after all, drunk or sober, murderous or meek, the mother of the little girl he loved. A man could not forget that so long as Mincy remembered it. Besides, old Claude was right. If the squaw got too cantankerous, they would just load her on the train and ship her back to Green River.

The important thing was how fine it was going to be down yonder in the Indian Territory. The wonderful outfit that Casebeer was buying in Kansas City, the wagons, plowshares, harrows, mowing machines, why, there was no end to the remarkable things they farmed with nowadays. Isom was certain now, as they at last headed southwesterly by wagon, that in Oklahoma all that Claude Casebeer had envisioned for them must come true.

The remarkable thing was that it did. For nine years, from that fall of 1875, until the drouth summer of 1884, "the Casebeer cotton farm" made money and good times for its owners and their hopes.

These were the harvest years, certainly, of Isom Dart's hard and hunted life. All that a man of his color could possibly imagine of bounty and reward, were his. Mincy, at eighteen, was a real frontier beauty, and also educated beyond the average. She had been transformed by boarding schools and tutors and was very nearly the "same-as-she-was-white" young lady of her Negro guardian's unchanging ambition.

The problem of Tickup had proved almost self-solving. Periodically put upon the train and shipped back to Wyoming without return fare, her native ebullience never failed. Not once did she take offense at the obvious shabby treatment, but believed to the end that Isom Dart was her greatest admirer. Why else would he send a simple Indian woman on so many wonderful journeys on the Iron Horse?

How she managed to get back to Oklahoma within a few months of each expulsion, she never explained. Neither did she falter. Even when the partners put her upon the "Katy," the Missouri, Kansas and Texas Railroad—which ran through the Cherokee country from Kansas City all the way to Dallas, and by branch lines to any other place in Texas within reason, even to Old Mexico—Tickup was more than equal to the challenge.

It took her seven months to return from one side-jaunt on the combined trackage of the Fort Worth and New Orleans Railroad, Houston East and West Texas Railroad, and the new spur line to Galveston and the Gulf Coast, but she made it back to Oklahoma, as usual, and on schedule, with the first of spring and the new grass.

Mincy, a gay enough creature considering her bone-tough early life, did not possess any startling intellect, and so she never questioned this constant loading of her train-doting mother onto the railroad cars.

As for Casebeer, he accepted the challenge of his odd family with faith and good will. He ran the farm insofar as the Cherokee countryside was concerned, always paying his share of the crop to the Indian landlords in full amount and on the exact date, and was completely accepted in the near all-Indian township. Both he and Isom Dart were well liked. Indeed, both were more popular with the Cherokees than was Tickup, who got off on the wrong moccasin in Manawota, the principal settlement. In the attractive and prosperous Cherokee community, the squaw attempted to peddle door-to-door the wares which had supported her in style in Idaho and Wyoming and Colorado. The Cherokee housewives, far from appreciating this competition, nearly lynched the visiting businesswoman. She was rescued only by another ticket to Wyoming, and the intercession of Casebeer, who made a notable oration at the town hall meeting of protest on the subject of interracial relations and peaceful solution of all problems. The warpath, the white man said, had long become overgrown with grass, and plowed up into corn and cotton furrows, so let there be reason and understanding between men, and especially between women.

The Cherokee ladies agreed only on the stipulation of the railroad ticket, promising that the next bid the Shoshone solicited in Manawota would be sealed with a tomahawk between the eyes.

As for Isom Dart, the culture of the civilized Indian community was a revelation of continued happiness. He was more than accepted in Manawota, he was respected. A people of great skill in animal husbandry, the Cherokees appreciated the ex-slave's endless knowledge of horses and cattle. There was another reason for the good relationship. During the War between the States the Cherokees had been sympathizers with the South. Before the war they had also been slaveholders. Hence, the Negro was no mystery and no problem to them, nor was he any oddity to the community. It was an atmosphere reassuringly familiar to Isom Dart. In a sense he had come home when he arrived in Manawota Township.

After he had been there only long enough for Casebeer and himself to lay out their fields and get in their first crop, he informed the white man of his feeling. "Old Claude," he said one day, "do this here fine land and these here quality Injun folks looks daft to you?"

"Daft?" frowned Casebeer. "What do you mean, daft?"

"Well, suh, when I got well follering old Billy Buck's nursing of them Wyoming gunshot holes, he ask me what it were I wanted most to do, and I tells him 'to go home.' He look at me like he do a sun-blind horse, and he say, 'Man, you're daft! You ain't got no home'!"

"Well?" demanded Casebeer impatiently.

"Well, here we is home, ain't we?"

The white man nodded slowly. It was a good feeling to know that his Negro friend truly felt this way. It let Casebeer know that his debt to Ned Huddleston—whatever its nature from the Texas posse guilt—was now discharged. Isom Dart had a home. Claude Casebeer had given it to him. Now surely Ned Huddleston had died in Wyoming of those gunshot wounds, and his ghost would rise no more to haunt the conscience or contaminate the memories of the resurrected Isom Dart.

"Aye," Casebeer said softly, and after the thoughtful spell. "Here we are home, Isom. And thank God for that."

"Yes, suh," agreed his companion, and the two men walked together, shoulder-to-shoulder, across the rich-turned earth of their fields, toward the snug farmhouse in the cottonwood trees on the rise overlooking the river.

# 58.

It was a morning to make a man glad that God had thought up Adam and Eve and the whole idea. This was surely the sort of day where you had to know Somebody was running things up there. A day like this just didn't happen; it was caused on purpose.

Isom Dart stood on the corner of Main Street and Sequoyah, hub intersection of Manawota, Oklahoma, surveying the kingdom of good into which his white partner Claude Casebeer had so successfully introduced him. Everything Isom saw looked fine to his grateful eye on that mid-summer morning.

The banker nodded to him; the storekeeper waved; the black-smith and the butcher spoke friendly greetings. The saloon-keeper, swamping out for the new day, smiled and asked his pardon for the moment's blocking of the boardwalk by his push-broom's small mountain of stale sawdust. Even the undertaker unfroze his face at Isom's courtly bow and cheery morning's word.

But most of all the big Negro farmer's eye and heart were taken by the sight across the intersection of Mincy talking to two of the town's three white girls, all chatting as happy there in that summer sunshine as though they had good sense, or did not know a dark hide from a light one.

"Praise be," he murmured to himself, "there is the real money in the bank."

He tipped his hat to two Cherokee ladies going by, and they dimpled bronze cheeks in gracious reply. The town marshal, coming past, stopped to inquire how Isom saw the drouth, so far. They augered it a little, deciding that that year's crop would not make cotton, but that these dry spells did come and had to be taken with the good years and averaged out. When the lawman had gone on and Isom was about to turn into the bank, he heard the delightful giggling of young women and he looked across at Mincy and her companions. The cause of the female commotion was not far to seek. And, in the first glance of it, Isom understood that that yellow-wheeled rig was *something;* and the boy driving it was cut to fit the high style of both the buggy and the bright-coated sorrel mares which drew it.

Blue, the buggy was, sky-blue. And the lacquer of its many coatings made the color shine with more nacre than an oyster shell. The wheels, creamy-jonquil yellow, were spoked into rubber-tired rims of brightest Indian vermilion. The top was the blackest patent-leather and shiny as stovelid polish. With its varnished hardwood dashboard, brass running lamps, step irons, whipsocket and seatgrip trim, well, that rig was like nothing seen before that day in Manawota, Oklahoma.

The matched sorrels—racers by their lean elegance and hot-bloods from their lathered nervousness—were also of a class not common to Manawota. Yet for all the sauce of team and buggy, the driver topped the outfit like a diamond stickpin. He was a dazzler, handsome as a spaniel pup, all-male as a Morgan colt, pleasant as the morning sun and, by the instant tittering of the three young females which greeted his flashy arrival in Manawota, a lady-killer from the first gleam of his white teeth and carefree toss of Texas-cut dark curls.

"Quality," said Isom to the kerosene streetlamp which shared the corner with him. "Southern quality, mistuh; yes suh!" Then quietly, with pride. "You knows it any place!"

Across the way, the newcomer responded to the blushes and dainty posturings of the young Manawota ladies by wheeling the sorrel strutters two times around the intersection at the high gallop. His piercing Confederate rebel yell, shrill mustang whistling to his wild team, together with the dust and pebbles spewed by the spinning rims of the yellow-wheeled rig, brought the morning's normal traffic to a panicked halt. Then he sent it into disordered rout by driving the sorrels up onto the boardwalk of Sequoyah.

Women screamed, children yelled, strong men cursed and dogs went yelping for the nearest shelter. The dashing stranger spun his rig to a halt within whip-touch of the overcome young ladies, leaped to the ground and swept off his tall white Stetson.

"Ladies, I thank you!" he greeted them. "Permit yourselves the pleasure of my acquaintance. Madison M. Rash, my lovelies. But you may call me Matt."

He re-donned the big hat, reached with the tip of his buggy whip to tap the shy-tucked shoulder of Mincy Casebeer. "Especially you, honey," he said, and unleashed the sunglare of his smile, all around.

Before Mincy might faint dead away, or at least vapor partially in ordinary politeness, the lady-killer's triumph was cut short by the appearance of one not so young and nowhere near so verging on the swoon.

"Look 'honey,' " growled Marshal Jim Eagle Blackowl. "You get them damned sorrels off this boardwalk inside ten seconds or you're going to jail. You auger it one second and you'll be in the hoosegow long enough for that bear grease in yore limpid locks to turn green. Now you git, Mr. Madison M. Rash, and you keep them hosses in the street where they belong."

He wheeled to the excited girls.

"Was there any insult flung, young ladies?" he asked.

Mincy and the others denied fetchingly that the handsome

stranger had employed word or gesture that might impugn the morals of an alabaster statue. "Why," said Clarissa Mae Childress, "he was a perfect gentleman and I think you're perfectly horrid, Marshal, to say such mean and ugly things to him and, moreover, Jim Eagle, you needn't call for me for the dance tonight, as I wouldn't be seen with such an ill-mannered representative of the law and of the welcoming spirit of Manawota." The other girl, Annabelline Chockie, joined in the attack, and Jim Eagle was glad enough to see the Texas charioteer come to side him with true southern grace.

"Now, now, ladies!" cried the tall and sun-tanned youth. "The Marshal is surely right and it was only your combined beauty which addled my head so bad. Marshal, accept the Rash apologies for raising all this dust. I hope I will see you at the dance tonight, sir, and I know this Minerva of Manawota will be right where she belongs, on your arm!"

He bowed to Clarissa Mae, touched Stetson to Annabelline, locked eyes for three heartbeats with Mincy Casebeer, and leaped like Lochinvar in one magnificent bound to the buggyseat.

Backing the sorrels, he removed them from the walk with a nice hand for the reins, which made the watching Isom Dart admire his style all the more. With the team stepping precisely as a set of bobtailed hackney ponies, he sent it toward the corner of Main, and around that angle, out of sight. The instant he was gone, however, his raucous rebel yell echoed back to lift the hair of Jim Eagle Blackowl, and he was off down Main standing in the buggy's box scattering men, women, dogs, children and chickens from one end of Manawota to the other. Marshal Blackowl rushed for his saddled pony and gave valorous chase, but his Cherokee mustang was no match for the Texas steppers, and all that he arrested that glorious morning was a lungful of red Oklahoma dust.

Watching the equine race disappear into the haze down Main Street, Isom Dart chuckled and waved after the indignant town marshal.

"You never cotch him, old Jim Eagle. Hoo! hoo! That's a southern boy. You whupt afore you sinks a spur!"

# 59.

Mincy came to Isom that noon and asked if she might go to the night's dance at the town hall. It was a church affair and Isom saw no harm in it; he indeed believed such things to be only decent proof of his halfbreed ward's acceptance and advancement in the world of settlement folk at Manawota.

Casebeer, who was eating with Isom, inquired to know who might be taking Mincy to the doings. The slender girl replied that she didn't know yet, but would surely find someone. Casebeer could believe that.

Isom Dart's half-Shoshone waif was grown into a sure enough looker. A tiny girl still, she was only about five feet tall, graceful as a reed, yet filled out where nature filled out little girls who weren't little anymore. Her carriage, possibly because of her Indian upbringing of physical work and exercise, was of particularly eye-catching fluidity.

"She go tawny," Isom explained it for Casebeer. "Like a she-cat."

But with Mincy it simply wasn't a mere matter of very female body and bearing. The girl had an exotic face, oval, not broad like her Indian mother's, with an olive-bronze complexion; her eyes were almond in shape, set on the slant above high cheekbones and of a color to defy any ordinary palette's hues.

"Woods violet," said Isom Dart, recalling the tiny flowers of his Arkansas boyhood, and Casebeer could not improve on that. He would have said lavender or purple, if pressed. But neither color would have been as close as woods violet, nor anywhere near as pretty as the slanted, shadowed eyes of Mincy.

The girl was going to be trouble, Claude Casebeer was absolutely certain. It was a combination of her being shy on the one hand and bold on the other, taken together with the fact that Isom stubbornly did not want her to "marry a Injun boy," and

[205]

so persisted in warding off the several quite eligible Cherokee swains who swarmed about the dusky-faced halfblood beauty. It was the color bar in reverse, and Casebeer had argued with Isom about it, but the big Negro remained immovable. "How she going to be the same as she was white, iffen she ups and say the words with one of them Cherokee?" he demanded. No arguments of Casebeer's could penetrate the other's purblind determination.

The fact that the Cherokee were the most white-oriented of all Indians, that they had more Scotch and Irish and English names among them than they did Indian, made no impression upon the ex-slave. He loved the Cherokee, who had been so good to him, and he would do anything in the Oklahoma world for them that he could, but his girl Mincy was going to marry a white boy.

"Friend Isom," the white partner had said one day in final desperation, "you are talking like a nigger."

He had not used the word before and never did again, but Isom Dart knew exactly what he meant and how it was intended to be taken. Moreover, he knew that Casebeer was right in the accusation and he understood how it must have hurt the gentle fellow to make it.

Yet he could not yield. *Get over that river, Ned,* his old master had told him. *Get over that river and go free.*

Well, God had brought him this far, and over a lot of rivers, but never the right one. For Mincy it wasn't going to end that way. She *had* to get across.

Thus, when Mincy asked about the dance, Isom quickly gave his agreement. The girl literally ran out the kitchen door to her pony, standing saddled in the shade of the backyard cottonwood giant which spread its gnarled protection over the "Casebeer place." Vaulting to stirrup, she turned the animal in a quarter-spin, quirted it out across the river pasture toward the willows of the Kiowa Bend bottoms.

"Hoo, boy!" said Isom happily. "Ain't it grand what a little old yes can do?"

Casebeer nodded soberly, and got up from the table. "Not only grand," he said in his quiet way. "Likewise and sometimes mighty curious."

Isom dismissed him with a grin and a wave. Old Claude was a worrier. He would see the fly in the raisin custard every time.

But it was part of what made him a good partner, and if he wasn't as quick on people as old Isom, well, that was all right. Together they did just great.

Casebeer *was* a worrier. He went directly to the barn and got his saddle horse and set out by the river road, as though to go to the far field. His mind, however, was not on drouthed-out cotton. At the ford, he turned aside into the willows and tied his horse. Taking the footpath on the north bank, he worked backward toward the house and toward where the old wagon track came into the willows from the pasture. This was where they sometimes hauled water for the house when the well ran dry—as they were doing that summer—and it was where he thought Mincy had headed. The wagon track was out of sight from the house, but Casebeer simply had a hunch.

He had not reached the Kiowa Bend sand bar, a pretty little beach screened by willows, before he heard the laughter and giggling. He waited a bit, shaking his head and not happy. It pleased him not at all that he had saddled the right hunch. Yet he must make sure.

Coming to the beach clearing he made no more sound than any shadow trained in Pawnee and Comanche land. Perhaps he was a little rusty. After all, nine years had passed. A stick did squeak here, and a twig creak there and one dry-shag of bark actually cracked underfoot. But where it would have cost him his hair out where the horse Indians were, in this thicket of young love its price was only louder and more panting laughter.

He didn't watch it long.

Casebeer was not a family man. He did not yearn after women unduly, nor was he mainly set against them. Like any normal male at roam upon the frontier, he had known his share of company, but now Casebeer didn't have the time for dalliance, nor the temper either. Particularly, he had no moment for lady-killers. The studhorse frontier rough, the randy squawman, the drunken lout-at-lust, were not of his tribe, but he could understand them. What he could not abide was the settlement-haunting dandies who made the pursuit of women, particularly of innocent and stupid women, his sorry game.

The truth was that Claude Casebeer worshipped women. He did it in a removed and steady way, never with the courage to consider himself good enough for them, never with any under-

[207]

standing of the old law that warned they wanted to be treated rough, but always in frank tribute.

So it was he did not stand long in the willows watching the young rake from Texas hot-talk Mincy into the soft prairie grass beside the old down cottonwood at Kiowa Bend. Casebeer waited only time enough to be certain of what he saw, then went away very quickly and quietly, and sadly, too, for he knew that he must tell Isom and yet he could not tell him.

A way must be found to warn his old friend without destroying Mincy for him. The girl was Isom Dart's dream. How did you tell him that, to the Matt Rashes of the white man's world, she was still something less than their color?

# 60.

By nightfall of that first day Casebeer had thought of no decent way to tell Isom about Mincy and Matt Rash. In fact, he had about decided to say nothing. There just wasn't any way to tell an old friend that the pearl in his oyster was artificial, or only a grain of bad sand.

Besides, Mincy might come to in time and back off from the dashing Texan. Also, Rash wasn't much more than a boy himself, maybe just old enough to vote. He was a big devil, grown way beyond his years, and one of those youngsters who were "man enough" mighty early. But he was still not old enough to have gone sour. There was, Casebeer convinced himself, every good chance that Rash would ease up on the girl, at least enough to state his honorable intentions, if any.

No harm, in any event, in keeping quiet for the moment. If things continued to get out of hand, like that struggling down at Kiowa Bend, that was different. Then somebody would need to step in.

The dance that night did not reassure the anxious white man.

Mincy said nothing about her new beau. Isom took her into town, left her at the hall. At midnight, he and Casebeer went back to pick her up, and she was gone. They didn't have to ask where, or rather with whom. Plenty of green-eyed girls stepped forward to curl the lip and sniff out loud that it was Mr. Madison M. Rash who had borne off the dusky hussy. The boys were not much happier about it. Half of them had tried and made dry runs at the sensuous halfblood girl. Now this overgrown ranny from Texas whoops into town with his damned yellow-wheeled rig and his pearly teeth, and away he goes with Mincy like he'd been proper-courting her since she'd nubbined-out, and, well, by God, it was just too much!

It was, indeed, agreed Claude Casebeer. But Isom had his blinders on. He only nodded to the nasty jibes of the local swains, and their petty girl friends, and took Casebeer by the arm and said, "Come on, old Claude. I knows that little old gal. She'll show on time, and decent. Just flirttailing it a bit, that's all. I done told you a hunnerd time that she got that southern quality daddy behind her. That's high blood and run hot, but it don't run bad. Same go for the boy, onliest on him it's double."

Casebeer said nothing until they had gone out and gotten into the buckboard again. Then, with the team turned about and heading out of town, he let loose.

"Isom, I'll say it once and that's the end of it. All you can see in that Texas rowdy is that he's white and southern and what you call 'quality.' I'm letting you know I've seen something else. He had Mincy to meet him down by Kiowa Bend this noon and he took her into the grass there."

"*Whoa up!*" Isom hauled the team back on its hocks. "By God!" he cried. "Don't you talk like that, old Claude. Don't you dast say nothing more."

Casebeer could see the whites of his comrade's eyes rolling in the starlight, but for all his soft looks and peaceful ways Claude Casebeer was tough inside.

"Isom," he said, "I will talk and you will listen. I saw what I said I saw. I tried all day to think of a way to tell you about it without tearing you up. I couldn't figure it, so I said to myself that I'd wait. Likely Mincy would cool down and come to her senses, and same for the Texas Romeo. It would all blow past and nobody need be hurt. Least of all you, old friend."

He paused, and he could hear Isom breathing hard in the darkness. Then the tall Negro shook his head and muttered, "I knows, I knows, old Claude. Go ahead on."

Casebeer made it as plain as he could. Honorable young men didn't go to grass with proper-raised girls the first day they saw them. Neither did decent men, southern or otherwise, lack the common guts to come and call for a nice girl to take her to a dance. Good men of any cut or age went to parent or guardian of a girl and *asked*. When a man wouldn't do that much, he wasn't quality, he never heard of the word. He was, in fact, a pure and simple chaser. The only meaning the term "breeding" had for such hotspurs was that of a dog. They would try to get to any girl innocent or loose or just plain dumb enough to let them. Coming to Mincy, she qualified in two ways for Rash's recipe: she was both dewy-eyed and stupid. If such harsh talk hurt Isom, let him remember that he would be one hell of a lot worse hurt if anything bad came to Mincy from Matt Rash.

When he had finished, Casebeer reached over and took the lines out of Isom's slack hands. Clucking to the team, he drove the rest of the way to the farm. Isom never said a word until they had put up the team and wall-hung the harness and were walking to the house.

Then it was to show Casebeer that he still was trying to see a rambler rose where a cockleburr grew.

"Leave me sleep on it," he said. "You got to be wrong."

# 61.

Mincy came in that night at four o'clock in the morning. She was wild-eyed and mussed-up and would not talk to Isom Dart, who was waiting for her on the porch of the farmhouse. It was Matt Rash and the yellow-wheeled rig which brought her up the lane from the road, but the Texan had spied the glow of Isom's cigarette up on the porch and had taken off pronto. The girl went right on past Isom, up to her room in the loft gable. His plea, "Honeychile, honeychile, wait up—" trailed after her like a refrain or an echo, not the parental order or demand which it should have been; and the gaunt Negro sank wearily back into the old cane-bottomed chair, to roll and smoke another twenty cigarettes before the sun came up over beyond the river and the Dominick rooster crowing in the backyard sent him into his own bed, wide-eyed.

But Mincy was not all that came home that night. Unknown to Isom or Claude Casebeer, Tickup had returned. They found her in the morning on the back stoop, in a near coma, running a very high temperature.

Isom took one look at her.

"Lord, God," he said to Casebeer. "It's the spotted fever."

"Maybe not," said the white man grimly. "Put her in the harness shed on clean hay. I'll go fetch Doc Britt."

The squaw had come home from Wyoming some days gone. She had not been feeling well, she said, and believed it would benefit her to go down the river a piece and spend a week or so with a half-Shoshone woman friend, married to a Cherokee cotton farmer, whom she had found in Manawota the past summer. Now, evidently, not wanting to alarm or put out her hosts, she had stolen off and crept home, or tried to, when she discovered how sick she was.

How long she might have been "out in the woods," or if she had just left the Cherokee place, would have to wait. The immediate thing was the doctor's opinion, and this, rendered tight-lipped within the hour, confirmed Isom's muttered guess: "Smallpox and for sure."

They watched over Tickup until sundown, when she died. Mincy and everyone else, save Isom and Casebeer, were kept away from the Shoshone woman. When she was gone, Doc Britt, who had returned to see her, wrote out the death certificate and ordered the body buried immediately and deep, and the harness shed burned to its sills.

There was no argument. The grave was dug beneath Mincy's gable, where the girl could see it from her window, and where the grave itself could "see" the river.

"She loved moving water," Mincy said, "and green trees where the grass was good and kindling lay about. She would want to know that there's a good camping place nearby."

So quickly did the men work with the shovels, that the grave was refilled and shaped and the service read by Casebeer, all by the red light from the burning shed. It made an eerie sight, somehow filling Isom Dart with thoughts of far Wyoming, Brown's Hole, Charcoal Bottoms, and even farther back along the trail to Texas and *Comancheria,* to the rescue of Terresa from the Rangers, the treachery of the dowry of Dolores, all of that long-ago wildness of his youth in old Coahuila and along the Rio Grande. He shivered and was glad when Casebeer made the reading from his Bible quick and short. For the first time in nine years the jujubird was sitting on his shoulder. The *puha* feeling was in him strong. Suddenly Isom Dart was very much afraid.

An hour later the premonition was fulfilled. Casebeer found a scrap of paper on the kitchen table wedged beneath the Rochester lamp. He brought this now and handed it silently to Isom, where the latter stood on the rise beyond the house watching the moon lie silver on the river.

By this time in his life, the ex-slave could read in a limited sense—and this was a limited note:

"*Good-bye Daddy . . . Love, Mincy.*"

He read it aloud, like that, then looked at Claude Casebeer. It was typical of him that, with a hundred more obvious questions to ask, the big Negro put the only one for which the white man was not prepared, and the only one that cut through all that did not count.

"Which one of us," he said, "you 'spect she meant?"

Casebeer frowned and shook his head. "It doesn't matter," he said. "Come on; they've an hour's start of us."

Isom nodded wearily. "More like a lifetime," he said, and went with his friend, away around the corner of the house.

At the barn, they put the team to the buckboard. It was agreed, as they worked, that Casebeer would drive into town to find whatever trace of the lovers there might be in Manawota. Isom would stay at the farm and ready what outfit they would require, should they have to trail Rash and Mincy past the township. There was no question by either partner of the need to go after the young couple.

Mincy was only just eighteen. Whatever that Madison M. Rash from Texas had sold her on, was going to have to have the signatures of both her white and black foster-fathers, or they would surely know the reason why not.

They found out quickly enough on that last score. Casebeer was back from town almost before Isom finished diamond-hitching the camp pack on old Jeff Davis.

He was not alone in the buckboard, and Doc Britt's saddle mare trotted by a rein-tie to the tailboard.

What had happened was simple. Casebeer had gotten into Manawota before Rash and Mincy got out of it. He had apprehended them in front of the general store while they were laying in traveling supplies for the yellow-wheeled rig. A lecture to the Texan on cur-dog manners and a peremptory command for Mincy to get out of the rig and into the Casebeer buckboard, had followed.

Young Madison Rash, half again the size of Casebeer, had knocked the irate guardian down, stomped him into the horse apples of the gutter, cut him pretty good with a clasp knife. Then the deceptively mild Casebeer had come up spitting dirt and horse dung and taken into his younger opponent, full-out.

Bystanders had stepped in to halt the fray when Casebeer went for the second time into the refuse of the hitching rail. Doc Britt had been sent for, and in the confusion young Rash and Mincy had lit out in the yellow-wheeled rig. By the time the dizzy-headed loser had been whiffed around to his senses by Doc's pocket bottle of *spirits of carbonate of ammonium,* the elopers—give them the decent name—were long gone to Texas.

"Texas?" asked Isom, when Doc Britt finished the story. "You certain sure, old Doc?"

"Hell no!" fumed the physician, in no way appreciative of the night call. "I was only speaking figuratively."

"He means," put in Casebeer, for his first words, "that they are gone and no trace nor eyewitness word of in what direction."

Britt got his mare from the tailboard. "You'd best put Claude to bed for a day or so," he growled to Isom. "The damn fool should have stayed down. Those knife cuts could have killed him. As is, I want him quiet till my stitches set. He pulls them out, I'll bill him triple. Neither of you two has got sense enough to wad a birdgun load. Let that flirt-tail filly go for a good run," he advised. "It won't injure her. She'll come back to the barn if you'll let her. Goodnight, and don't bother bringing me any more of your business this week."

"Yes, suh," said Isom Dart, and gave him a hand up into the saddle. "Thanks, old Doc. You's a friend."

"You," snapped Britt unsympathetically, "are a fool."

"Yes, suh," acknowledged Isom. "Goodnight, suh."

"Go to hell," suggested the man of medicine, and turned his mare toward town.

There was a moment's silence between the Negro and Claude Casebeer. Then the latter apologized for his failure and said that he was sorry he had not let Isom come along and handle it himself.

"You could have whipped him," he lamented. "Damn it all, Isom, I was wrong. He was just too big and mean for me. God knows when we'll ever catch up to them."

Isom shook his head. "Don't fret, old Claude," he said. "We'll catch up to them, all right. We cut for sign first thing in the morning, and we stays on their trackline till it peters out, or we do. Leastways," he added significantly, "I does."

"No," denied Casebeer promptly. "We do."

"You heard what old Doc Britt say."

"Yes," gritted Claude Casebeer. "I heard him and I'm telling you the same as he did—go to hell."

"Hoo," said Isom softly, after a pause. "When old Claude set out to be a friend, he don't stand short."

"Not," answered Casebeer, "if he can help it."

# 62.

In the rose-gray of the dawn they set out from the farm. Isom drove, and in the back of the buckboard, padded and propped with bedding, rode Claude Casebeer. Neck-roped to the tail-

board, Jeff Davis ambled along. The white man looked unwell in
the early light and the Negro was anxious and introspective. In
the back, with Casebeer and the supplies, were two Winchester
carbines and half a case of shells. On the empty side beside Isom
Dart a sawed-off shotgun angled against the brake handle. Their
first move was to check the road, south and north, out of Manawota. The rubber-tired narrow tread of the Texas buggy was easy
to single out. Isom did not see it on the road either way from
the town. Leaving the main way he quartered the town to the
east and found nothing.

"Smart," he said to Casebeer. "Gone due west."

They circled around the town and, true to the Negro's guess,
found the rubber-tired track soaring off through swale and rise,
open grass and pin oak clump, right out over the open range
toward the buffalo and horse Indian country.

Marking the direction, Casebeer looked at Isom Dart and said,
"Well, old partner, I hope we brought plenty of bacon and
beans. It may be a spell before we see those two again."

"We'll see 'em," answered Isom.

They went on. And on. And still on. They held to the track of
the yellow-wheeled rig for six straight days. They crossed the Red
Fork of the Arkansas, into the Cross Timbers, fought through
that wild land of rough breaks, skeleton trees of unknown age,
catclaw shinnery and black-jack oak, came out on the North Fork
of the Canadian and saw beyond them the beginning of the great
sea of the short grass. Behind lay the lush blue-stem pastures and
the friendly settlements of the five civilized tribes. Ahead waited
only the stillness and the hazy blue of the beyond, and the inces-
santly keening whistle of the wind.

"Hoo," said Isom. "Back to the high lonesomes."

"You certain that you want to go on?" Casebeer's question
showed the natural drain of the long pursuit upon his own resolve. But it disclosed, too, an honest want to pull Isom away
from the arid track. The white man saw only despair in their
journey for Isom Dart. If they quit now, Mincy might remain at
least an unfinished dream for the big Negro. Casebeer feared that
if they went on, the dream would somehow finish itself, and Isom
Dart. "Isom," he repeated, when his companion did not answer
his question. "You sure you want to go on?"

"Hows I know?" said the other, shaking his head. "We ain't come up to them yet."

"All right," sighed Casebeer. "Have it your way."

They went on, and it was the same thing again, four days this time, straight out into the Llano Estacado. On the tenth day from Manawota, having seen nothing of their quarry and having lost, at last, the dimming trace of the rubber-tired buggy, they halted the second time.

"Well, Isom," said Claude Casebeer, "where are we?"

The gaunt Negro looked north and looked south. "I'd say we was almost out from twixt the Cherokee Strip and the Staked Plains," he replied. "Yonder off there, southly, is New Mexico. Bearing northly, you got Colorado. Another ways going to the west and we hits the old wagon road to Santy Fee."

"No, my God," interrupted Casebeer. "We haven't come that far."

"We is," said Isom, pointing. "Them's the Rabbit Ear Mounds poking up, on the right, and Point of Rocks doing the same on the left. Old trail run smack atween them."

They sat in silence in the whisper of the never-ending wind. Both men were taking stock. Both saw the same evidences of failure—the worn-out mustang team of the buckboard, the rib-bone weariness of the packmule, their own bearded, hollow-eyed and filthy faces—and both men reached separate, honorable conclusions.

"I'm done," said Claude Casebeer.

"I ain't," answered Isom Dart.

And that was the way it was.

They split the outfit carefully and with precise fairness. Nine years rusty or not, these were professional wanderers of the wilderness. Each knew exactly what the other would need and should have of their remaining supplies. The only arguing came with each man pressing the other to take more than his clear share, a sort of final graciousness typical of both.

They knew this was the parting. Lone, and lonely men both, until meeting and making their partnership, they did not have to *say* good-bye, they *knew* it. This was no "see you next spring," no "*hasta la proxima.*" There wasn't going to be any next spring, any next time. Not for Isom Dart and Claude Casebeer.

The big Negro insisted the white man take all of whatever

material things remained in Manawota, including the little money left in the bank there. It was not a great deal any longer. Good living and the expenses of schooling Mincy and traveling her mother, had depleted the original outlaw stake over the nine happy years. This summer's drouth failure should end the adventure, letting them both thank God for its goodness, and leaving them owing no man. Understanding this, Casebeer accepted the farm and its obligations.

For his return to Oklahoma he took the buckboard and the team. Isom, for whatever his journey, chose the old piebald mule. Each man kept a Winchester, and Isom took the shotgun, as well. "You'll need it more than I, most likely," Casebeer said. "I'm not hunting anything."

Isom divided up the supplies in Jeff Davis's pack, saddled the mule with his old high-horned Coahuila rig, made up his bed roll, slung his war bag from the Mexican horn and was ready. Minutes later, Casebeer departed.

Watching the buckboard dwindle across the tawny mane of the buffalo grass, Isom wept. "Old Claude, old Claude . . ." he said, and turned away.

Taking the war bag from the saddlehorn, he emptied it upon the prairie. In it, with his other treasures, was his old outlaw apparel: slouch hat, buckskin pants, hickory shirt, runover high Coahuila boots and carbine bandoleer. Stripping off the settlement clothes, he left them where they fell upon the sun-bright grass. Re-dressed in the bandit attire of the Brown's Hole days, it seemed to him as though nine years fell away with that pile of farmer's things left upon the dun-colored carpet of the prairie.

When he swung into the saddle, shotgun barred across the horn, and said softly to the old mule, "Let's go, Jeff Davis," Manawota, Oklahoma, was ten thousand miles away, not ten days, and the nine years were not nine years, but a forgotten lifetime.

# 63.

Going steadily west, casting as he went for a telltale buggy wheel track, Isom Dart made an unscheduled noon halt.

It was by the side of the old first wagon road to Santa Fe. There was a pleasant camp spot there, where the trail forded the shallow headwaters of Mesquite Creek, a far westering tributary of the North Canadian. Some desert willow, cottonwood and other shady brush made a sort of oasis there, in a country otherwise barren as a lunar scape. Coming to this place, Isom circled it warily, seeing it had prior tenants. But in the circling he met a creaking oxcart loaded with fresh buffalo meat; it was driven by a leather-skinned crone whom he would not have known in a dozen first glances, but who instantly remembered him.

"*Santos!*" cried the woman. "It's you—the Black One. *Bienvenidos, amigo.* Welcome home! What, you dark scoundrel? You don't know me? *Ai,* what an insult. You dog!"

Discovered, even seemingly claimed, Isom kicked Jeff Davis up to the oxcart, peering more closely at the grinning harridan in buckskin dress and Comanche braids.

"*Seguramente,*" he said. "It is a true thing, lovely one. I do know you from sometime. When was it?"

"*Nearly twenty summers gone, Negro,*" answered the woman.

Isom furrowed his brow, putting his mind along the backtrail. It came to him suddenly, not just from the hauntingly familiar face of the hag on the oxcart, but from that vehicle itself, and the cargo that it carried.

"*Sangre del Niño!*" he said. "The Comancheros! You're the wife of Gomez, the *jefe!*"

"*Angelina,*" answered the fat halfbreed squaw. "And you are Nedito. Do you think I would ever forget you, Black Man? Ah, you were something to see as a boy!"

Isom made a gracious wave, bowed from the waist. "And you,

Prairie Flower," he said. "You were more than only something to look at; you were everything to see. What has life done that is good for you and your people, *linda mujer?*"

It was a long time since he had used the Spanish. It pleased him, and Angelina Gomez, that it still flowed like sage honey from his dark lips.

"The language," said the woman, "is like the love. You don't forget the movements. What has life done for you, Nedito?"

He explained to her his new name and told her a lie of his good life since that long-ago summer, ending with the story of Matt Rash and Mincy, and of his own return, following them, into this land where the Comancheros had hosted him when both he and La Gomez had been prettier, and life another song than now.

"*Señora,*" he pleaded. "*Por favor.* Is there not some news you may give me of this yellow-wheeled buggy and the two I have described who would be in it? I implore you!"

Angelina, listening with a sudden intentness, frowned. "Perhaps," she said. "Gomez himself may want to tell you a thing. I don't know. Why do you not ask him? He comes there, behind you, over the rise."

Isom felt his neck hairs lift. Gomez coming behind him? Gomez from whom he had stolen the priceless gray Entero? Whom he had humbled in his sleep not only to this woman, his wife, but to all his tribesmen and women? *Que tal!*

He cocked the hammers of the shotgun, swung the twin muzzles ever so little to cover the fat Comanchero woman.

"Call over my shoulder to Gomez," he said low-voiced. "Warn him that this *escopeta* has triggers finer than the soft-spot hair beneath the chin of the stallion which I stole from him. Say it will go off, if old scores are still kept to account in his memory. *Quidado, mujer!*"

All of this was in Spanish, of course, and Angelina, rather than being disturbed, threw back her head and laughed. "Gomez!" she shouted. "Come here and see who has come back to visit you. An old friend. One from very ancient times. A real *compadre.* Hurry, you fat pig!"

To Isom, as the hoofbeats of Gomez's horse, and of several other riders, drummed in behind him, the mountainous squaw muttered, "Ease the *escopeta* away from my navel, fool. I will say nothing of such nonsense to Gomez, you understand? Better learn who your friends are, Nedito. It's unkind to aim a shotgun into a friend's belly-button. Am I correct?"

"*Señora belinda,*" said Isom, sweeping off his battered sombrero, "you are more correct than the stars!"

Next moment Gomez was up to them and had recognized Isom and was embracing him as though the trail-worn Negro were an own-brother returned from the dead.

Nothing would do but what Nedito should stay with the Comanchero camp on Rabbit Ear Creek. This could be a day or a week or forever, but it must at least be for this same night. What? Hard feelings over the stolen gray stud? After half of a man's grown lifetime? Pah! What was a horse between old friends? Gomez didn't even remember the brute's name. Was it Santiago? Chico? Cuchillo? What?

"Escudo," said Isom. "His name was Escudo."

"A lie!" Gomez yelled instantly. "It was Entero!"

They looked at each other a moment, enemies. Then the Comanchero threw back his fat head and roared until his belly grew sore from being punched by his saddlehorn.

"Come on, *hombre!*" he shouted to Isom. "God's blood, but we shall have a *baile* this night to deafen those old Rabbit Ears. Don't say a word. Tie that sorry mule to the cart and ride up there with my woman. We will go ahead and prepare the welcome. *Hi-yee-hahhh!*" With the yell, Gomez galloped off with his buffalo hunters, up the old first road to Santa Fe.

Isom turned to exchange looks with Angelina. The squaw grinned, pierced ear to pierced ear.

"A position for you, eh, Nedito?" she suggested. "You don't know if you are going to a fandango or an ambush."

Isom considered it a moment only. "*Señora,*" he said quietly. "I never did know."

At the camp, the guest was glad enough to get a fresh buffalo roast for the noon meal. He also could not help but be interested in the stories recounted by Gomez and the others; such as the rise of Quanah Parker among the Kwahadi Comanche, Quanah being the little half-white son of the old chief Peta Nocono, out of the white woman, Cynthia Ann Parker. Did Nedito remember Nocono? He headed the band which accosted him with the stolen Entero. Remember that band with Pin Oak Jack? Sure, sure.

And old Pin Oak, he was still alive and well. A strange thing, too. Not long ago, a Kwahadi had come to visit the Comanchero of Gomez. He had seen Pin Oak that spring, and guess what old Pin Oak had captured out of a band of wild *mesteños?* Hah, in a thousand years, Nedito could not imagine it. Well, Pin Oak had not so much captured this relic of another day; the relic had more actually wandered into the Comanche camp and surrendered. Aye, even the years had not covered the old saddle marks on that one's withers. A gray, yes a gray—almost white with the snows of time. Hah, you fool! Of course it was Entero! What other horse would have the intelligence to come into a camp and give up when he could no longer run fast enough to stay with the band?

*Ay de mi!* what memories.

Did Nedito recall a time—was it in the summer of seventy-one?—well, anyway, the time that he came back to Texas, or at least back to the Llano Estacado, looking for that same gray horse? Old Pin Oak Jack maintained that Nedito had visited with him that summer. He said it was down on the Rio Blanco, in the Arroyo Frio, where the Kwahadi had a big encampment that year, one of the last really good buffalo years. Pin Oak told a Comanche lie about the Rangers of *Tejas* running Nedito all the way from that camp to a place not far from here—the headwaters crossing of the Rio Canadian—and of Nedito outwitting them at the river, crossing in among a herd of longhorn cattle driving north. Well, if it weren't a Kwahadi camp-fable, then perhaps Nedito would be made happier to know about the old horse, and about Pin Oak Jack saying that he would feed the ancient bone pile in respect of his old friend Nedito, who had fooled the Rangers, and care for the rheumy-eyed old he-horse until it lay down for the last time.

Isom, not without a tear, assured Gomez and the Comancheros that Pin Oak Jack was not spreading camp lies. He also told the New Mexican buffalo hunters that indeed his heart was made warm by the old ghosts from the past, especially by the story of Entero, but that in all truth his soul was too burdened with sorrow at the moment for him to convince his charitable hosts of his sincerity for their kindness.

Here, Angelina interrupted to tell briefly the reason for the return of the big Negro rider. "I told Nedito," she ended with a shrug, "that perhaps Gomez would have a thing to say to him of this matter." She turned to her fat husband. "Was I right or wrong, *jefe?*"

Isom felt a sudden turning in the spirits of the noontime feasters. All were watching Gomez.

"Do you mean about that *pobrecita* yonder?" the chief said. "That one we passed?"

Most of the Comancheros were pagans, praying, if at all, to the old Comanche gods. A few, however, were of the True Faith, converts of the mission *padres*. These few, Isom saw, now crossed themselves.

"What would you say?" asked Angelina. "We all saw the strange wheel tracks leading away from there, did we not?"

"Jesus God," said Isom Dart. "No, no, it ain't so . . ."

Gomez, understanding a little English, bobbed his thick-fleshed jowls. "I am afraid that it is, *hombre. Lo siento mucho.*"

The Comanchero chief, a cautious pagan, crossed himself, then tossed a pinch of dust to the Thunderbird, most feared of the Comanche gods.

As Isom's heart sank within him like a cold stone in the quiet of dark waters, Angelina moved around the fire to his side. "Come," she said, putting one great suety arm about his defeated shoulders. "I myself will go with you. The others may remain. In a time like this, a man will want a woman to hear him weep."

"A true thing," said fat Gomez. "The men and I shall stay here. *Vaya con Dios, Nedito.*" Then, not thinking how it would sound, "Take a shovel, woman."

# 64.

As they went down the old trail in the oxcart, Isom saw the dark birds circling. Angelina turned the bulls aside, went over a spine of rocks, down an ancient buffalo trail into a pocket of willow beyond. There was a spring there and some little grass. Isom could see the old, as well as the recent, signs of camping. It was here that the buzzards wheeled. Even as he and the Comanchero woman creaked downward in the cart, several of the fleshy-necked birds lumbered upward in their surprise.

"They are not heavy," said Angelina. "They have not been on the ground long."

Isom nodded. It didn't matter, really.

At first they did not see it. Then a kit fox of the desert, bat-eared and curious, scuttled at their appearance, the movement of the tiny beast bringing their eyes to what had engaged his nose.

"Ahhh, Lordy," said Isom. "Pore, pore, pore chile."

"*Que dice?*" asked Angelina.

"*De nada,*" answered Isom. "There is death here, all right. You brought the shovel?"

"Don't you want to go nearer and be sure? Perhaps it only seems to be the one you seek."

"It is the one. Only a child. See how small she lies there."

"*Si,* and no blanket even. Just that filthy shred of checkered rag beneath. God's name!"

Isom looked and saw that Mincy lay upon what was left of the buggy's lap robe. He remembered the plaid pattern distinctly. He could see it again in his mind, folded neatly and hung upon the bright brass dashboard rack.

"Here is the shovel," said Angelina.

Isom took the implement, climbed down from the cart. "You won't come with me?" he said. "Perhaps a woman could place her as she should be?"

Angelina shook her head. "No, *hombre.* It is why we left her ourselves. We saw the dark birds flying and came over these rocks, knowing of this spring and this old stopping place, thinking some ancient Comanche brother had come here to die. It was in our hearts to give him some food, a blanket, what comfort we might. You know we don't turn out our very old ones. Only the *Komantcias* do that."

"You said you left her then? *Por que?*"

"You will see," said the Comanchero squaw.

Isom went around the spring to the pathetic huddle of the human form which did not seem real there in the rank grasses of the hidden spring. When he had come to stand over Mincy he saw, as Angelina had said that he would.

The girl's face was mottled with the markings which were unmistakable. Her throat and chest bore the same gruesome blotching—the spotted sickness. Mincy had contracted smallpox from her mother and had come down with the dread malady on the trail with Madison Rash. In the young face was terror and suffering and the dread of death and of dying alone. And she had died alone.

Isom Dart examined that campsite more carefully than he had ever studied any sign in his life. The oldest horse droppings in the area of the spring itself—those which must be the leavings of the Matt Rash sorrels, which could not be confused with the droppings of the Comanchero mustangs farther away in the rocks where Gomez had halted his followers the previous day—those freshest signs of the sorrel team were *four days old.*

Mincy had moved about, crawled to the spring for water, made unmistakable markings in the dust of life after the Texas dog had left her. The vultures having been to see her only this same noontime would have been proof enough. Had she died before Rash departed, the dark birds would have been down and there would have been other even more savage marks than those of the smallpox upon the small, frightened face. As it proved, however, even these mute evidences of guilt were not required. Angelina Gomez, observing the big Negro's sifting of the site, called over to him from the rocks where the oxcart waited.

*"Hombre,"* she said. "If you seek to know how long she suffered, she still lived when we came yesterday. She heard us coming, but could not see us for the fever. It was only briefly that she moved, struggling to raise up, and to see, to look for who it was that came. But it was not us that she saw, only death. He came with us, over the rocks here. When we knew it was the spotted sickness, drawing near enough to see the signs on her body, then she was still. It was all in those few moments of our finding her that she died. *Lo siento, Nedito."*

Isom found a soft place in the iron breast of the prairie and made the hole as deep as he could. There was no shroud, and so he placed her upon a bed of pulled sweet hay within the earth. A fragrant blanket of the same cloth would cover her. But before that, he took from his hunting shirtfront the tiny buckskin medi-

cine doll Mincy had given him on that sad day at High Creek
Bench, when Squawman Croad had cut the pride and the dark
skin from his body.

"You give it to me, honeychile," he whispered. "You give it to
me with your life. You give it to me with your love. I gives it
back the same ways." He put the doll into the cold hands, against
the rigid breast. The slim fingers and his own gnarled ones were
wet with the tears which fell with the medicine doll and with
Mincy in the grave at Hidden Spring.

"One time you weep for me, little Injun gal," he said. "You
put your little finger on them whip cuts and the tears stand in
them violet eye to break this old black heart. Break it the same
way that it's breaking now. Oh, God, baby gal, cain't say no
more, cain't cry no more. But oh Jesus, honey, how I weeps inside
. . ."

He remained on his knees beside the only being who had loved
him, big hands knotted, dark head lowered. The sobs which
wracked his body were terrible in their soundless grief. Angelina,
seeing them from the distance of the oxcart, could not bear their
evidence.

"*Nedito. Hijo mio,*" she called. "Enough, *hombre.*"

He raised his head, looking over at her.

"Come on," she said. "Let us be away. God will surely guard
this place. Life continues. Make the sign of the cross to be safe,
*amigo,* and then leave. *Por favor.*"

Isom got to his feet and finished the work. Drawing the cross
upon the mounding of the earth with a stick, he placed a cairn of
red desert rocks at its head. Then he picked up the shovel and
came away.

At the oxcart he halted and looked back, still uncertain.
Angelina spoke to him quickly, yet with dignity.

"One time each year," she said, "we Comancheros pass this
way. It is the time of the early showers. They bring the tiny
flowers, *hijo,* springing from every crevice, every pocket of the red
earth. In that time, passing hereby, blossoms will be plucked and
left there where your child sleeps, and a prayer said, Indian and
Blackrobe, both. This is the promise of Angelina Gomez, your
friend who weeps with you in her heart. Will you not come
now?"

Isom climbed into the seat beside her, put the shovel behind

[225]

them. "The heart will always remember Angelina," he said to her in Spanish. "God spare your house."

The Comanchero woman turned the bulls, prodded them back up the slope. "Sadness, sadness," she sighed. "And life so brief, so dim and swift in the burning, only as a bit of sheep's tallow in an old tin cup."

They had crested the rise once more, giving view back onto the hawk's-shadow loneliness of the grave. Looking thus over it a final time, staring at the trackline of yellow-wheeled rig which spindled away from it, and from Hidden Spring, Isom Dart's deep voice answered.

"That's so," he said in English. "And yonder goes one life ain't no more wick to burn."

# 65.

A summer rain had softened the plains. The track of the yellow-wheeled rig lay imprinted with the nakedness of a  new brand. For the most part Isom could read it without dismounting, or even slowing the ambling gait of old Jeff Davis. When it did grow faint on rocky ground a bit of quartering found it again. There was no place in that virtually timberless outland where a wagon or a buggy track could hide.

And the sorrels were faltering now. Shod when they left the Indian Territory, still showing shoe marks as far in the flight as the abandonment of Mincy, the sign of the buggy team now bore no trace of iron. The feet were splaying, and Isom found three of the discarded shoes pulled and thrown aside by Rash. Ahead the elevation increased to an outcrop of stone. There could be but one end—a man was what his horses were, and the horses of Matt Rash were done.

"Hoo, mule," said Isom Dart to Jeff Davis. "We cotch 'em tomorrow. Keep rambling."

But they could not wait to come up with the yellow-wheeled rig next day. Indeed, as they went on, the broken roughlands began to seem familiar to Isom and he soon realized that the next valley held the old Trincheras Trace, an Indian road to the buffalo country. More important, in its westerly terminus, it bore upon the bustling Colorado settlement of Trinidad. Should Rash reach this haven, he might be lost to his Negro pursuer.

The problem was whether the buggy team, flayed of hoof or not, would be able to make superior time to Jeff Davis on a traveled track, such as the Trincheras Trace. In the unmarked wilderness already traveled the mule was the easy match of the sorrels. Now all was changed, or would be, should Rash come first to the Trace.

"Old Jeff," said Isom, where they paused to boil the noon coffee, "he don't make it today, he never do. And he ain't going to make it today. Come sundown on the old Trincheras road, we going to be there a'waiting for him."

Jeff Davis walled his eyes, wrinkled his whiskered snout, and started to *scrree-hawww* his agreement. Isom spilled his coffee while leaping to seize him by the muzzle and prevent the brass-lunged bray from erupting into the solitude of the Trincheras hills.

*"Ho-shuh!"* he ordered. "You make a sound, old mule, I butchers your tongue out."

Whether convinced or uncaring, Jeff Davis settled for a disdainful grunt, and went on with his noon-halt browsing of the rabbitbrush and buffalo grass.

Mid-afternoon brought them to the spine of the last ridge. Below lay the valley and the tiny dun-gray thread of the ancient Indian roadway. It was an apprehensive moment. Yet in ten minutes of intense scrutiny in the glass-clear quiet of the high country afternoon, Isom made out no dust devil on the distant track. As still as it was, any wheeled rig would have put a hanger of fine haze into the air that would be unmistakable to the owlhoot eye. Rash had not reached the road. He was somewhere in the tangle of foothills between where Isom Dart lay on the ridge and the fanning-out upon the valley's floor of those hills.

"Old Jeff Davis mule," said Isom, "we is got him."

Isom could plainly see the goat-track trail which Rash had been following; the track plunged down off the ridge to be lost in the lower hills and then emerged to make a Y-fork joining with the Trincheras road to Trinidad. At the fork lay a high jumble of rocks, buttressed by thick brush crowding closely onto the flanks of both trails. Beyond the rocks ran the Picketwire River. It was a very lonely place, designed by nature for a confluence of outland paths; and it was a natural ambush.

Isom Dart shifted his grip upon the sawed-off shotgun, ticked Jeff Davis in the flank. "Go 'long, mule," he said. "Mister Madison Rash is did for."

In that sort of steep going it was no trick for the Negro rider to circle in the hills to the west of the goat-track trail and so come to the Trincheras Rocks ahead of Matt Rash and the yellow-wheeled buggy. He muzzle-wrapped and hid-out the mule in the scrub beyond the main road, hard by the fork. The blood-red of the sundown was just staining the high ridge when he took his place in the rocks with the shotgun, and when, a mile over the valley floor, he saw the dust cloud of the yellow-wheeled rig come out of the hills.

# 66.

Matt Rash was tired. He was so tired his bones ached. The sun, westering over Trinidad and the Sangre de Cristo Range, was flat in his eyes. Coming free of the last of the hills and into the valley, the glare of it was like a great red eye staring into his weary brain.

"Son of a bitch," he said. "I hope to God that's the last of it."

The sorrels, at the sound of his voice, laid back their ears, as worn down as the man who drove them. Next moment, however, the ears were alerting forward, as the dusty nostrils flared to the scent of the fresh water on the quickening breeze of evening.

"Coo-ee," said Matt Rash, noting their livening. "Go along

easy now. That's water sure enough. And rocks and brush and firewood for certain. We'll camp yonder on the stream. That'll be the road to Trinidad. We're home."

He held the sorrels in, for, used-up as they were, they wanted to trot. And Matt Rash didn't care for them to do that. It was yet another long day's drive to Trinidad, and the Texan had reason to save every step the sorrels had left in their game hearts.

He sent a long over-shoulder look to the hills in his rear, as he brought the yellow-wheeled rig free of them; and gave a second long look back when he had covered half the distance of the flat toward the Trincheras Rocks and the river.

For the past three days he had been followed. No, it wasn't that for certain—he may have been followed any number of days—but he was certain of the last three.

The feeling had come on him the second day out from the place he had left Mincy. During that day and the next one, he had figured it was only his conscience tagging him, maybe even catching up to him a bit. But, hell, what was a man to do? Nobody stayed healthy messing around with that spotted fever. When the kid had gotten dog-sick on him, then told him of her Shoshone squaw mother coming down with her death of the smallpox only a short while before, what was there left to do? With the pox you went two ways. You either caught it and died, or you got the hell away from it and prayed. Well, he had gotten away.

He shook his head, the matted curls caked with campgrease and neglect. "Goddamit," he growled. "I didn't ask her to bring *that* along!"

Why, the entire idea had been a good time—just a long spin out on the prairie. Had the kid stayed healthy, nothing would ever have come of it. They'd have split the blanket somewhere along the line, when it got too frayed for him, and she'd have made her way back home the same way she'd made it away from home, on that blanket. By God, he hadn't promised her anything but what he'd given her, a fast ride and a hard one.

She was crazy-wild, that kid. Bad as a pure Indian. All that shy stuff and ducking and coloring up. Christ, she'd torn into him like a cat. All he'd had to do was touch her and . . .

He broke off his thoughts to curse again, and take a third swift look behind.

[ 229 ]

All clear.

Well, that was something. Either his shadow had quit, or was fallen by the wayside. It didn't matter. Past the river was Trinidad.

Funny, though. He had laid back a dozen times on his own trail to catch his follower, and never had a decent sight of him. Whoever it was, was plenty slick at tailing. Probably Indians, or maybe a couple of renegade white men living along the owlhoot. And it was just possible that Matt Rash was shadow-jumping. How could you say somebody was following you when you never saw anything on your backtrail?

It was the Indian kid. Had to be. She was following him. He was letting her do it, that was, by letting his mind go back and fetch her up to him. Now that was a wrongful thing. He had done all any man could for her. That was a good place, a safe place, where he had left her. It had shade in the day, warm rocks at night, good water all the time. For a little old breed girl who was going to die anyway, it was as good a place as any.

The hell with all of that.

Sure he had liked her. And sure she had clung to him like he was half again as good as God. So what of that? What *mestizo* kid wouldn't do the same thing, given the same shot at a white man of quality? He was ready to say he might wish he hadn't brought her away from Manawota. It wasn't in him to feel good about the poor little devil being taken so puking-sick. He wasn't any damned animal. If he could have wished her back in Oklahoma on her cotton farm, he would have done it. But, by Christ, if a man wished in one hand and spit in the other, he'd sure enough find out in a hurry which hand filled up first. No sir. Matt Rash didn't catch that little old Indian girl the smallpox, and there wasn't one goddamned thing he could have done for her after she took it. *"The hell with it!"* yelled Matt Rash, into the stillness of the mountain sunset. *"Goddamit, forget it!"*

He grew more calm, as the rocks of the river neared.

Ah, Jesus, but it was going to feel grand to get into that stream and soak off some of this Colorado muck. He was full enough of dust and sand and blackdirt and camp-smoke grime to be a damned horse Indian buck. There sure would be a flow of water in the stream, from the way the sorrels had winded to it. Most watercourses this time of year in that region ran nothing but yellow sand and rocks, with maybe a lizard or two and a tuft of bunchgrass for variety. But there was good brush along that channel ahead, looking bright green in places. That was live water yonder. Maybe the luck of Madison M. Rash was looking up.

He was into the deep shade of the rocks then, out of the low red slant of the sun.

He hadn't noticed from farther out in the flat how very close and high the outcrop flanked the road. It was very nearly like a miniature pass, dark and quiet and narrow. Damn. Funny how gloomy it was in there. A man no sooner sighed with relief to be out of that damned sun, than he was looking ahead for it with sudden urgency.

Nerves. Nerves pure and simple.

God, why did the gloom and the rocks and the stillness and the crawl of the lonesomeness in that place make him think of that other place?

Shadows. Shadows in that place. Shadows in the other place, too. He was just too damned tired. His eyes were seeing things that weren't there and never had been there and never would be there, or anywhere. It was coming in out of the late flat sun, into that purple hole through those high close rocks, that choky, thick and blind-gut brush. He'd see better in a minute.

And he did.

The sorrels, not intent on anything but pulling through the rocks to the river, literally squealed with fright and reared going sideways and back into the buggy, snapping the tongue. In the instant that he fought the horses, keeping them from going down, Rash took his eyes from the road and the shadows in the rocks. It was then that the deep soft voice came to him from the center of the roadway ahead and, whirling, the lines still tight-wrapped in his hands, he saw the tall gaunt scarecrow standing between him and the river and the sunset in the Trincheras Rocks.

"Don't you move," said Isom Dart, and in the echoing silence of the order, cocked the outside hammers of the shotgun and raised it to blow away the life of Madison Rash.

# 67.

Death was there. It lay poised beneath the twin hammers of Isom Dart's shotgun. Not even the wind moved in Trincheras Rocks as the gaunt Negro stood thirty feet from the yellow-wheeled rig. At the distance the buckshot charges would shred Matt Rash. The pattern of the lead pellets must cut away his life. He could not twist nor spring aside. The Texan was dead when Isom's black fingers closed upon the triggers. But they did not close.

Before the ex-slave stood his life's enemy, the white southerner, flayed naked of plantation armor. Gone were the overseer's whip, the field captain's gun, the dogs, the leg irons, the lynch pack of fellow pale-eyed white men, nameless in the dark which hid their vile justice.

This white man was *his*. He belonged to Isom Dart. And Isom's fingers would not close upon the triggers, even so.

But in the instant that eternity thus held its breath for Madison Rash, the southerner had recognized the voice from the shadows of the rocks as a Negro voice—a speech deference known to him and to his kind since the slave ships plied from the Congo and the Ivory Coast to Mobile and Biloxi.

"Nigger," he said. "Put down that birdgun."

*Nigger*, the man said. The tone of the word, the absoluteness of its use, stayed again the tightening fingers of Isom Dart. They would not contract that last quarter-inch which would erase all that stood between him and the breed of Madison Rash. Jesus God, he thought, is this the ending of it?

Isom Dart had come a lifetime from Siloam Ridge and the Arkansas slave boy Ned Huddleston. He was thirty-five years old. It was passing twenty springs since Fort Sumter and the guns of April. In the terrors of that dark journey, Isom had killed. There was no accounting of the men who had died where Isom Dart walked. Too many times the price of his own life had been that of some fellow man's. Death was the easy wage. And there in his hands at the crossing of the Picketwire he held its instant payment to the man who had debauched Mincy. Yet Madison Rash stared at Isom Dart through the murky shadows of those rocks at day's end, at trail's end, at life's end for one of them, and he said the word and it was Isom Dart who was destroyed.

In the buggy, waiting through the stillness where a brave black man died, Matt Rash understood his victory.

He wrapped the lines of the sorrels about the buggy whip bracket on the dashboard of the yellow-wheeled rig. Easing down to the roadway, never taking his pale eyes from Isom's dark face, he walked through the dust of the Trincheras Road across the distance which separated him from his assassin.

A dozen strides. Not hurrying, not delaying. In that moment, a final desperate resolve to complete the vengeance which was his, rose up in Isom Dart. A last valiant flame burned deep inside his heart. Its fire reached his frozen trigger fingers, with the white man but three, and then but two, dust-deadened steps away.

But the Texan did not halt his stride. The two steps became one, and even as that closing stride was taken, Isom Dart stepped back a pace.

"Don't come no fu'ther, Mister Matt," he said; and the odyssey of Isom Dart was ended.

Rash nodded and reached out and took the shotgun from his hands. He broke open the weapon, picked the shotshells from it, dropped them into the dust, gave the empty gun back to Isom. There was no hatred in his voice, no disdain. He had recognized the tall Negro in coming up to him in the evening shadows. To the extent that such a man might feel such an emotion, there was even the confession of original sin in the words of Matt Rash.

"I'm sorry," he said, "about the Injun girl."

Isom's long arms lost their life. They seemed to melt from the position of holding the returned weapon on Madison Rash. He stood with the shotgun dangling, shoulders sloped, arms hanging at sides. Something more than the moment's determination to murder had drained from the ex-slave.

"There wasn't nothing," said Rash, "that I could have done for her."

"You could have stayed with her," said Isom Dart, the words as lifeless as the dangle of his arms.

But even that small rebellion, that last hint of an equality of exchange between his world and that of Madison Rash, was enough. The voice of the southerner returned from its brief, awkward brush with compassion.

"Boy," said Rash, "you're plain lucky the way things are. Now you understand me, Uncle, I'm weary and wore down and I won't say it twice: You go and get your horse and you get on him and you get the hell over the river, yonder, and you keep going."

In the pause, the sorrels whickered and stomped, restless to get on to the water. The eyes of both men flicked toward the yellow-wheeled rig, then back.

Rash was not wearing a gun. His rifle reposed in the buggy out of practical reach. Isom's glance could see no other weapon carried by or available to his enemy. The shroud of evening lay deep upon Trincheras Rocks. No watchman prowled that lonesome ground save for the rustle of the sundown breeze, stirring again. In its hidden oiled scabbard, inches from his hand, the Spanish blade which had been his inseparable friend from Fort Worth jail to the Tip Gault surround, waited upon the will of Isom Dart.

And waited.

Matt Rash stood inside the sweep of the powerful arm, a dead man but for the command of conscience, or of courage, which would speed the slender *cuchillo* into his vitals.

But Isom did not strike.

The order for vengeance, for justice, would not leave the brain of the ex-slave, locked there by a past whose phantoms would not down, whose ghosts arose to cry out *nigger!* and to fall upon their knees before the shibboleth of southern quality. The tensing fingers fell away; the Spanish witness was not called.

Isom, nonetheless, lifted up his head. His voice was low, but it was the old deep voice, and there was an odd calm in it which surprised Matt Rash and made him unsure.

"Yes, suh," said the tall Negro, and turned away.

In the bouldered brush he found Jeff Davis and climbed upon the old mule, guiding him out onto the dusty road. They shambled toward the crossing a seeming silhouette of despair and sorrow, a scarecrow of a black man in a floppy hat, a lop-eared piebald packmule, harshly wedded symbols of brute toil and human shame.

Yet at the very lapping of the water's edge, Isom drew rein and, pausing, looked back. He saw Matt Rash watching him. He sensed the anxiety, the tension, of the regard. Did the white man know? Had he guessed the truth?

Back there, Isom could have killed him in the glinting of a sunbeam. Either with the gun or knife he could have let out the white man's life into the puddled dust of the Trincheras Road. Instead, he had given over the one weapon, stayed the other. And all that he had surrendered in so doing had been the bitter, burned-out ashes of a lifetime's hate. Had he fired the gun or plunged the blade into the bowels of Madison Rash, he would have been no more a man nor less a brute than the Texan. But he had risen above, and forever above, Matt Rash. In the final accounting it was not the white man who let the black man go free back there. It was not Matt Rash who had taken pity upon Isom Dart. It was Isom who had won the victory. It was the black man who had walked away knowing what Isom Dart knew now, and thanked a just God for: the chains of the past did not shackle him, they shackled Madison Rash.

Isom sat a lengthening moment looking over the stream. He did not see the Picketwire, but that other distant shore beyond the Rappahannock. He was again beside the stilling limbs of his old master, dying with the twilight of Second Manassas, and he heard once more the words of freedom ringing strong across the almost twenty years and twice a thousand miles away: "Go over the river, Ned. Over the river is free!"

They were not the words written upon the paper Colonel Huddleston had given him with his freedom. They were other words, spoken in some separate tongue. They called through the caves of darkness and despair, carrying from the heart of one man to the heart of another, bringing light and bearing love.

They had guided Isom Dart to this shore and would guide him yet to the other.

So much no man could take away.

Black against the Colorado sunset, the scarecrow rider grew tall. His hand moved to threadbare shirtfront, came away, cast its yellowed paper burden on the current of the near-bank shallows. The ancient letter fluttered briefly like a stricken bird. It whirled to deeper water, bobbed downstream, was gone. Isom Dart touched Jeff Davis, bony heel to waiting flank, dark eyes alight and looking far.

"Go 'long, Mule," he said. "There's one more river to cross . . ."

## ABOUT THE AUTHOR

---

Will Henry has written over a score of books based upon American history, particularly that of the great westward expansion and its effect upon the horseback Indians of the plains. He was born and grew up in Missouri, where he attended Kansas City Junior College, and has subsequently lived and worked throughout the western United States. Residing in California at present, Mr. Henry continues his research into regional lore and legend which is the basis for the unique Henry blend of fiction and fact. Nine of his novels have been purchased for major motion pictures. Several of his works have won literary awards, including four of the coveted Spur Awards of the Western Writers of America, and the first of the Levi Strauss Golden Saddleman Awards for his classic story of Chief Joseph, *From Where the Sun Now Stands*.